LEGACIES OF CHERRY RIDGE

Copyright © 2011 Craig Stevens

ISBN: 978-1-61434-711-8

All rights reserved. No part of this book may be used or reproduced, stored in a retrieval system, or transmitted in any form or by any means (electronic, mechanical, recording or otherwise), without the prior written permission of the author—except in the case of brief quotations embodied in critical articles and reviews.

This is a work of fiction inspired in some instances by persons and settings within the author's experience. The resemblance of any characters to persons living or dead is entirely coincidental and unintentional.

Original Cover Art by Betty Stevens
Author photo and cover design by Rita Stevens
Book design by Book Locker

To order additional copies of this title contact your favorite local bookstore or visit www.Booklocker.com

The author invites commentary via email: rcspub@nycap.rr.com
www.rcspublications.com

Printed in the United States of America on acid-free paper.

First Edition

LEGACIES OF CHERRY RIDGE

Craig Stevens

Good health & prosperity!

Craig Stevens

This story is dedicated to my patient wife Rita, loyal and heroic Gretchen, and my late father.

It is also dedicated to the offspring of small towns across the country. It is further dedicated to sufferers of clinical depression and anxiety who can maintain a sense of humor and enjoy an ultimately uplifting tale. These two groups are not mutually exclusive.

Prologue

About midway through this story Christopher St. James has suffered a panic attack and remains in a deep state of depression and anxiety. His friend Meghan tells him to sit at his computer and write. She knows it is writing that rights his balance.

Chris complies and starts out to describe the characters, quirks and dark side of the otherwise forgettable upstate New York small town in which he was raised. He thinks he despises the town; yet fate, or maybe serendipity, keeps returning him to it.

Soon his tale evolves into a chronicle of the events that began in that town in one sense a few months earlier, in another sense generations ago. In time it becomes increasingly clear that he himself is one of the Legacies of Cherry Ridge. The legacies do not involve curses, vampires or anything supernatural or surreal ... so far. They are of the sort born of culture, tradition, environment and maybe genetics. Add a stimulant or a catalyst and ... and the result is this, his story.

Chapter One

It Wasn't Quiet and Dull for Long

I awoke disoriented. The bed felt softer and lumpier than usual. There was something odd about the ceiling. The crack in the plaster that greeted me each morning was absent. Did I finally fix it? No. Okay, I am not at home. So where am I? Cherry Ridge. The realization made me sigh with resignation.

Gretchen lay beside me. She had not yet stirred so I slowly eased my way out of the bed. I stumbled to the blinds and peeked out. The early morning August sun made me squint my eyes.

After satisfying the usual bathroom needs, I took the hated pills: two for cholesterol, one for blood pressure and one for depression/anxiety. Plus a small aspirin and a fish oil jellybean. In my mind, I was way too young for such meds, but my doc had said otherwise.

While dressing I called out to Gretchen: "Hey, Bonehead, how about going to the diner for breakfast? Do you want to see Millie and Willy?" Gretchen rolled over, passed gas and twitched her tail.

By the time I had my sneakers on she was waiting next to her leash. As usual, she raced me out the door. She relieved herself and that led to a doggie smile and tail wag of satisfaction. Then she accepted the Breath buster she fully expected. She chewed it while I attached her leash. I said: "Let's walk around the house before we head out."

I wanted to circle the four-unit, two-story building. My father had inherited it a few years earlier. He was about to sell his house and move into one of its apartments when he died. As the executor of his small estate, I had made frequent journeys from my home near Albany to empty out his home and put it up for sale. I had planned to promptly sell the apartment building, too. I wanted to shake the muck of Cherry Ridge off my shoes for good, and I mean good. It was where I had been raised, but it is also where I where my shadow of gloom had begun to take shape. Every reluctant visit brought back the memories.

There was no quick escape. In a lousy, low-price market, the house lingered; so, I moved a few basics into the empty apartment and used it when I had to come to town. Wouldn't you know? As soon as I did, my dad's home sold. I closed the estate still owning the apartments.

The grass was freshly mowed. There was no trash on the grounds, the paint and windows looked good; the tenants who were seeing to the building's maintenance in return for reduced rent were following through.

"On to Millie's, Gretch," I said. We headed down to the sidewalk and turned toward Ridge Street.

I tell Gretchen that she walks with me like my grandmother did when I was a boy: slowly with great purpose and deliberation. Taking mild weather walks was pleasure for each of them. Neither missed anything of interest along the way, although, truth be told, what they considered of interest differed. They used different sensory organs. Gretchen tended to pause for new smells, where Nanna stopped to note the flora. Each enjoyed encountering both two- and four-legged creatures and, when possible, engaging with them. I think my grandmother was the first and maybe the one and only squirrel whisperer.

It was early in the sleepy town so we encountered no one. Save for the distant buzz of the occasional car or nearby bird there was no sound. A rare breeze had cleared the humidity and now it was still. A hint of skunk lingered in the air, which was probably why we didn't see any furry creatures about. During last night's walk, Gretchen had bolted through the backyard after a skunk. Or so I thought at the time. As bright as she is, Gretchen has never learned that skunks and dogs don't mix. She had already one smelly incident, yet she didn't fear another.

Since we hadn't been to Millie's in some time, I reminded Gretch of her special relationship with Millie. I didn't need to. Each time I said "Millie" I could see it registered with her and she quickened her pace.

In the spring more than two years earlier, we had been at the state park when a young girl fell off the wooden bridge and into the rocky Cherry Ridge Creek. Gretchen bolted then, too, leash and all, and dove into the cold, rushing water. True to her Labrador heritage, she grabbed the little one by her clothing and pulled her to shallow water. There, two or three others and I secured the girl and summoned help. The toddler had a broken arm and some abrasions. Several bruises emerged later. Eventually she would fully recover. A bystander caught Gretchen's plunge and the ensuing rescue on a phone video. Later it went, as they say, viral on the Internet.

Gretchen's celebrity was a mixed gift. For a brief time the demands were excessive. Fortunately, in the days of abbreviated news cycles, her fame was fleeting outside Cherry Ridge, but not to Millie, who is the rescued little girl's grandmother, nor to the rest of Cherry Ridge's residents who cherish Millie's family.

Legacies of Cherry Ridge

Gretchen remained a hero. Willy Logan, Millie's husband who heads the Chamber of Commerce, led a movement to honor Gretchen. The mayor, the little girl's other grandfather, presented her the key to the village, the first time in anyone's memory such an honor was bestowed. Local wags couldn't help joking that there was only one key and finding it was the hardest part of the preparations: few people locked anything in Cherry Ridge.

The awarding of the key was more than ceremonial lip service. Gretchen received invitations to be a special guest at every major village event. In fact, the public reason we were present in Cherry Ridge was to attend the annual hot air balloon festival. Moreover, she was the only dog not only allowed but also cordially welcomed to venture into any place open to the public. On the occasions when we took advantage of her privilege, she often was offered gifts, usually, but not always, food.

The Diner

We used Gretchie's prominence at Millie's Diner whenever we were in town. It was nearly impossible for us to pass by the establishment without risking insult to the Logans. Typical of a dog, Gretchen did not mind milking her status for food; even it was a simple Milk Bone. She would and could eat almost anything, anytime, anywhere. It had become my job to help her maintain her health, figure and some dignity.

Millie's Diner is properly called The Cherry Ridge Inn, as the worn sign out front proclaims; but for three generations it has been called Millie's Diner in honor of its founder. She was Millie not for her first name of Mildred or Millicent —in fact, her name was Esther. She was Millie because she had been a milliner. Her daughter Ellen had become the next Millie. I know that the current Millie's real name is Arlene only because she had long ago been my babysitter. It could be very confusing to outsiders.

Millie's Diner has a wonderfully rich history full of diverse tales. At one time it housed a speakeasy. At another, it was a haven for gambling. Fights were once common. Stabbings in the early days. At least two shootings, one early on and one only a decade ago. Big business deals and political decisions. Romances blossoming and romances ending.

The building had first been an inn with a tavern anchored by an enormous, handcrafted mahogany bar. While the back bar had been removed to install a more modern grill and food preparation equipment, the Millies had taken great care to retain as many of the old features as possible or replace them with modern equivalents. The red oak floors remained. The deep red leather booths on each side of the entry doors and along one entire wall had been reupholstered many times. The tables down the center still had bentwood, ice cream shop chairs. The Seeburg jukebox, a mid 1950's addition, still played selections from Willy's vast collection of 45-RPM records. Next to it was a modern CD player, but it was only used to "re-broadcast" radio shows from an even earlier period.

As to the food, it was largely vintage, small town diner food. Nothing Greek about it, as so often is the case with diners. While there were some concessions to modern tastes, the best selections came from the breakfast menu and the lunch specials: fresh-baked hams, locally made sausages, and baked goods from next door. Meat loaf and old-fashioned blue-plate specials. Good soups, good gravy, great coffee. And perhaps best of all, fountain cokes (with cherry or vanilla if you like), seltzers, sodas, floats and sundaes. Willy Logan called himself the last of the soda jerks. Millie said he was half right.

We cut the corner at the library. The stoplight changed over from blinking red to three colors. There was opening activity at the service station across the street. Out of one of the bays came Ed Peck: "Hey Gretchen, hey Chris," he roared. "Good to see you back in town. Goin' to Millie's? I'll be over for a coffee in a jiffy." "Hey yourself, Ed. See you there."

The diner is in the first structure past the library. The four-story, brick building with stone columns is typical of its 1870's origin. Its architectural uniqueness lies in three brass gargoyles, each overseeing one of the three sections of the building. Ask nearly any resident of Cherry Ridge about them and the answer will be a blank stare and something akin to "Huh? I hadn't noticed them before."

The three sections yield three ground-level storefronts. The diner is in the center. To the left is the bakery which Millie and Willy Logan also own. To the right is an erstwhile formal dining room. In the current recession, it is more a meeting room. The Rotary, Lions, Jaycees and others gather there for luncheons. In the evenings, when the diner serves only a limited menu, the meeting room hosts card and game players. The upper floors contain apartments, all vacant save one, and a couple of offices.

The Logans' youngest, a teenager, was outside sweeping as we approached. He lit up when he saw Gretchen approaching. He pulled open the door and shouted: "Mom, Gretchen is coming!" He bent down to grasp Gretchen as she trotted to him. "Hi ya, girl," he said, "How ya doin'?" I remembered Randy as a shy kid so I didn't take offense when he didn't speak directly to me. He did hold the door fully ajar and usher us in with a flourish.

We had barely entered when Millie greeted us. We exchanged a few pleasantries with her and several of the patrons. The pleasantries included numerous pets and pats for Gretch. There were several familiar faces and a couple of names came to mind, but there was no one of close acquaintance. In truth I had very few personal ties in the village, whereas my late father knew nearly everyone.

Millie led us to the middle booth directly across from the flip-up opening in the bar/counter. She said that she had heard we were in town and noted that Willy was in the bakery. As to the first I noted that word gets around fast. As to the second I asked if Willy was making apple fritters this morning. "One apple fritter coming up," she said. "What else can I get our favorite customers? The ham is really good this morning and we have some homemade turkey sausage that Gretchen might like."

Gretchen's ears perked up when she heard the words turkey and sausage, so we knew that was a good choice. I agreed that a slice of ham along with a couple of eggs over easy with rye toast and OJ would do me fine. And, of course, some of Millie's eye-opening coffee.

In less than a New York minute, Millie came back with the coffee in a mug with my name on it. There were scores of similar ones lining a wall. She also had a water bowl inscribed "#1 Citizen" on one side and "Gretchen" on the other. I asked her if she had time to sit with us and bring me up to date on the local news. I knew there was no better source. She could be more detailed than an historian with a Ph.D.

Millie reported the recent marriages, deaths and births. She told me that Karen Shannon came back to town, her "tail between her legs." Something different, I thought. "Her ex is doing time for a 'Fonzi' scheme." I tried to picture what that might be. "I remember you two were an item in high school. She's living in the house next to her parents with her two kids."

"No, we weren't," I said while thinking that it was maybe true if only in my teenage dreams. "The Warren house? The one with the bomb shelter out back?"

"Yeah, I think that's right! I remember hearing stories about the bomb shelter, but I didn't know if they were true. Do you know for sure?"

"Pretty sure," I said, "I was outside the entrance when I was a kid." The place was known to "radiate" if you count teenage heat.

She told me that "Bung" Byers had died a few weeks earlier. I was probably one of the few people who could have read the obituary of Clair Jonathan Byers and known that it was Bung.

Bung was representative of a class of small town characters and eccentrics. He had been a daily presence on Ridge Street since before I was born. Wearing the same dark blue suit and blue tie he would move station to station along the two commercial blocks. At each stop he would hoarsely comment on the state of the world in general and Cherry Ridge in particular. His audience was anyone who listened. Few did. Kids mocked him and others avoided him. "In a way I kind of miss him," said Millie, "but I won't miss his spitting and the remains of his filthy cigars."

Millie went on to say that a new antique shop had opened across the way, about the fifth to take space in the former W. T. Grant's. The oxymoronic juxtaposition of "new" and "antique" amused me. She said the bank had changed its name again, and that Ed Peck had changed from Mobil to Sunoco. Coincidentally, as I was saying I had noticed that when I passed him earlier, Ed came in. I heard someone ask him if he was getting better mileage. He came by, stuck out his hand and then gave Gretchen a hearty, two-hand grasp.

By then, Gretchen had polished off her turkey sausage. I had eaten an enormous fritter and I was well into my ham and eggs. Millie described several changes and additions at the school: new bleachers at the football field, a new elementary school principal, a few new teachers, a new guidance counselor and a couple of coaching changes. Although Cherry Ridge is small, it takes its sports seriously. Several graduates had earned athletic scholarships and a few had become professional players or coaches at some level. It was a way out.

"Oh!" said Millie, "I haven't told you what might interest you most. Mel Reeves is only publishing the paper once a week, on Friday instead of Tuesday and Friday." I showed some surprise. I hold well-edited, small newspapers in a special place and Mel published such a paper. He was a throwback to the old-school editors of a century ago.

Millie explained: "Mel said that Mel Junior convinced him to make the change. Junior has been working with Mel during his break from college—you know that he is attending Northwestern, right? He said the paper would be more profitable if it published just once a week. The one edition is bigger, more pages. Mel Senior called it 'edition by subtraction.' I didn't get that at first."

Inevitably, I run into Mel when I am in town. He is as close as I ever had to a mentor. He encouraged me to write articles for the paper when I was in high school. I made a mental note to make sure I see him this visit.

It was getting busier so Millie excused herself to help the staff. A couple of patrons stopped by to fawn over Gretchen. Willy finally got free long enough to encourage me to come by when it was quieter so we could talk some politics and sports. He also said he had some new dandelion wine he would like me to try.

I was about to bid the diner adieu when Millie returned. "Chris, you like odd things, right?" I nodded and said, "I guess. It depends." "Well, there is kind of an odd character in town." "Odd how?" I asked. "Well, maybe not really odd, but peculiar." I didn't see the difference so I waited for Millie to go on.

"About two weeks ago this guy started coming in every morning at precisely the same time." Glancing at the clock she said: "In fact he is due in about half an hour. The first day he came in he asked for porridge and bangers. Ginny told him we could do hot oatmeal and that we had link pork sausage and turkey sausage. He asked for the oatmeal, pork links, two soft-boiled eggs and rye toast and tea. He's ordered the same thing every day since. Ginny thinks he is from down under, but I think he's a Brit."

"Could be either or South African or a New Zealander," I said, "I guess he is kind of different from most of your usual patrons, but don't you have others who come in at the same time and place the same order?"

"Well, yes, there are Sam, Donna Wilkins — a course she has the diabetes — and a couple of others, but there is more to tell. He seems to wear the same clothes — not many come in here for breakfast in a suit and tie 'cept for old Doc Gamble and sometimes even he doesn't in the heat of summer. But maybe this guy has more than one of the same color? He always brings a newspaper, he always sits in the back booth that no one ever wants, and he talks to no one except the waitress. Milt says he is staying at his motel. Says he has a rental car. Says the guy keeps his room like it's been unused. Nobody seems to know why he is here. Maybe he's lookin' at property, maybe even the Hillside Castle. The rumors never end about the castle. Wouldn't that be somethin'? Whaddya think?"

The "whaddya think" caught me off guard. I didn't want to tell Millie that her imagination was running away from her. "I dunno, Millie," I said, partly lapsing into local speech. "Maybe he's waitin' for something or someone. Maybe he just likes your food. Could be anything. Could be nothing."

"Well," Millie said, "If you are still here in 20 minutes or so you can see him yourself," and then, going back to her original characterization, she added, "He's an odd one, he is."

I told Millie I sensed that Gretchen needed to go outside, but that I would be back for another cup of coffee. She said her daughter (probably the next

Millie) was due in any minute and that she would hold my booth for me. Millie was heading over to the bakery.

Gretchen did her stretchin' on the lawn of the library. I sat on the Malcolm J. Walker bench and for the umpteenth time wondered who Malcolm J. was or is. I was always forgetting to ask someone. Les Bowman, an 80ish friend of my father, came by walking Tessie and Nigel. For a few minutes Gretchen had a couple of little guys to cavort with. Les repeated some of the news I had gotten from Millie and added a bit more. He literally pointed out that Ed Peck had changed to Sunoco. Les asked if we were going to be in town for the hot air balloon show and I said that that was the plan. He said to look him up; he would be selling tee shirts for the seniors' center fund drive. I asked him who Malcolm J. Walker is/was. He said, "Hmm. Good question. You got me by the short hairs."

When we returned to the diner I could see the coffee klatchers were coming in, mostly seniors, mostly male. Then Officer Curt "Chub" Simmons came rushing in, clearly agitated. He called out: "A dozen ham and egg san'wiches and a dozen coffees, all regular. Right away!" "To go or eat here, Curt?" came the snickering reply.

Portly Curt was about to answer back when he spied us. "Chris, Gretchen!" he said. At least this time I got first billing. He came over quickly and plopped down across from me. The booth shook in response. My small hand got lost in his big fist. He was bursting to tell somebody something. I was going to be that somebody.

Curt was one of the athletes who had gone on to college success and played a few years of minor league football. Dumb as a box of hammers, the locals would say, but soft and sweet inside like the jelly donuts he favored. A knee injury brought him back home permanently.

He immediately began to argue with himself. "I shouldn't say anything," he said haltingly, "not yet, but I know I can trust you and it'll soon be all over town anyway ..." He leaned over as his whispered story came out rapidly: "There's been an, uh, incident. Over near your building. Right behind it in fact. Young woman, teacher we think. Well, maybe, we aren't sure. The chief and the whole force is there. They're waitin' for the sheriff's forensic team to arrive. Chief sent me here to get san'wiches and coffee."

Curt's words confused me. "Whaddya mean you aren't sure? Was a woman hurt or what?"

"We dunno. There's blood all over the place but we can't find a body! Look, Chris, I gotta get back. Keep it to yourself, buddy, right?"

Curt hovered at the counter, nervously eating a bear claw. He had to wait another couple of minutes for his order. I heard one of the patrons say: "What's with Curt? It looks like he's about to pee his pants." To which another replied: "Oh, he probably hasn't eaten since breakfast."

For a minute or so I thought about the shocking news Curt had told me, then I noticed the old Westminster clock. As I expected, no check came my way. I put three 5's on the table and said: "C'mon Gretchen. It's almost nine, the bank will be opening."

I waved so long to everyone in general and to no one in particular. Once outside Gretchen stopped as if to ask which way we were going. I was eager to get to the bank, but my curiosity about "the incident" took hold. "Let's go back to the apartment. We can take the truck to the bank." Nearly always agreeable, Gretchen led the way. Instead of the leisurely pace we had taken to get to the diner, we strode along briskly on the return. My companion seemed to enjoy the pace.

On The Way to the Bank

Instead of continuing on to Poplar, our street, we turned on to Hemlock. Hemlock was the site of the "incident." That had us walking directly toward the sun, already three hours above East Hill. The brightness made it hard to see the "castle" Millie had referenced. It stretched along Castle Ridge two-thirds up the hill. I put on my sunglasses. The glasses helped me see the gathering of vehicles three blocks ahead. They were on both sides of the street.

I could see half a dozen official types standing by or sitting on the cars close to the house. A few were finishing sandwiches and drinking coffee. Curt had made his distribution. Mel Reeves, Sr. and Jr. were both there, armed with cameras and recorders. They were trying to overhear what Chief Charles Broadhurst was asking Icky Stone as Icky sat astride his classic Columbia bike, streamers, bell and all.

Quite a contrasting pair, those two: the gray-haired, uniformed former federal agent who had retired to his wife's hometown to become Cherry Ridge's Chief of Police and the unkempt "notorious Cherry Ridge pervert," Icky Stone.

Icky was in his late 30's. He worked around town as a nighttime janitor. When he was a pre-teen some yappy young girls thought it fun to claim he had tried "to look up their skirts." They called him Icky and the name stuck.

Worse, though, was that from time to time unsupported claims were circulated against him. He was accused of lurking, loitering, public exposure, public urination and peeking through windows. The evidence was always sketchy at most, and formal charges never came about.

My dad, who had lived two doors down from where Icky lived with his mother, thought he was a decent, misunderstood kid of limited intellect. Dad would say "The Ickster" was an odd duck, but he was good to his mother and was the first one on the street to arrive when a neighbor needed help with snow or leaf removal. "Anyways," Dad would say, "Cherry Ridge has more odd ducks than even ones."

A somber crowd of some 25 to 30 ducks was earnestly quacking and gawking from the side opposite the point of interest. Some of them had cameras. A couple of Cherry Ridge's finest were keeping them at bay. Meaning, basically, they were involved in the speculations. Curt was one of them. We managed to slip behind most of the crowd. I only recognized a couple of faces and exchanged nods of greeting. Unlike at Millie's, Gretchen drew little attention. When we reached the corner to cross the street Curt caught up with us.

"The lady's name is Cassandra Cross. Mrs. Morgan said she moved in yesterday. She was at her sister's overnight so she had Icky give her the key and help her move in. She didn't have much stuff. Mostly baby things. Mrs. Morgan went to greet her when she got back this mornin'. She found the door open, looked in, saw blood everywhere, and called 911. Nobody knew about the boy until Mrs. Morgan asked about him. They found him hidin' in a closet upstairs. Jeff heard cryin'. I guess they missed him the first pass through. Mrs. Morgan took him to her place to clean him, feed him and get him into some clothes. She'll look after him 'til Child Services can get here. Chief has been on the phone with Principal Kline. Kline said Miz Cross called in yesterday to say she had arrived and she had an appointment with him this afternoon."

Spitting out so much so fast left Curt out of breath. I said something unmemorable about what he had related. Then he said, "Uh, Chris, we need to talk with all the neighbors so I hafta ask you if you heard or saw anything unusual last night or this morning." Curt got out a notepad.

"No, I don't think so. We got into town, got here, about 6:30. I picked up a pizza at Morelli's on the way in. About 7:30 or so I took Gretchen on a walk down to the stream. We were back by sundown. We settled in and I was asleep by ten … Oh, wait, there may be one thing. Just before I turned in I let Gretchen outside the door to pee. She bolted into the backyard. I think she was agitated by the smell of skunk in the air. I called her, but she didn't stop until she reached the hedgerow that separates the lots.

Let's see, I think I heard a metal clang like a trash can being toppled. Coulda been the skunk. There were porch lights on at the house but I didn't see anyone. Sorry I can't tell you more, but I was worried at the time about Gretchen getting sprayed."

"That could be useful info, Chris. The Chief will probably want to talk with you. You'll be around, right?"

I told him I would be in town at least through Saturday and I gave him my cell phone number.

"Thanks, Chris," he said, "I have a feeling it's goin' to be a really sad day. We gotta find a body."

Reference to the cell phone made me dig it out of my pocket. I hate the things. I only carry one for emergency use. Since I had given the number to Curt, I figured I better turn it on. Notice of a message popped up. I fumbled with the buttons. I heard Maggie's voice.

"Boss, your phone is never on! It is soooo frustrating. Anyway, I hope you are having a good trip. Some guy named J. Pierpoint Wadsworth, Jr. called," she said in a mocking imperious voice. "I told him you were out of town for a few days, but I didn't tell him where you'd gone. He said you should call him if you need assistance, whatever that means. Okay? Seeya."

A Look Back

Maggie is the young woman I hired a couple of years back, shortly after I started St. James Public Policy Research. Raven-haired Maggie O'Connor stands about 5' 11", over 6' in sneakers, her preferred footwear. She had been a high school standout in soccer, volleyball and softball. Her soccer play had earned her a college scholarship, but in the summer before her junior year she was the victim of an uninsured drunken driver who died in the crash. She suffered multiple injuries including near destruction of one knee. Competitive by nature, she endured two years of therapy and rehabilitation while completing a degree in math and accounting.

A few years later she had entered unannounced into my excuse for an office — shabby would be a compliment to it. I noticed she had a bit of a limp. "I didn't see anyone outside," she said, "Are you Mr. St. James, the person I see for this job? I'm Maggie O'Connor." She was holding a folder and several pieces of paper.

"Yes, I'm Chris St. James. Do you have a resume?"

"Yes, and here are my references." Then, seeing Gretchen lying a few feet away she said: "What a sweet Lab girl you have there. What's her name? Can I pet her?"

After I spoke her name, Gretch got up and approached Maggie's outstretched hands. "We have a Pekingese, Gretchen." I was about to say that's not a dog but an animated toupee when she added, "But I always wanted a big strong athletic dog like you."

I asked her to be seated in the one other chair in the room. I scanned through the paperwork. "Meghan," I began.

She interrupted with "It's Maggie, Maggie O'Connor."

"Okay, Maggie," I said, "You would appear to be overqualified for what we have to offer. It says here you have honor grades at Siena and a couple of years working for a top New York City accounting firm. I'm looking for a jack-of-all trades: a bookkeeper, receptionist and I can't pay all that much. You must have been making much more in the city. Do you know what we do here?"

She said she had done an Internet search and learned only a little about our fledgling enterprise. "It seems like useful, interesting work. I read some of what you have written, too."

"And?" I said.

She didn't comment on the writing. Instead, she said: "The thing is my mom is in a wheelchair. I came back home when she was stricken and I need to be able to look after her, take her to doctors' appointments and such. But I also need a job. I can keep books, I can answer phones, I can do anything needed. I took a few poli sci courses. I'm good with computers. I can do research. I have had a couple of good interviews, but as soon as I ask about some flexible time they turn me away. I understand companies want people to be present but I really don't want to go back to waiting tables. I came in hoping a small company could use me and be understanding."

Her desperation was obvious, but her forthrightness was refreshing, and there was something about this young woman that sparked my interest. Besides, I was no slave to a clock and if she could do the work, I'd have no problem with her being absent from time to time. I certainly was. I asked her if she would like some coffee. She said she seldom drinks coffee, but she would have some if I did.

I asked her how she liked it and poured her a cup. She took a sip and tried not to make a face. "I know," I said, "It's not very good."

"I can make better," she offered confidently.

We talked for another twenty minutes or so. I learned that her father, a police detective, had died in the car accident in which she was injured. He left a modest pension. Her mother had been a nurse. When Maggie finished college she went off to pursue her career. Now she had two brothers in college and a mother in need. Somewhere along the line I confirmed that we could be flexible with her work hours, so long as the necessary work got done.

"What do you think, Gretchen? Should we consider this young lady?" Gretchen had already made up her mind.

I excused myself and went out to confer with Vincent who had come into the outer office a few minutes earlier. Vincent DeSantis is my second-in-command and my only full-time employee at the time. He looked in at Maggie, smiled and shrugged.

When I returned to my desk Maggie spoke up. "Can I call you Boss? I can start tomorrow."

She didn't ask about the pay or benefits. Nevertheless, I offered $2,000 more than the budget called for. She accepted. A few weeks later Vincent told me she'd noticed the discrepancy in the accounting records. Vincent said he told her not to be concerned, that I was a soft touch.

The caller to whom Maggie referred, the nobly named J. Pierpoint Wadsworth, Jr., is the son, obviously, of J. Pierpont Wadsworth, Sr., the catalyst for why I had a second and more important reason to be in Cherry Ridge. Three weeks earlier the senior Pierpoint called me at home at almost precisely the time a courier delivered me a package bearing his law firm's name. He said a friend of my father's was giving me a piece of property in Cherry Ridge. He asked if I had access to a facsimile machine. I said I did and that pleased him. He then asked me to review the contents of the package, sign where indicated and fax the papers to the number listed.

I asked cautiously: "Who is making this 'gift?' What is it going to cost me? How do I know this isn't some kind of scam?" J. Pierpoint Wadsworth, Sr. replied: "I am very sorry, didn't I say? Angus Ferguson is your benefactor … and it is no scam, he is a very serious man."

I thought, Angus Ferguson? Then dawn broke. "Could you mean 'Scottie' Ferguson?"

To which Pierpoint replied: "Yes, of course, you would know him by that name."

I did. Scottie was indeed a friend of my dad's. When I was a kid, Dad had taken me a few times to Scottie's rough old camp in Brampton Woods outside of town. Over the many years Dad would occasionally mention he'd had a visit from Scottie. And I'd had a fairly long conversation with him right after my dad's funeral. I remembered it was friendly but a bit odd.

I figured the property I was being given must be Brampton Woods. My guess was that it was worth very little. As I recalled it was mostly rugged, wooded hillside land. I could probably sell it for a few thousand dollars to a hunter, maybe one of those that came down from the city to hunt turkey or deer.

While talking with Pierpoint I opened the envelope. The documents looked legitimate. There were counter signatures and witness signatures and stamps of various sorts. The papers certainly did not look like a printed version of a Nigerian e-mail fraud.

The conversation continued for a few more minutes. Pierpoint said Scottie had fallen quite ill and that doing so had triggered actions that had been in the works for some time. The dates alongside the signatures of one Angus Ferguson made this ring true. Pierpoint said that while the gift would hold up should Scottie die, it would be legally cleaner if he, Pierpoint, had signed documents in hand before such an event.

After clicking off the phone I sat down and read the papers with care. "Maybe I will get stuck with an unpaid bill for back taxes or something, but what the hell, Gretchen, let's take a chance that this is for real." I signed the papers and faxed them off.

Ten days later, the senior Wadsworth called me at work. Scottie had died peacefully at age 92. There would be no services. He asked if I was willing to fulfill one of Scottie's wishes. I said I would if I could. "Good," said Pierpoint, "He wants you to scatter his ashes over his mother's grave. It's on the property he gave you. I will have the ashes delivered to you by courier. I will also send you the deed to the property and a means to get into the property." At the time I thought that meant a key to a building or a gate, not the means to open a safety deposit box.

At the Bank

We reached our car without further interruption. Actually, the vehicle was not a car, but a big Chevrolet Silverado pickup. When I saw it on the lot I decided it might be more useful than the small SUV I had intended to rent in lieu of my little hybrid import. It was harder for Gretchen to get into, but she seemed to like riding higher and a little closer to the front seat. I liked that the high seat backs would deter her from jumping into the front, something she always did when I left her alone for even a few minutes. That would mean less hair to clean out later. Gretchen shed year around like the guy in the dandruff commercial.

We parked in front of the bank on Ridge Street. There were plenty of spaces available. It was close to 10 AM and yet the village seemed to still be mostly asleep. We were across from the New Moon Theatre. It was only open on weekends and the scheduled attraction was a second run. Years back the line of people waiting to get in could stretch three or four stores down, sometimes even on weeknights. The old theater held many memories. I probably learned as much or more there than in all the books I have read. There was that night in the balcony with ... but I digress.

I told Gretchen that I didn't want to test her privileges in the bank so I was going in alone. The Chevy was cool and the windows were halfway down. Her eyes stayed on me as I strode toward the bank.

Once inside I identified myself and asked to speak to the manager, a dour, sour Mrs. Kennedy. She had taken over many years ago when the then manager, my dad's oldest brother, had retired. Her office was just inside the entryway. I could see Gretchen through her window. She was in the front seat. Mrs. Kennedy noted that she hadn't seen me since my father had passed. She said she had received the proper paperwork from Pierpoint and all I had to do was to show identification, complete two transfer forms and fill in the signature cards. This took less than five minutes.

Mrs. Kennedy called her assistant, Lauren, and asked her to show me to the vault and deposit box 101. Lauren settled me into a small cubicle within the depository, then excused herself. On the table before me was the largest box they had available. It was far more than needed for simple keys to a gate or a locked cabin. Maybe there were a few keepsakes inside that would prove interesting.

I raised the lid gingerly. Immediately a sea of green struck my eyes. Greenbacks to be more specific. Stacked bills filled two-thirds of the box! My heart leaped and I started to shake. They were stacks of one thousand, five hundred and one hundred dollar bills. In one corner lay a flat envelope with my name on it. I opened it to find a folded sheet of paper and two DVD's. I unfolded the paper and read the handwritten words:

My dear Chris,

You have begun the journey I have set out for you. Where it takes you is in your hands. You will find an explanation when you view the DVD. You can do that at the camp. What you have found in this box and all that you find at the camp is now yours. There is no key to the camp entrance. When you go there Julia will let you in.

In case you have forgotten how to get to the camp, turn past Holy Sepulcher Cemetery and keep going until you reach the end of the road.

Beware the snakes.

Scottie

My mind raced from thought to thought. Could all this money be mine? I looked around me to make sure I was alone, as if I were a thief fearful of being caught in the act. If it really is mine, why would Scottie give it to me? And who is this Julia and why would she be at the camp when I go there? It was all really too much for me to take in.

In addition to the money and the envelope there were two velvet bags tied with leather cords resting upon a pile of documents. I opened the larger of the two. Even now, in hindsight, I am at a loss to describe how I felt. Astounded is inadequate. The bag held scads, maybe hundreds, of large diamonds! I pulled at the knot of the second bag. It held a small handgun, a .25 caliber Beretta as I determined later. I was nearly paralyzed. What's happening? Am I dreaming? What do I do?

I tried to gather myself. Lauren had said to buzz her when I finished or if I needed help. I hit the buzzer much harder and longer than necessary.

It occurred to me that thousand and five hundred dollars bills had not been in circulation for many years, so they had to be very old or fake. I removed one bill of each denomination and flipped the lid to close the box. Lauren arrived promptly. I handed her the bills. "Would you please verify that these are real?" I asked.

"Certainly," she said before looking a bit stunned to see the thousand-dollar bill. The bill seemed to prompt her to add, "It could take a few minutes."

"Could you also look out the window and see if my dog is okay? She is in the truck at the front of the building."

"You mean Gretchen? Would you like me to bring her in? I am sure no one here will object."

"Well, that would be nice, if you don't mind, and if she is willing to come in with you. Her leash is on the front seat. The truck isn't locked."

I lifted the lid for the second time. I half expected to find it empty, but the contents were still there. I leafed through the documents while waiting. I knew nothing of financial instruments but they appeared to be mostly bonds. I heard Gretchen's paws on the marble floor in the distance. In seconds she bounded in beside me. On her heels and in her heels, Lauren couldn't keep up. I thanked her. She said Mrs. Kennedy was doing the verification. They don't see 500 hundreds and thousands. I spread my hands apart and asked her if she could find me a container about "yay big" and she said she would.

I sat back, transfixed by the box. I had always had a reverse snobbery about money. I had tried to convince myself that it meant little to me, a common way of coping with having very little. Now with so much right in front of me I was having trouble restraining my impulses. I wanted to shout to the world: "I am rich, big time rich!"

Mrs. Kennedy came in with Lauren. Mrs. Kennedy was holding the bills; Lauren was carrying a box. "These bills appear to be good, Mr. St. James," said Mrs. Kennedy with a big smile. "We would have to send them out to be 100% sure. Would you like to make a transaction?"

She had called me *Mr. St. James* — the money had already had an impact.

My first impulse was to deposit all the cash into an account. That could take considerable time if Mrs. Kennedy decided each big bill needed checking, and she would be right to do so. Then I remembered reading somewhere that collectors would pay far more than face value for thousands and five hundreds. I decided to deposit only the hundreds.

The total came to exactly half a million dollars. I had a thing for doing mental calculations. The hundreds had occupied about half the space all the currency occupied. At face value the remaining half of thousands and five hundreds had to be worth five and 10 times the hundreds, respectively. Add in the diamonds, about which I knew nothing, and I guessed that the value of the contents of the box might exceed ten million dollars! It was like winning the lottery without buying a ticket. And tax-free at that!

A half an hour later Gretchen and I emerged from the bank with a brand new money management account, some temporary checks, the stack of Scottie's papers, a thousand dollars in cash and the all-important DVD.

On the Way to the "Camp"

We drove two blocks and parked in front of my family church. For many years my church attendance has been sporadic. I have issues. Christianity has had the perfect guide for over 2,000 years and the same time to get it right; still it hasn't. Way too many institutions and individuals pick and choose from the Bible to justify their own agendas. My tendency is to follow the New

Testament as the best source of what is right and adhere to my Eleventh Commandment: Thou Shalt Not Be a Hypocrite.

Nowadays I am more likely to drop in on a midweek afternoon than a Sunday morning. I feel that God, my grandmother and now my dad are able to hear me better then. I like going into a dim, muted church to give thanks, ask for guidance or simply meditate. This day I had reason to do all three.

I walked across the old bricks as I had hundreds of times before. I reached for the door handle and pulled. The big mahogany door didn't give. Locked! I tried the adjoining handle. Also locked. To protect against vagrants, thieves? I wasn't in some urban slum. What the hell good is a church if it can't be entered?

I was upset. No, I was angry, a feeling I rarely experienced. I started toward the rectory next door. Then I thought, what good will it do? Was I going to find someone to open the church just for me? Not likely.

Instantly I was transported back nearly a decade, back to when my wife of two years suddenly announced she was leaving. She had found someone else. Shocked and humbled, I had gone to a church then and found it locked. That time I did go to the rectory where I was summarily told to make an appointment.

Yes, I have issues, some profound and philosophical, some very personal.

I returned to the pickup and I saw the warm eyes waiting for me. I got into the back beside Gretchen. "I need to talk, Sweetie."

Gretchen extended a paw and dropped her head on my lap. It was nearly noon when I finally realized even good listeners can need a pee break.

We stopped at the drive-up window of a hamburger joint at the end of the village. My breakfast had been more than ample but I wasn't sure when I would get a chance to eat again. I ordered a cheeseburger with extra onions — Gretchen wouldn't care if I ate onions — and a plain one for the Bonehead. No, no fries with either. With the burgers and a shake I pulled into a parking spot. We ate in silence. I poured water from a plastic container into Gretchen's travel bowl and placed it at one end of her seat. Lying flat, she extended both her front legs to first embrace and then tip the bowl. After a few lapping sounds we were on our way.

It wasn't far to the right turn off the main road. I slowed as we passed Holy Sepulcher Cemetery. I told Gretchen we would stop by the gravesites later. The road narrowed to one lane and turned to gravel at the end of the cemetery. Before us were heavy woods. It was as if we were entering a tunnel.

I took off my sunglasses. Two signs announced "Private Property." We were entering Scottie's land. Hmm, my land.

The road began to rise. The wooded drop-off to our right grew deeper and steeper. I could no longer see through the trees to the valley to the north. Bird warbling and squirrel chattering announced our intrusion. Gretchen had her head out the window looking for the pesky squirrels and chipmunks.

We had to drive slowly to avoid numerous fallen branches. Still, it wasn't long before we stopped. We had gone maybe a quarter mile. Straight ahead the road was no more than an old logging path continuing along the drop-off deeper into the woods. The main road, such as it was, turned left and more steeply up the hillside. Guarding it was a very serious looking gate attached to a small concrete building. Going around them would not be an option.

Built into the building was something that looked a bit like an automatic teller machine. I approached it gingerly. I was maybe three feet in front of it when I was startled to hear "Please state your name." I hesitated. The disembodied voice repeated: "Please state your name."

"Chris St. James," I replied.

"Welcome, Christopher, I am Julia," came the response. "Please put your hands on my screen." I did so. "Thank you. Now look into my screen. Thank you again. Is there anyone with you?"

I told "her" Gretchen, my dog, was in the truck.

"Fine," said Julia, "I will now open the gate for you. Do you want me to open the gatehouse? The entrance is inside the gate." I said no. "Fine. You will find me at the end of the road."

Scottie's "Camp"

Another half mile later we were at that end to the road. We had traveled higher, but at times we nearly leveled off on what seemed to be tiers or ledges. There were many twists and turns as the road sought the best way around or through to the next level. Now we seemed to be at the last tier, maybe 150 feet below the crest of the hill. To the left was a narrow debris-strewn walking path. To our right there was a gap in a thick row of evergreens. We eased through the opening and came to a stop. There before us were two large buildings and several smaller ones.

It was nothing like I remembered. The camp of my youth was little more than a shack. In its stead was a compact, formidable structure built tightly to the rock wall behind it. Its roof was covered with solar panels except in the center where a cupola stood. The building's sidewalls were punctuated with a single row of small thick blocks of glass. As I stepped out of and away from the truck I could see a wing on one side.

A large, two-story building rested about 50 yards farther down at the edge of where the woods began again. It was wide enough to have four double-car doors. Between the two large structures was a series of solidly constructed sheds.

Gretchen whimpered. She didn't like the gravel under her paws. She moved toward the evergreens, found a bare spot, and deposited her breakfast. At that moment, we had different priorities. I walked across the gravel on to the narrow deck that fronted the house. The door looked like it could stand up to a bomb. Maybe that was the idea. To one side there was a box similar to the one on the gatehouse. "Julia, it's Chris St. James and Gretchen," I said as I approached. "Can you open the door?"

Julia immediately responded, "Yes, Christopher, I have voice recognition."

The door slid to one side. I took a deep breath. Gretchen had reached my side. "C'mon, Bonehead, let's see what we find inside Scottie's version of Farnhan's Freehold."

Due to the great contrast with the glaring sunlight, the inside registered as nearly solid black. Passing the threshold seemed to trigger the indirect lighting surrounding the room. It took a few seconds for my eyes to make an adjustment. There seemed to be but one large room.

The first thing I focused on was something hanging above the center, some kind of pull-down stairway leading to the cupola. To the right of the center were kitchen fixtures. To the left there were shelves, cases and a long dark sofa. More immediately to my left was a workstation. Without further examining the room I strode toward it, looking for a way to play the DVD.

"Are you there, Julia? I want to play a DVD."

"I am here, Christopher. Insert the disc into the slot on the right of the monitor."

My hand trembled as I located the slot and inserted the DVD. The monitor changed from "Standby" to "Encrypted File." Julia underscored the situation orally. I said "Julia? This is Chris. Open the file, please."

She responded: "Opening encrypted file."

A date ran across the screen. It was about 18 months ago. Scottie's face appeared nearly full screen. Then he settled back into an armchair and began to speak in a matter-of-fact tone.

Hello, Christopher. You seeing this would give me great pleasure. Maybe I am somewhere where I am taking that great pleasure. I assume you are in the camp and viewing this with Julia's help. Indeed, Julia can help you in many ways. She is a magnificent creation, if I do say so myself. Talk to her like you would a person. She can be stiff at times, but you will learn to cope with her.

I should begin by saying that I set up the camera and arranged all this without any assistance. That should prove I am competent. And I am under no duress unless one counts the duress of time.

Scottie sipped from a glass and cleared his throat. He looked old, but how should I describe him? Feisty is the best I can come up with. Certainly he was still a big man.

I trust you like the camp. It is different from when you visited with your father as a child. It is now all yours including everything you find in and on it, along with a few other things that are elsewhere, like what you found in the bank.

You are no doubt asking yourself why I have given you these things. It is a bit complicated. Our lives are intertwined more than you know. You do know your father was my friend. He was my only real friend in Cherry Ridge and he always made time for me when I came to town. He was a lousy fisherman, but a decent and honest man. We always had a good time when we were together.

What you probably don't know is that his mother, your grandmother, took me in for a time when I was a youngster and had no place to live. She was always very kind to me and to my mother. I have come to regret not repaying her when she was alive. I was too busy ... I was always too busy doing more important things, or so I thought.

You will remember our talking for a while after your father's funeral. I was very pleased to hear what you said earlier during your eulogy. I regret not having a relationship with my son so that he would speak of me as you did your father. I also could tell how much you loved your grandmother. Afterwards I began to take more interest in you. I had already seen to it that you got the grant to start your business . . .

"What?" I said to the screen. "The grant? The Magnus Foundation grant? You were responsible for that?" I was stunned.

Scottie continued to speak and I was missing words. "Julia, stop and back up 15 seconds." Julia did as I requested.

It is easy to give you the camp. The little rented shack where I lived with my mother was on the property. When I got the chance, I bought it along with the whole damn hill. About three square miles. The history of the property showed that some of it belonged to your grandmother's ancestors back in the early 1800's. They tilled the south side. You will find a stone cross where they likely worshipped. I think they were swindled out of the land. By giving it to you the land is back in the right family."

Scottie paused as if his thoughts had gone elsewhere. *"I learned a lot about you and I decided you are the one to redeem me. Chris, I spent a very full life, but not a good one. I accumulated a very large fortune, not always by the most ... by the most, uh, ethical means. If I did any good with the money it was by accident.*

I failed as a husband and father and in countless other ways. Now I am giving you a blessing ... and a burden. The blessing is great wealth. The burden, too, is great wealth, the responsibility that comes with it, a responsibility I never understood, but I am confident you will.

A longer pause.

Pierpoint has worked hard to assure that this gift took place before I expired. 'Expired,' that's Pierpoint's word. Like a license that has run out and can't be renewed.

Another sip from the glass.

He is confident that it is protected from the scavengers who will come after my estate. My offspring—save one—cannot be trusted, but Pierpoint can be. He is a dull man, but he is capable and scrupulously honest and I have paid him millions over the years. Turn to him if you need to, but rely first on your own instincts.

That's about it. I wish I could see the look on your face now and as you explore the property. There will be surprises. Leave no stone unturned. I wish I could watch you over the coming years. Maybe I can? No doubt I will soon know.

One more thing, no, two. There is single malt Scotch sitting on the counter. Raise a glass to me, no, not to me, to the future good you will do for me. And there is a Morgan in the barn. Your dad loved that car. Crank it up for us, will you?

I stared at the darkened screen for I don't know how long. My heart was pounding. My body was shaking. I took in two or three deep breaths. Thoughts swirled through my head. Am I in some extended dream state? Had I been drugged? Is this fantasy? Slowly I slumped from the chair onto the carpeted floor next to Gretchen. I hugged her close. She looked at me with her big eyes. I said: "Sweetie, I'm scared. I'm not sure what is happening but I am pretty sure our lives have changed forever." I decided to find the Scotch.

The 30-year-old Glenfiddich was bracing, especially neat. I rarely drank, especially since my military days. There had been far too much of that in my family. Nevertheless, I could appreciate smooth whisky, a friendly St. Emilion or a well-brewed lager. I poured a second shot into the water glass I had found in the cupboard. This time I ran the tap water. It looked clear so I poured some over the whisky.

I surveyed the room. It was sparse. The workspace bordered on a series of cabinets against one wall. I could see that one case held weapons. In front of the cases was a large brown leather sofa with a blanket resting on it. These items faced the kitchenette where I was standing. Sink, refrigerator, cook top, microwave and a few cabinets. I opened a few doors and found very little and nothing unusual. There were several more cherry wood boxes containing the same rare Scotch and a few bottles of XO cognac. Scottie had good taste.

There was a small island with cabinets, a countertop and a single stool. A television monitor resided in the island directly across from the sofa. No oven, no dishwasher. In the front corner opposite the work space there was a wooden table, simple pine by the looks of it, and a single chair.

The entire back third of the room was empty. To the left of the kitchen area there was a wide doorway. I assumed it might lead to a bedroom and a bathroom. I entered and found a toilet, a sink, a shower stall and laundry equipment to the right. The rest of the space, to the left, was taken up with a sophisticated array of technology: household mechanicals to one side, computer equipment to the other. Between the two areas there was a windowless door with a peephole through which I could see the storage sheds. There was no bed, no sleeping area.

I turned my attention to the cabinets across the way. There were only a handful of books at the top. Nearly all were scientific reference books. No dictionary, no Bible, no anything to indicate Scottie's reading preferences. There were eight framed, signed, glossy photos. I immediately recognized a young Willy Mays, Satchel Paige, Winston Churchill, and Ernest Hemingway. I couldn't identify the others.

There was a framed snapshot of a young girl, maybe 13 or 14 years old. There was a photo of four men and a woman in front of a yacht. The first two letters of the yacht's name appeared behind the people: HA. Maybe Hawaii? Pairs of initials had been hand printed alongside each of subjects. I assumed AF stood for Angus Ferguson. There is no way I could recognize him. The picture must have been taken 50 or more years ago. I removed both photos from their frames and looked at their backs. There was nothing written on them. All they said was Kodak paper.

The large, two-level, glass-doored cabinet of rifles and shotguns was not a surprising find in a woodland camp. The presence of two assault weapons in it was. I moved to the second piece, a highboy of drawers of varying depth. The highest and the one below it contained a variety of handguns. Some were older revolvers, most were semi-automatics. I gingerly picked up one, then a second. Both were fully loaded.

Except for the bottom drawer, the rest of the cabinet contained ammunition, holsters, and cleaning tools. The bottom drawer, the deepest, was nearly filled with letters, address books, notebooks and what looked like journals or diaries. I was tempted to settle on to the floor and begin reading. The first two letters I grabbed were written in French, the third in what looked like Russian. It was the same with the journals. No linguist, I moved to the third cabinet.

In the top drawer were architectural drawings, schematics and sketches. The drawings on top seemed to be for the building I was in and the barn. The next drawer was not nearly so full. On one side were vehicle titles and transfers; on the other side were tax and historical documents related to the property.

The next drawer had my heart pounding once again. It contained layers of velvet trays holding gemstones: diamonds, emeralds and rubies. All cut but none in settings. Hundreds of them. Tiffany himself would be envious. I was stupefied.

Finding more greenbacks in the two bottom drawers was almost anti-climactic. I was already overwhelmed.

After a few staggering minutes I called out: "Julia? Are you listening?"

Her reply came immediately: "I am."

I began to engage her in conversation. It quickly became clear that she was far more than a sophisticated security system. She had an advanced level of artificial intelligence that I had only seen in movies. She was downright scary. I began to question her about her identity, capabilities and functions.

She called herself an "Angus Model 7," the successor to an "Angus Model 6," named Uncle Andy. Uncle Andy manages the garage and its activities. The garage, she said, contains vehicles on the first floor and Angus' workshop on the second. I asked if I could see inside the garage and she said I could. Her monitor broke into two sections. One showed a variety of vehicles, the other a well-lit, elaborate array that looked more like a laboratory than a tinkerer's shop.

I asked her what would happen if she had a malfunction. She said she routinely runs system diagnoses on herself and all the camp sub-systems. She said that her clone and replacement parts are in the utility room. She said the camp is fully independent: the camp and its state-of-the-art systems are entirely "off the grid."

Was Scottie a survivalist? A paranoid schizophrenic? I surely did not know. The one thing I was certain about was that Angus "Scottie" Ferguson was a man of achievement and mystery, and I was almost certain that more mysteries were to come. In essence, he had told me just that.

At the end of my dialogue with Julia I made a facetious reference to Star Trek. I asked if she had a "Prime Directive." To my surprise, she said she had four. I asked her to state them. She replied: "1) Obey the commands of Angus Ferguson; 2) Protect the Property; 3) Avoid detection; and 4) Obey the commands of Christopher St. James."

No doubt the last had been recently added.

I had lost track of the time. More than two hours had passed. I asked Gretchen if she wanted to go out. She had clambered on to the sofa and was more-or-less asleep. Her tail twitched when I spoke to her; otherwise, she made no effort to move. Afternoon naps were her specialty.

I made a decision. "Julia? Can you make a phone call? I would like to speak with J. Pierpoint Wadsworth, Sr." Before I could tell her the number, it popped up on the monitor.

I told Pierpoint that I was calling from the camp. I told him about the DVD. He said he had a copy and had viewed it. He didn't directly mention the wealth Angus had talked about, but he reiterated that everything in the camp is mine. I told him I had found some documents that I didn't comprehend (a vast understatement). He also advised that I should hire an attorney so there would be no conflict of interests.

He then said the estate would take time to go through probate. "We are talking about an *estate* worth at least a billion dollars. I emphasize estate because I don't know how much Angus gave you, squirreled away or whatever. And I don't need to know. I was his attorney for nearly forty years but I can't say I really knew him. I know almost nothing about his early years. He was truly a man of secrecy. Perhaps you will learn more about him."

Pierpoint said Scottie had bequeathed a portion of his estate to a grandchild, but Pierpoint's people had been unable to locate her. There would be the heavy estate taxes and any challenges brought by other family or third parties. The extent of Angus' family was unclear. Another portion of the holdings was to go to employees. A third portion was to go the Magnus Foundation, which Angus had begun funding five years earlier.

A single bequest was to *me* with a specific caveat. The bequest was the ownership of Auracle Media, which Angus had acquired only a year ago. The caveat was that I would be willing to head the Magnus Foundation. Since these and other holdings would require management during the interval before probate, a judge's order would be required to assume leadership.

I ended the conversation knowing I had acquired even more wealth and more responsibility, but I had learned very little more about my benefactor.

I felt very alone and isolated. Mom and Dad were the last of their generation and they were gone. My one sister had preceded them. No one had heard from my older brother in many years. The last time Dad knew his whereabouts was when Mom was near death. He called from some place in the Middle East. When I had settled Dad's estate his share was set aside.

I had never been a social magnet, but I had had some good, close friends over the years. My best friend from Cherry Ridge had died in a useless war. My service friends had scattered like my college friends that followed. And then, when my erstwhile marriage ended I had gone into a sustained funk that effectively cut me off from whatever social network I had.

At present, the best I could say is that I had good relations with my professional acquaintances, but I didn't hang out with or confide in any of them. There was only Gretchen. It would be fair for an objective person to say I was a depressed but functional loner. I decided that had to change, but now the prospect of doing so was muddled by the money. How could I know another's friendliness wouldn't be based on my wealth?

I asked Julia to call Maggie, a decision that I guess had been brewing all along.

"St. James Policy Research," she answered, "How can I help you?"

"Hello, Maggie, it's Chris. It's good to hear your voice."

"Huh?" she said, "You hear my voice almost every day."

"Yeah, well, this is kind of a different day. A lot has happened."

"You okay, Boss? You sound, uh, different yourself."

"Maggie, I need a really big favor. I need your help. I need you to come out here to Cherry Ridge right away for two, maybe three days. I know it can be hard with your mom and all, but you will get a big bonus ... and a big raise, too. If you need someone to stay with your mom I will gladly pay for it. Trust me, this will be a good thing."

She didn't hesitate: "I trust you, Boss. Tonight might be hard. Is tomorrow morning soon enough? My brothers are still home from college. They can see to Mom, but I may have to rent a car. We're sharing mine right now."

"Rent yourself the best car you can, Maggie. I mean it; the sky's the limit. Book a room in the Ridgeview Motor Inn. It's decent. If it's full try Milt's Motel. Bring some hiking clothes and that nice new summer suit you wore the last time we had VIP's in the office."

"Okay, I can do that. You noticed the suit, huh? Will you keep your phone on? I'll call you later, tonight, when I have things arranged, if that is okay."

I said, "Definitely, Maggie, the phone is on and will stay on. We'll talk later." We ended the conversation there. She hadn't asked me why I needed her to come. I guess she meant it when she said she trusted me.

I suddenly felt very tired. Despite the enticements of learning more about the place, about Julia, about the garage contents, all I wanted to do was get outside, get in the truck and return to reality. I left everything as it was except for the open bottle of Scotch. That came with me.

Reality was Ed Peck's Sunoco station and the Cherry Ridge convenience store next to it. I gassed up. I picked up some food items. We returned to the apartment. I was feeding Gretchen her dinner when my cell phone rang. The call was from the Cherry Ridge PD. Could I come by the station in the morning and speak with Chief Broadhurst? We agreed upon 10 AM.

I was trying to divert my mind by watching Rachel Maddow on television when Maggie called. She said she had made the preparations. She wanted to know if I had talked with Vincent. I said no, but that I would get in touch with him in the morning. I told her I had a 10:00 AM appointment. I told her to call me when she got to town and to head for the Cherry Ridge Inn next to the library on Ridge Street.

She asked, "Is there anything else I should know, anything else I should bring along?"

I said it was too complicated for the phone and that I would fill her in the next day. She could bring along a camera if she had one handy.

She said: "You know your phone has a camera, don't you?" then added: "Whatever is going on you sound really stressed and beat. You should get some sleep."

I said that was my goal, right after taking Gretchen out for her evening walk.

Chapter Two

Restless Night

I slept fitfully. Visions of pirates with swollen treasure chests, cloaked secret agents meeting in dark alleys, and fiendish talking computers flashed before me. The specter of an aged Scottie Ferguson kept turning into a snarling demon covered in vipers. "Redeem me. Redeem me. Beware the snakes. Beware the snakes," the figure repeated over and over again.

Finally, some clarity took hold. It was 5:15. A.M. I was agitated and sweating. The single sheet I had covering me was on the floor. So was Gretchen, probably miffed by my tossing about.

I tried to orient myself to my reality. What could great wealth mean? My mind did not go to big houses, travel, yachts. It did go to ending my worries about house payments, property taxes, and health insurance. There would be no more hemming and hawing about spending a few dollars. No more job insecurities, no nasty job applications, no need to go anywhere I didn't want to. No need to make a living!

I could have simpler luxuries: hire a masseuse, a cook, a chauffer. I could become eccentric and grow my hair like Howard Hughes or eat lobster and cherry pie three times a day. I could wear a new pair of socks everyday, like Jerry Lewis was said to do. If I wanted to. But except for maybe the masseuse I didn't want to.

These were simple things that would barely make a dent into the staggering amount of money I now had. It was way beyond my needs and limited desires. What would I do with it? What would, what could fulfill Scottie's desire that I redeem him as if I were his personal Christ?

My God! I had the power to intervene in people's lives and change them forever. Me, virtually alone! Is that a good thing? Shouldn't people be allowed to lead their lives, fall, get up and start again? Is there some magic formula that could tell me to give them this much but not that much? There were no simple answers. I took some satisfaction in realizing a lesser person might say to hell with Scottie's mandate altogether, but I also knew a greater one might know the answers. I stumbled into the shower and let the cool water wash over me, all the while trying to be sure the preceding 24 hours had really happened.

I thought I might as well eat something. I made some toast and opened the peanut butter and jam I had purchased the night before. Naturally, I dropped a well-slathered slice on the floor. Why must it always fall jelly side down? That's surely reality. I employed the bachelor's five-second rule, scooped it up and made two sandwiches. I poured a glass of milk. I turned on the TV to TCM and settled on to the couch. Gretchen urged me to make space for her. I did. I reached for my laptop and opened the e-mail. I decided I would write Vincent (don't call me Vince or Vinnie) DeSantis.

Vincent De Santis and the St. James Policy Research Center

I had lucked upon Vincent De Santis in a curious way. It was closing in on four years ago, about two weeks before the first Tuesday in November. I was clearing the debris left on my doorstep by electioneering canvassers when a tall, heavyset young man with wild, dark curly hair approached. He had his own collection of flyers and was wearing a partisan button. He called out genially, "Sir, nice day isn't it? Can you spare a few minutes?"

"I can if you have a spare campaign button," I said, "I collect them."

"I don't have a spare, but you can have mine. I can get another."

In the next half hour or so we sat on my steps sharing a couple of beers. I learned much about Vincent, including why he didn't want to be called Vince. His mother had named him after her favorite saint, Vincent de Paul. From time to time she would remind him "You are Vincent of the Saints, not Saint Vinnie."

In a less than saintly manner he was living with his girlfriend while he completed his dissertation in political philosophy. He didn't really like the political wars, but he had some family connections so canvassing was a way to earn some extra money.

He was refreshing to me. He wasn't driven by a particular ideology but rather by the study and explanation of how ideologies reify and take hold. Some of the things he said could be taken as to the right, others as to the left and some were midstream. I liked him and I, too, had studied political science so we talked with some ease.

We parted with the agreement that it would be good to continue talking some time, but neither of us suggested concrete plans. Consequently I was surprised a few weeks later when he reached me by phone. First he wanted to be sure I remembered him. When I said I did, he said he felt he had an almost final draft of his dissertation. "Maybe you would read it some time?" he asked.

I told him the only dissertation I had ever completely read was my own. The next day a copy of his manuscript was inside my storm door. It was no Patterson page-turner, but over the next few days I managed to get through it more easily than I had expected. Fundamentally, it was a treatise centered on the role of government based on the difference between wants and needs. It was strongly influenced by Herbert Marcuse whose writings I had dipped into.

Vincent wrote with unusual clarity for an academic. He didn't linger over obvious points and he didn't pad his content with marginal references. That was good because I had never grasped the literature at his level and lesser-known references would be lost on me.

Several weeks later Vincent called to thank me for reading his work and to tell me that a couple of my comments had been helpful. He owed me at least a dinner or a bottle of scotch.

I asked him if he had landed a job. He said no, the economy was taking its toll on new hires. He could only find adjunct work. He was concerned that he would have to turn to family connections and take a state job, but even that wasn't plausible given cutbacks and layoffs.

I decided to take a chance. I told him that I had recently landed a sizable grant to establish what I was calling St. James Policy Research Center, a name suggested to me by my sponsoring foundation. I told him I would need an assistant director. I told him I could pay him a little more than what a first year assistant professor would make.

He didn't reject me out of hand so for the next half hour I gave him the background:

Some months earlier I had received a letter from the Magnus Foundation asking me to apply for a grant specifically to do policy research. It was more or less a Request For Proposal but somehow it read like it was written for me.

At the time I was scrambling to make ends meet. I was teaching two courses at two different area colleges as an adjunct instructor. I was doing policy research for two clients referred to me by a professional acquaintance. And I was trying to pick up dimes and quarters doing general freelance writing.

At first I thought it was a joke or maybe a scam. RFP's just don't get addressed to unaffiliated individuals with little professional standing. I checked to be sure there was indeed such a foundation. When I learned there was, I called a contact number and I was assured the request was legitimate.

At minimum, I thought, I could fill out the response. If nothing more it would be a good exercise in grant writing. I had done a few in the past with mixed success.

It took me less than a weekend to put the submission together. I had already formulated an idea where a center would strive to do historical, bibliographic, non-partisan research on various sorts of public issues, from the grassroots to the tall trees. My thought was to employ advanced graduate students to perform the detailed research, and then collectively produce reports.

I sent the proposal off on a Monday morning. On Friday I received a registered letter confirming I had "won" the grant. A few notes even enhanced the funding by including items I had neglected. An enclosure outlined what I had to do to manage the finances and file reports. The money would begin to flow as soon as I established a proper account. And it did.

I had found an office site, negotiated for office equipment and I was in the process of trying to solicit a staff. An ad was to come out in the next edition of "The Chronicles of Higher Education" and other publications.

It was almost as simple as that, which, of course, was astounding. Such things don't happen.

Vincent felt the same way. I could tell he was dubious about it all. Still, he said he would think about. An hour later he called again. I remember his words: "This is weird, Chris. But I tend to believe in serendipity but it is only good when you recognize it. I will take a chance. When do I start?"

Vincent,

Please don't accept a job until we talk. Trust me, I am going to make you a life-changing offer you won't want to refuse. It is serendipity all over again, in a bigger way!

Maggie won't be in this morning. I asked her to drive out here for a few days to help me out. Big stuff is happening. And I mean BIG! I will fill you in Monday if not sooner.
Chris

Again, I was asking to be trusted. Reaching out was not something I did easily.

I raised the volume on the TV. The African explorer was talking about shooting elephants in his pajamas. That line always made me chuckle. Gretchen had begun snoring. I leaned against her and tried to get lost in the antics of Groucho, Chico and Harpo.

Mel Reeves, Chief Broadhurst

Once ready to meet the day, I drove to Millie's without Gretchen. I left her behind because I figured the place would be hopping and I had to see Broadhurst at 10:00. I had to park half a block away. Millie's was indeed busy, but neither Millie nor Willy was visible. Everybody had something to say about "the incident on Hemlock."

I was trying to pay for a bagel and coffee when Mel Reeves motioned to me. Our history dated back to when I first entered high school. I had shyly brought him a story. Instead of gracefully showing me the door he had sat down with me, read it, edited it, and printed it. For the next several years he took my writing seriously. Sometimes he would be critical, but he was never harsh. He taught me how to be my own critic, and rewrite until I got it right. I was a year out of high school when I stopped writing for him. It wasn't his decision and it wasn't really mine. It was, I know now, the depression.

Mel was wearing his usual: stained white shirt, red suspenders and a red bow tie. A classic throwback to an era that predated him. In cold weather he would wear a grey fedora. It called out for a placard that said, "PRESS." After the usual bantering, Mel got into it.

"I saw you talking with Chub yesterday. I can't help but ask if you saw or heard anything."

I responded by summarizing what I had told Chub and asking if there was anything new on the case, specifically, had they found the woman.

"Maybe what you heard was the attacker ... No, they haven't found her. They can't even be sure of her identity —no ID papers, no blood to match with— but I can't see where it could be anyone other than the new teacher. Broadhurst is beside himself. It's his first real mystery and I don't think he has a clue to what happened or why. I did learn that Mrs. Morgan said there were drapes missing. The theory is that the perp rolled the body into them and carried it off."

"Perp," I thought. That's TV for you. "What about her car or prints?" I asked.

"No car, no weapon, no personal effects other than a suitcase with some clothes and the kid's stuff. No photos. Icky said the car was a blue SUV. He said he doesn't know cars, just bikes. He said she was really nice. Gave him $20 and asked if he would come back and help her when her stuff arrived. The sheriff's forensic crew dusted for prints and took Mrs. Morgan's and Icky's, but nothing's been learned as of this morning. Of course, some people are pointing at Icky. They say if they'd locked him up years ago this wouldn't have happened."

I had no particular reason to defend Icky. Still, I found myself saying: "Icky didn't do it. He isn't capable of doing something like that."

"Yeah," Mel said, "I agree with you. Still, people talk."

"They shouldn't," I snapped, "He's as much a part of Cherry Ridge as any of them. More so than some."

Mel seemed rebuked. "Well, yeah … It's good to see you, but I have to get to the office. The mayor and Broadhurst both asked if we could get an edition out early to calm people down. Some people are worried there's a slasher on the loose —well, there probably is at that."

"It's good to see you, too, Mel. As it is, I have to see Broadhurst myself and then go out and check out some land."

"Whoa right there, buddy. What's this about seeing Broadhurst?"

I told him I had gotten a call and that I thought he wanted to follow up on what I'd heard the other night. I said Broadhurst offered to come by, but I thought it better not to have the Chief's car outside my place. As he said, people talk.

I started to leave when Mel said: "Did you say you are buying land here? Is there a story in it?"

I said I already have the land, Scottie Ferguson's Brampton Woods.

"Whoa! Scottie Ferguson! Now there is a name I have not heard in a very long time. Didn't know he was still alive. Didn't know he owned those woods. Give me the story."

"Later, Mel," I said, "I shouldn't keep the chief waiting."

I walked the block and a half to the village building and entered the door marked CRPD. I was a little early but Broadhurst didn't make me wait. I had only met him once, back at the time of Gretchen's heroics. He showed no sign of remembering that.

He offered me a seat. I placed my driver's license and business card on his desk. His expression suggested he thought that action was odd; nevertheless, he picked them up and looked at them. "This is your home address? You don't live here in Cherry Ridge? Officer Simmons says you grew up here, went to school with him."

I wasn't sure if he was asking me or telling me. "That's right. I keep an apartment in a building I inherited from dad, and yes, Chub, er, Curt, was a year behind me in school. We played ball together."

"You are here for the balloon thing? You're here early."

"Yes," I said, "and for a personal matter." Despite having said the matter was personal, I told him what it was: "I recently acquired some land outside the village and I want to take a look at it."

"Your place at 60 Poplar backs on to 57 Hemlock" the Chief said flatly, looking at a notepad, "That is where the incident occurred. Officer Simmons' notes say you were at your apartment the night before last and heard and saw something that might be of use to our investigation."

"I don't know how useful it is, but as I told Curt, I had reason to be in the backyard and I heard what sounded like a noise from a trash can and I noticed the side porch light was on."

What time was that?"

"I guess it was about 9:30, give or take five minutes."

"You know that because?"

"I made sure my dog had peed, went inside and I was in bed a few minutes later. The last time I looked at the clock it was 9:50."

"Are you sure it sounded like a trash can? Could it have been a car door or something else?"

"I guess it could be a number of things but it sounded like an old metal trash can."

"Okay," he said dismissively. "If you think of anything that might help us you will contact us, right?"

"Sure," I said.

"Oh, one more thing," he said, echoing Columbo, "Do you know Ms. Cassandra Cross?" I said I had never heard the name until yesterday.

I pulled out my phone as I left the cop shop. I had it off while I was inside and, sure enough, Maggie had called. "Boss, I thought you promised to keep your phone turned on? I am on my way into the diner. See you there."

Maggie Arrives

Millie was at the front register as I entered the diner. She motioned me near and in a teasing, sing-voice said: "There's a pretty young girl waitin' for you. She seems reeeeallly nice."

I wondered if I blushed a bit when I said defensively: "She works for me, Millie."

Millie rejoined: "I bet she does!"

The place had thinned out some since I was in earlier, but it was still chatty. Courtesy of Millie, Maggie was in the same center booth I had been in a day earlier. She smiled when she saw me. She was dressed for the weather in cargo-style shorts, a white tee shirt emblazoned with a jazz festival graphic and her ever-present sneakers. This day they were tied with pink laces. Her hair was pulled back in a ponytail, not unlike July 4th when I was at her home and played volleyball with her and her brothers. I had never been so glad to see her.

"I'm sorry you had to wait for me. I had to keep an appointment with the police chief."

"You what?" she said. "Are you in trouble with the cops? Did you get a ticket?"

"No, no trouble. I just needed to talk with them about an incident that happened near my apartment. I think they are talking to everyone they can."

"You mean you know something about the murder of that woman? That's all everyone here is talking about."

It took me a minute to explain my peripheral connection to the incident. Millie came over and asked what she could get us. Did the young lady want another raspberry iced tea? Maggie said she was okay. Millie lingered as if she was expecting something. An awkward few seconds passed before I realized what she was waiting for.

"I'm sorry Millie. Millie Logan, meet Maggie O'Connor. Maggie is the executive vice president of my new company." Maggie's eyes lit up.

"It is very nice to meet your Maggie," exclaimed Millie, "Executive vice president! At such a young age! How wonderful."

Now the usually unflappable Maggie was flapped. She was blushing. Millie cast me a wry glance as she said, "Well, I will leave you two to conduct your business. Just sing out if you need anything."

As soon as Millie was out of earshot, Maggie queried: "Executive vice president? Of what? When did that happen?"

Instead of answering, I motioned to her to follow me outside. Once on the sidewalk I said, "This place is full of big ears. It's best we talk in private. We need to fetch Gretch. Then I can fill you in on everything. Where's your car?"

She pointed to a spiffy convertible with its top down. "You said I could rent anything I wanted to," she answered with a touch of uncertainty.

I responded a little too enthusiastically: "Great! I bet you look really good in it … See that black pickup? That's what I am driving. Follow me, it's only a few blocks."

I pulled up alongside the square block of park opposite the apartment. Maggie pulled up behind me. I told her it looked like rain was coming so she had better put the top up. She pulled a bag from the car and joined me. "So this is where you grew up?" she asked, pointing at the apartment building.

"No, this is the building my dad inherited shortly before he died and then it passed to me. Look across the park. Do you see the house on the corner, the one with the wrap-around porch? That was my parents' place for their last 20 years or so. I was out of school when they bought it so I only stayed there on visits. When I was growing up we lived in a couple of different places." Turning back toward the apartment I continued: "This isn't much of a place, but it's better than motels in most ways."

I was fumbling for the door key when Maggie said: "Speaking of better than motels, I haven't had a chance to tell you something, Boss. I had no problems making arrangements to get here, except for one thing." She paused.

"What's that?"

"Well, does this apartment have an extra bedroom or at least a comfy sofa? Both the places you told me to check into are full up, something about people coming in for a balloon festival. Unless you know of some place else, the nearest vacancies are 10-12 miles away. I uh, I don't know how you feel about it."

I opened the door. "Gretchen will protect me," I said. "It is part of her job description. We'll work it out."

Gretchen was blocking the open doorway. She didn't look like much of a deterrent what with Wally, her stuffed walrus, in her mouth. She never traveled without at least one of her brood. Carrying one in her mouth was her petulant signal to me that she was anxious; but in an instant, seeing Maggie changed her angst to ecstasy. Gretchen was never hesitant to show her affection to someone she cared about. Maggie was barely in the room before she was on the floor rolling about with Gretch. It got pretty noisy. Finally, I said, "C'mon Gretchen, you probably have to pee."

"Me, too," said Maggie. I pointed to the back of the apartment.

Once settled in I tried to tell Maggie all that happened in an orderly fashion. She listened intently and nearly silently until I got to the findings in the safety deposit box. "Omygawd!" she shouted, "Omygawd! You *are* rich!"

I told her that is only the start of it. I told her that when I got to what I thought would be a shack in the woods I found something more like a survivalist's compound with gobs of money and valuables stashed in it. I told her she would see for herself in a short time if she were willing. "Sure I'm willing. I can't wait," she said, "Can we go right now?"

I was eager to go, too, but first I needed her to answer a question or two. I explained that it was important to keep everything private. I told her I feared the consequences of it getting out in public, kind of like what some big lottery winners face. Would she keep what she had learned and would learn in confidence? She adamantly said she would.

Next, I asked her if she was willing to have her life change. I told her not to answer hastily. There could be many demands on her. "Does this have something to do with what you told Millie? That I am the executive vice president of your new business? What new business? Is it for real? I don't know why you'd want me, but count me in ... so long as I can take care of my mom ... and you don't ask me to kill somebody or something. You won't, will you?"

I laughed at the last, then turned serious: "There are many reasons I want you ... for this job, Maggie," I said. "For one thing you're smart. You know things I don't. You can do things I can't. This is all going to get very complicated, no doubt more than I can imagine. Most of all, I believe I can trust you. Gretchen trusts you. Gretchen has great instincts about people ... .How about a salary of $100,000 a year, full benefits and a company car for starters?"

"Omygawd, Chris, do you mean it? So much? I could, I could just kiss you!" It was the first time she had ever called me Chris. She threw her arms around me in a bear hug and did kiss me ... on the cheek. "Gretchen, you have the bestest papa in the whole wide world."

The money and all had made at least one person happy, at least for the moment. To bring us back to earth, I suggested we make some sandwiches to take with us.

The three of us were loading ourselves into the truck when Mrs. Dumbrille came out of the adjoining apartment. "Chris," she called out, "I haven't had a chance to talk with you since you arrived. Have you heard what happened at Martha Morgan's?"

I said I did. I said it sure was a tragedy. I said I was late for an appointment and that I would catch up with her later. Mrs. Dumbrille could turn a one-minute dialogue into an hour-long soliloquy. Inside the truck I tilted the mirror. I could see her eyes following us as we pulled away. She definitely was not looking at me.

I turned on the street that parallels Ridge St. Our conversation veered back and forth between the possible murder and the "Scottie Matter." As we neared an intersection, I said, "That brick building on the corner was my grade school."

"It's really old," Maggie said. "St. Joseph's. 1893. Were you there then?" she giggled. "Is that your church across the street? It's a pretty church. Were you an altar server?"

"Yes," I replied, not mentioning the anger the church had prompted a day earlier.

Moments later I pulled into the village's one small strip mall. I handed Maggie a list and a hundred dollars. "See if they have this stuff and anything else you might think we could need. The office-type supplies at the camp are almost non-existent."

A few minutes later Maggie returned saying, "Cool store. I could have looked around for half an hour. Here, try this red licorice. It's really good."

It began raining as we reached Holy Sepulchre Cemetery. The cemetery made Maggie reflect: "Every time we passed a cemetery when I was a kid my dad would say 'That's a popular place, people are dying to get in there.' He'd laugh as if he had never said it or heard it before." Then she giggled again.

As we entered "the tunnel through the trees," Maggie continued to think about her dad. "He would have loved this. He loved nature, the woods."

"You must miss him a lot."

"Every minute, every day," she said, " Oh, look, there's a ground hog!"

"They call them woodchucks out here, Mag. A ground hog is sausage or that creature in Pennsylvania."

"Yeah," she said. "Bill Murray."

"Yeah, and Andie MacDowell looking her best." Like you, I thought.

Maggie Sees Scottie's Place

Julia challenged us as we got out of the truck near the gate. Maggie was immediately impressed. I told Julia who she was, Julia said her usual "Fine" and asked that Maggie go through the screening. This time I asked Julia to open the gatehouse. Inside were a snowmobile, an ATV and containers of gasoline. "I guess it's good to know these things are here." I said.

"Do you know how to operate them?" Maggie asked.

I replied: "No, but we can learn, can't we?"

Once outside the camp, Maggie noted a couple of things I had ignored the previous day. She pointed out small trickles of water coming down the side of the cliff. It appeared the trickles came together under the graveled parking area then flowed into a pond or pool on a terrace well below where we stood. "Cool," she said.

Julia let us in. I gave Maggie a 30-second tour before excusing myself to use the bathroom. I figured she would check out the computer or the cabinets, but when I re-entered the main room I didn't see her. The center metal stairway had been pulled down and she was atop it. "Boss, have you been up here? C'mon up, there's room for two."

I climbed the open stairs gingerly. As I neared the platform at the top Maggie moved to one side to make room for me. "Where did you find the binoculars?" I asked. "They were just hanging here. Have a look." Although it was raining, I could see the outline of Cherry Ridge in the distance. I could see the castle to the northeast. I could only imagine what a clear sky might offer.

I scrambled down to find Gretchen looking up, wondering what we were doing. When Maggie hit the floor she asked: "So where is all the loot?"

I first showed her the drawers of money. Her eyes widened. "Are you sure it's all real?" she exclaimed.

"I have no reason to think it isn't," I responded. "Look at what's in here."

"Omygawd, omygawd!" she whooped, seeing all the gems. She began to barrage me with questions. They all boiled down to "Where did it come from and whaddya going to do with it?"

To which I said, "That's what we have to find out."

When she'd calmed down, we turned to the paperwork in the cabinets. "These bonds could be worth millions, Boss. They are bearer bonds."

I looked at her quizzically as she continued, nonstop. "That means they are negotiable. They accrue interest. Anyone who possesses them can turn them into cash. They are probably old. Back in the 1980's or 1990's, I forget which, the government outlawed new ones, but the existing ones remained good. Some countries still allow them. It is going to take a while to find out what they are worth. Probably the best thing to do is take a few samples and get them checked out." I agreed, so she selected a few and put them in an envelope and marked the outside.

I asked her to turn her attention to Julia. Julia balked until I instructed her to assist Maggie, including opening encrypted files. Within minutes smart Maggie and super smart Julia were fully engaged.

Every so often Maggie would say something like "awesome" or "very cool." Occasionally she would hit the keyboard. Occasionally she would call out with some finding she had made. She would note it and move on. I was meticulously unloading the weapons when she cried out: "Boss, come quick! I think I hit the mother lode!"

She had. She had found a list of Scottie's numbered bank accounts. They were numerous. Most resided in Switzerland, Austria, and Liechtenstein. A few were in the Caribbean. One was in Costa Rica. Maggie said she didn't know much about them, but she thought that the money could be moved without identification or signature. She said that some could be entirely anonymous while with others only a few senior bank staff would know the account owner's name. Clearly, Scottie had gone to great lengths to make a great portion of his wealth unknown to anyone — until now. Maggie seemed more excited than I was. That was because I was next to numb.

We were laughing about getting greedy and finding still more valuables when Maggie said: "Yeah, there must be a vault somewhere." In a stern but joking tone she commanded: "Julia! Tell us where the vault is."

We both laughed even harder until Julia responded: "The vault is in the back of the building. Shall I unlock it?" "Yes!" we said in unison.

Through the magic that was Julia, the center panels on the back wall moved forward, then slid to the sides, exposing a door much like the building's entry door. It then slid open. I nearly tripped over Gretchen as I chased after Maggie to see what was inside.

At first I thought Scottie had cut into the cliff to make his vault, then I realized it was a natural cave. I had known since childhood that there were caves in the area. I had even explored a few but none went far into the hills and none went downward like Howe Caverns. When we were kids we called them bear caves or fox dens.

We both stopped short of entering and looked at each other. Clearly, Maggie was more intrepid than I. "Is there a flashlight?" she asked.

Before I could answer she stepped into the black void. Instantly lights came on. They extended at least 40 feet into the hillside. I followed her. The cavern was a good 10 feet wide and seven feet high but to me it was uncomfortably small. There were fissures all around and a hissing sound. I remembered Scottie's caution: "Beware the snakes." Is this where they are? Did Scottie have some kind of defenses like in an Indiana Jones movie? "Be careful, Maggie," I implored.

My imagination was running away with me. There were no snakes. No creepy-crawlies of any sort.

"No food in the camp, huh?" Maggie said. "It looks like there is enough here for an army." Along one wall there were shelves holding tightly sealed containers of staples and dried foods. Along the opposite wall were stacks of plastic-wrapped cartons of toilet tissue, matches, candles and other paraphernalia. Everything was carefully labeled.

At the very back, where the roof curved downward, tarps covered whatever was there. I was beginning to feel a bit claustrophobic and wanted to turn back. Before I could, Maggie pulled at a tarp. Light reflected off a wall of yellow. Of course, I thought, what valuable had been missing from this odd chest of treasures? Gold.

Maggie wrested one of the bricks from the stack. This time she remained calm. "I think a standard brick of gold bullion weighs about 30 pounds," she said, "That's about 480 ounces. Do you know what the price of gold is today? Something over $1500 an ounce, I think. If I'm right, each one of these babies is worth over $700,000!" We didn't even try to count how many there were.

We returned to the main room strained for more we could say about our discoveries. They were overwhelming. Gretchen was oblivious to them and to our roller-coaster behavior. Job one for her was to get outside and pee. As I reached the door with her, Maggie asked if she could use my credit card. I got it out asking "How can you use it here?"

"Julia." she said, "We could do with doing something down-to-earth. This place needs some things and I am going to buy them on line. Trust me." The magic words.

The rain had lessened. It was humid, muggy. Gretchen seemed to need a little time so she wandered the property, avoiding the gravel. A rabbit made an untimely appearance and was quickly chased into a hole. Gretchen came back to me smiling. Yeah, she can smile, especially when she gets the best of a four-legged creature, or me for that matter. When we were finally back inside Maggie handed me my card. "Good timing. I am almost done," she said.

"So, are you going to tell me what you are buying?"

"There are no beds here. You just might want to spend the night some time, right, and all there is is that stiff leather couch. You can sure tell there has never been a woman in this place. So I made an executive vice presidential decision and ordered what you need."

"What, from where?" I asked, "How is it going to get here?"

"I am ordering from Sears. A queen-size bed, a double bed, mattresses, box springs, linens and blankets, a dresser and two nightstands. And towels and stuff for the bathroom and kitchen. And before you say it, none of it will be delivered here. It's being delivered to your apartment. Then we can bring it up here ourselves in your truck. I got the order in soon enough so that it should be delivered by noon tomorrow." She was very satisfied with herself.

"How much did you spend," was my knee-jerk reaction. "About $4,500, but does it matter, Mr. Moneybags? Besides, I have always wanted to buy 400 thread count sheets. Come feel the quality."

"Okay, as Julia seems prone to say, 'fine.' How about using that computer for something else? Can you use that cardstock to make up some temporary business cards for yourself? Just your name, title and 'Serendipity Ltd.' on it. Maybe a phone number if you can get Julia to come up with a secure line that she can re-route to your cell. I bet she can do it."

"Serendipity? Something good that happens accidentally. I like the sound of it. Do you want some cards for you, too, and maybe Vincent? He is going to be in this, isn't he? What title should I give him?"

She was racing ahead of me but I said okay, use the same phone number for all of us and give Vincent the same title.

As to my choice of the word serendipity, I thought the word fit up to a point. Everything seemed to be happening by accident. It would remain to be seen if the accidents would all be happy. Besides, I simply liked the word. It sounds classy beyond its meaning. Take out the "dip" and you have serenity, another nice word. I like "S" words like slush, swish, sluice, sleuth, sensual, salacious, saliva, salamander, and sufferin' succotash. Some are onomatopoetic; others are simply fun to say.

We had not stopped to eat and it was getting late in the afternoon. I got out the sandwiches and the drinks. Gretchen and I chomped away while Maggie multi-tasked. Until then I hadn't realized how quick she was with a computer. When the cards were finished, she handed me one. Gold lettering on black. I could not help but think how symbolic her choice of colors was.

We had been talking about checking out the barn. As the three of us walked toward it, Maggie said: "This is feeling so surreal. It is like a dream and a trip to Disneyland rolled into one. Thanks for letting me be a part of it, Boss." She paused. "It's not like I am anxious to leave, I'm not at all; but, do you think I can get back home by Saturday night? I need to let Mom know."

I said: " I don't see why not. You can go anytime you feel you need to."

"It isn't that I need to, but Friday is my birthday and Mom will want to have a party Saturday night. I already told her not to plan for Friday."

"Oh, I wish I had known! But if you do stay through Saturday morning, Gretchen and I will take you to the balloon festival."

"I'd like that. Big balloons on my birthday. I'll call Mom tonight. Can I tell her I am getting a promotion and a raise?"

"Sure, but try to keep the lid on the details, okay?"

Legacies of Cherry Ridge

By comparison to what we found in the main building, exploring the barn was a trip to a museum. After instructing Uncle Andy to let us in we found there were eight classic cars to match the paperwork we had found earlier. I don't think they were chosen for their high value, although each one would cost me, the former me anyway, more than I could afford. Four were American: a yellow '64 Studebaker Avanti, a red '56 Corvette, a red '07 Chrysler Crossfire, and a white '55 T-Bird. About the last, Maggie said, "That's like the one the mystery blonde drove in American Graffiti." I was surprised she would know the car or the film.

The four others were imported sports cars: a Porsche, the '54 Morgan 4-4 that Scottie had referred to, a Jag, and a soft top 1977 Triumph TR-7.

The last was promoted as the "shape of things to come." I'd had one briefly, a well-used one, when I was about 22. Someone had compared TR-7's to bad boyfriends: they never work, they smoke, they cost a lot of money, and they leave you flat right after you've fallen in love with them.

I thought finding the cars was out of place. It was obvious Scottie had done much to avoid drawing attention to the camp. Driving flashy cars that would stand out on any street was a contradiction. Then again, maybe they never left the grounds. I was pretty certain that, with Maggie's help, that would change.

In addition to the cars, the first floor also contained shelves of spare parts, mechanic's tools, a car lift, and a big Dodge Ram Hemi pickup with an unattached snowplow rig. Plus another snowmobile and an ATV. Maggie had to sit behind the wheel of each one of the cars. She wanted to find keys and see if any started, but I stalled her. "It is probably going to be a pain to get them registered, inspected and roadworthy," I said. "Don't be so negative," she said, "We can get it done."

A quaint, old-style lift took us to the second floor. It was the kind where you pull down on a rope to start the platform rising and pull up on it to descend.

The second floor was amazing in its own ways. There were four sections of different sizes. One held the once popular Shopsmith, a multifunctional machine, along with other woodworking tools. Another held metalworking tools and welding equipment. The third was devoted to equipment one would find in a chemistry lab. The final section contained electronics. All had cabinets and shelves containing parts and materials. Each had a long worktable with drawings and reference books. The chemistry area included a water supply and built-in basins. I wondered what concoctions Scottie had devised in this building?

Maggie, Gretchen and Me at the Apartment

It was past Gretchen's normal dinnertime, and she began doggedly hounding me. We decided we had been at the camp long enough. As we drove back across the gravel road, Maggie said, "I'm with Gretchie. What's for dinner? How about we stop and pick up some steaks and potatoes? I can cook, ya know."

Gretchen had her regular dinner, then waited impatiently aroused by the aroma of broiling beef. It turned out Maggie could indeed cook. She sautéed mushrooms and onions to spread over the Delmonicos. I even ate the broccoli she insisted on putting on my plate. It wasn't bad with the cheesy sauce she had made.

Gretchen got more than her share. She had two people to mooch from. Nevertheless, she still wanted to play the biscuit game. It was a simple one. I would break up four middle-sized Milk Bones into small pieces and hand feed them to her. No matter how many pieces I made, Gretchen would not stop expecting them until she had gotten all four. If I stopped at three and showed her empty hands, she would persist on pestering me. Only after she was sure she had gotten four and I showed her empty hands would she feel satisfied.

Maggie found the interaction amusing, but less so when Gretchen turned to her and slapped her bare leg with a paw. "Gretchen, that hurt."

"Gretchie, mind your manners," I said, "I think she wants you to give her a Milk Bone." I grabbed one out of a bag and handed it to Maggie. "Be sure you break it up." She did and all was well.

We had not spoken about the sleeping arrangements. I broached the subject. "There are some boxes in the back. Stuff from my dad's house. I think there are some linens and stuff. I'll change the bed and make up the couch for me."

"Let me do it," she said, "Why don't you take Gretchen for a walk before it gets too late?"

"Too late" was not in our lexicon when it came to Gretchie's walks. We had been known to wander about in the middle of the night. We both liked the stillness and the night air. Nevertheless, not having to change bedding was certainly an inducement.

The rain had finally halted and it occurred to me that Maggie might need some time without the two of us, so we stayed out quite a while. When we returned the couch was made up. Maggie was using her phone. She waved to us as we entered.

"Yes, mom. A promotion and a raise ... No I can't tell you any details right now, things are moving fast. What? ... Yes, it is nice here. Very quiet. Gretchen is a lot of fun. Chris, he's not so much fun." She cast me a sideways smile. "Just kiddin,' Mom. He's been the perfect gentleman ... Mom, let's not get into that ... No, mom, I'm not. You sure you're okay? Well, Dylan is reliable, but Sean can be so irresponsible . . .Good, I will call you tomorrow. Luv ya."

"Is everything okay back home?" I asked.

"Yes," she said. "She wants to know more about everything, but I didn't tell her much, like you said."

Cautiously I asked, "Did you tell her where you are staying?"

"Oh, yeah, no problem with that. She thinks I am safe because you're probably gay."

"WHA, WHA, WHAAAT???" I stammered. "Why would she ever think that? I'm not effeminate or ... " I didn't know what to say.

"Easy, Boss," she said. "It wouldn't matter if you're gay. And there is your lady friend from Philadelphia, right? Alexandra something? So I know different. It is just that Mom has this theory that if a man is close to 40 or more, lives only with a dog and has never been married, he must be a real loser, gay, or have serious commitment issues."

I let the reference to Alexandra pass. "Well, straighten out your mom, will you?" I sputtered, noticing the pun after the fact. "Besides, I have been married."

"You were married?" she said unable to suppress her surprise, "I didn't know. You've never said anything. Does Vincent know?"

The proverbial cat was out of its proverbial bag so I felt compelled to give her a brief summary of the events I had tried to bury. When I finished the story she said: "I have kind of wondered if maybe someone had broken your heart. I'm sorry you had to go through that."

"Maybe not so much my heart, Maggie, but certainly my trust," I said. "By the way, I don't think Vincent does know. And if you were to say I had a broken heart you know what he'd say? He'd say 'You need a new heart, Bob.' Get it?"

"Yeah, he would." she said, "He's funny, but sometimes he doesn't know when to stop."

Past *my* distant past, I probably should have let the conversation move on. Instead, I said "What about you? It only seems fair that you tell me some deep dark secret about your romantic past or present."

She giggled. It was not her joyful giggle but a self-conscious one. "No present, I'm too busy." I waited.

"There was this guy in college, Roger. He was a basketball player. Maybe you heard of him. I guess I thought he was the love of my life. After the crash he was there every day for about two weeks, then not so much. Then not at all. Mom and my brothers hate him for leaving me like that. But I figure if he couldn't take the bad with the good, I am better off for it."

"What about your time in New York, that must have ... "

She waved me off with her hand. "Just a bunch of greedy creeps on the make. Can I try some of your Scotch? Maybe it will help me sleep."

"Sure," I said, surprised at the request. I wondered if I had triggered a bad memory. "I'm going to get ready for bed myself. Once you're settled in I'll find out how this couch sleeps."

"No," she said, "I'll sleep here. I'm younger than you." I suggested we flip for the bed. She won and chose the couch.

A little while later I heard yelps, so I looked out from the bedroom. Maggie and Gretchen were bouncing about the living room. Gretchen was making playful growls and Maggie was laughing. She was wearing pink bunny slippers and Gretchen thought they were playing keep-away with stuffed animals.

Pragmatism

Maggie showered and dressed before I knew what day it was. When she heard me rouse, she called out that Gretchen had been out to pee, but still seemed to want something. I told her where to find the Breathbusters. She asked about making breakfast. By the time I was dressed, she had turned deli meat, eggs, cheese and onions into giant omelets. Good omelets. I noticed she was wearing the bunny slippers. "Gretchen now understands they are my stuffed animals, stuffed with my big feet," she said.

I asked her if she brought her suit and, if she had, would she mind changing into it. Ideas had been percolating in my head. I told her I wanted her to look spiffy, take the convertible and visit a real estate office, maybe two. I told her I wanted her to inquire about the ownership and possible purchase of the castle. "The castle? You're thinking of buying that old pile of bricks?"

"Maybe," I said, "It has some potential." I gave her a little more history as best as I knew it.

"Don't you think it is kind of rundown and creepy? There may be bodies up there, ghosts and who knows what."

"Do you believe in ghosts, Maggie?"

"Of course I do, I'm half Irish," she said.

"And the other half?"

"I'm a Polcat," she replied.

"You know polecat is another name for a skunk, don't you?"

"Yeah, but that's what my Dad called Mom, as in 'his little Polcat,' Polish Catholic. What about you?"

"English ... "

"That I can tell," she said.

" ... And German on my dad's side and English and Irish on my mother's. So I am a mutt, like Gretchen."

"Gretchen is no mutt; she's a pure sweetheart."

"And I'm not?"

We developed a plan for the day. Gretchen would stay the morning in the apartment. Maggie would visit with realtors. I would deposit some of the cash into the one other bank in town. I would also visit a different realtor, the one who handled my dad's house, and put the apartment building up for sale. We would then reunite at the apartment and wait for the Sears store to deliver. Next would be lunch at Millie's to catch up on the gossip. Then we would head to the camp for the rest of the day.

I was unknown to the bank manager, a recent arrival in town. He seemed discreet and tried to show little reaction when I gave him a million dollars in cash to deposit. He tried to advise me about investment options. I said maybe later, but for the moment I only wanted to make a simple deposit.

My stop at the realtor's didn't take long. They had all the information they needed. All I had to do was give them an asking price. They would fax a contract to my office.

I arrived back at the apartment just as the Sears guys were putting the last of the packages on the porch. Mrs. Dumbrille was present. She had agreed to sign for the delivery. I asked the guys if they would put the load into the pickup. There was hesitation until I said: "There's 50 bucks in it for each of you." They worked quickly. Mrs. Dumbrille tried to pump me for information. The most I told her was that I would be taking the stuff to a friend's camp.

I decided to give Vincent a quick call. He was eager to learn all he could but I put him off. I told him I had come into a lot of unexpected money that was going to mean changes. I asked him to keep quiet about it until Monday. He agreed to.

"By the way," Vincent said: "I took a call from Alexandra. I told her you were off for a few days, out at your hometown. She told me to tell you it was your loss. She didn't ask for your cell number. If she had I would have told her you never turn it on. Okay?"

Alexandra had been my friend—I guess that is the innocuous word—since college. We were completely different personalities but somehow we had maintained a relationship. I didn't see her during my brief marriage and I only heard from her a couple of times during her two marriages. Nevertheless, we would end up connecting again. She was a great remedy for when my bouts of depression would set in. She had a certain "naughty girl" charm that was only exceeded by her physical attributes.

For her part, I could only think she liked having a "Saint" James to cavort with. Before I got Gretchen I would sometimes visit her in Philadelphia where she worked in publishing, but I had only done so once since then. That didn't deter her when she was determined. She would cajole me into encouraging her to come to me.

It was 11:30 when Maggie arrived. She was glad to see the truck was loaded with the stuff. She wanted to know if I had hoisted it in myself.

While changing out of her suit, Maggie reported that both the real estate agents she had spoken to brought in their owners/managers. They seemed more than excited. I said they should: she looked like money in a town that has little of it.

She'd learned that the castle was in private hands and not active on the market. Both agents had provided about the same information. The asking price some years ago was $1.4 million, but it had last sold for about half that. Both sources said ideas for it had been tossed around but none had come to fruition. One agent said its needs are "mostly cosmetic." He spoke realestatease. I knew better without seeing it. Damage from water, vandalism, graffiti, and creatures. Maybe some theft.

The second said it was structurally sound but needed TLC. She thought the castle was quite a building for the right buyer and the right use. More realestatease, but a little closer to reality. Maggie left the second by saying they should find out all they could and call her ASAP.

"So it went well. Good." I said. She added that both agencies wanted to know about Serendipity. "I told them it was a private company led by a rich eccentric who was looking to make some investments."

So now I'm an eccentric! "Eccentric? When are you going to call me Scrooge McDuck?"

"Who?" she asked.

The booths were full when we arrived at Millie's. Both Logans were busy. One of the staff, Betsy, showed us into the seldom-used anteroom.

"What's good here?" Maggie asked.

I replied: "It's not haute cuisine, but it is all pretty good. They use good, fresh stuff. They haven't had a case of ptomaine or E-Coli or salmonella in weeks."

"Ha, ha, you're funny, not," responded Maggie.

Maggie was looking around the diner. "This sure is a cool old place. It's like an old movie set. They even have an old jukebox. Does it work?"

"Indeed it does," I said, "It gets used when it isn't noisy in here. Willy has several jukeboxes. He's a collector. He can take them apart, fix them and put them back together. He has more old records — 78's, 45's and LP's — than anybody I know. You can ask him anything about music and radio — so long as it was before 1970 — and he will have an answer for you. I think he has a web site now, but I have never looked at it. I should."

"Jukebox, that's a funny word," said Maggie.

"It comes from juke joint, a dive, the kind of place where the boxes first became popular."

"How do you know stuff like that? Did Willy tell you?"

"Probably. I like old things, old radios, old radio programs. Willy used to tell me about them. Not many people my age are interested."

"Willy isn't that old, how come he cares about that stuff?"

I told her Willy had been around records from before he could walk. His father had owned the local music shop where he also taught piano and guitar. When the shop went out of business Willy kept most of the stuff. Willy and Millie were long married by then. "I think Willy would have gone off to play his guitar or work in radio if it hadn't been for her. They were high school sweethearts. Really good people."

"How nice," Maggie said.

We were wondering where our waitress had gotten to when Maggie leaned toward me. "Don't look now, but those two people who just came in are people I talked to this morning. They'll recognize me."

"I don't think so, Maggie, you look very different now than an hour ago and it has been my experience that Cherry Ridgers are not all that observant. Put your reading glasses on and we will do some eavesdropping."

The pair of agents sat down with another couple. I recognized one as a local attorney. We couldn't hear much of what they said but it wasn't long before we heard "castle," "decay, "bricks," and "flashy young woman with a snappy car." It wouldn't be long before it was all over town that some outsider had inquired about the castle.

On our drive to the camp, Maggie asked me again about my interest in the castle. I admitted that although I had grown up in Cherry Ridge, I had never once been in it. It was in its death throes when I was in my teens. Some kids had taken swimming or dancing lessons there. Some had even gotten a part-time job, but I had not been one of them. Still, it held an odd fascination for me.

I told her maybe it could be a site for seminars or a research center or some kind of school. Maybe it could be a center from which to dispense the Scottie fortune. It couldn't hurt to investigate, could it?

I felt kind of odd when I said this. For two decades I had been trying to put Cherry Ridge beyond the reach of my rearview mirror. My parents' presence, then the lingering apartment and even Gretchen's notoriety had kept me bound. Now the Scottie thing had brought another tie, and what was I doing about it? Thinking about taking on even one more link and a big, dirty historic one at that!

Maggie was asking something about whether I really did plan to give most of the money away and how would I decide whom to give it to. Isn't there something I've always wanted to have? Finally, she said, "You aren't listening to me, are you?"

"I'm listening," I said, "Outside of owning the Yankees, I just don't have any answers. Not yet."

"You may not have enough to buy the Yankees, but you could buy the Mets. They stink! And I am a Mets fan."

As we toted Maggie's purchases from the truck, I found it nice to be doing something simple and practical. We worked easily together. She was willing and strong. At one point I noticed her wince. I asked her if she was hurt. "Oh, it's nothing. Sometimes my knee plays tricks on me. The docs said it would be prone to arthritis. It usually goes away quickly."

I couldn't help but look at her scarred knee and wonder about the other scars she had. Her long hair usually covered one on her neck, but with it pulled back it was visible. Just a trace of one ran across her forehead. I suspected there were more. She never talked about them, what she went through or the accident itself. No doubt the scars ran deep.

Maggie was musing about giving the place a name. Initially, Scottie's Camp didn't do it for her. We bandied about various names, but none led to an Eureka! moment. I mentioned "Farnhan's Freehold." It was lost on her, before her time. I tried to outline that wandering story about religious, race and Armageddon-like events until I realized that the only real similarities lay in the survivalist-like compounds. We finally decided that if it came to needing a name it should be Scottie's Place.

The bed frames went together quickly. We arranged the mattress and springs and placed the dresser and night stands. Maggie said, "Why don't you go find something else to do? Stare at the diamonds. Take Gretchen outside. I can finish in here." I was beginning to wonder just who was The Boss.

Reflections on Cherry Ridge

Gretchen and I wandered down by the pool of water. The sounds of frogs jumping made her curious. Although we were lower on the hillside, the change in angle allowed me to see more of Cherry Ridge through the trees.

It was not a rustbelt town. There wasn't that much metal. Maybe a dry-rot town? Except for the brick stores on Ridge Street and a few scattered churches, old wood dominated.

Historically and until post World War II, Cherry Ridge was a bustling village with potential. Now most of the business structures were empty or reduced to containing second-rate enterprises. The old mills were long gone, the handful of early 20th century factories were gone or abandoned. The housing was aged. Most of the few large homes had been cut up into apartments. The area population had remained fairly constant, but that was because newer homeowners had built on the hilltops and hillsides where family farms once flourished.

Local employment was limited. Many residents commuted to work at canneries, state prisons, colleges, and other endeavors. Only the presence of a growing regional hospital kept the local economy on life support. When I was a kid there were four to five doctors in town. The hospital now had over 50 affiliated physicians. Several were Asians, something new for the area. At least, the throwbacks might say, "they are educated professionals."

The area was still redneck, in the ominous meaning of that word. It was still virtually lily-white. In my youth, the migrant workers stopped coming to work the farms so there were no blacks except for a church sexton. There were no Jews, no Hispanics. Only a handful of Italians were in the mix of English, Irish, Scots, Germans and Poles.

The culture remained stagnant. Despite modern highways and communications, in many ways Cherry Ridge had not gotten out of the 1950's at best. It was still conducting an annual Minstrel Show, complete with blackface, into the 1960's. It was still common to hear derogatory terms used and demeaning jokes told. The expression "free, white and twenty-one" was part of the lexicon. I think I was in my early teens before I realized that "being jewed" was not the right way to say one was bargained down on the price of some commodity.

No outside race, ethnicity, religion, lifestyle or political orientation was exempt. Moneyed people and large corporations were also targets. At the other end of the economic spectrum, most Cherry Ridge poor were accepted, but outsiders in poverty were "lazy or trying to live off the system." Cherry Ridge practiced equal opportunity prejudice and bigotry. Ignorance was bliss.

In fact, community values had worsened in the mid and post 1960's when the pandemic drug culture began to claim its rural victims. To the credit of Chief Broadhurst, that sickness was confronted. Symbolic of his actions were road signs at every entrance to the village. They were harder hitting than the typical "Drug-Free Zone" signs one sometimes sees. Broadhurst's said things like "If You Are Carrying Drugs, Turn Around" and "Entering Cherry Ridge. Drug Traffickers Will Be Prosecuted to the Fullest Extent of the Law."

After a few arrests, even the resident, pot-smoking Baby Boomers took him at his word. Furthermore, Broadhurst took curfews seriously. He saw no reason for the youth to be on the streets after midnight so he pushed the village council to enact a law that included few exceptions.

I found myself doing one of my random mental calculations. I estimated the town's total value at less than half a billion dollars. Given what I had already determined, Scottie's gift to me was way beyond that. Scottie had bought the whole damn hillside. It was conceivable I could buy the whole damn town!

More Practicality and a Little Fun

We went back inside. Maggie said: "Whaddya think? I should have bought a couple of chairs and some other things, and you need some color on these walls, but this looks less like a prison cell and more like a place a civilized person can live in."

I looked around. Colorful linens had been added to the kitchen area and a lamp stood alongside the couch. Of course, the new sleeping area was the main attraction. "What are those contraptions?" I asked.

"Oh, those are the Walls of Jericho, like in the old movie. They provide some privacy. See, you can squeeze them in if you want to. One of us or both of us could stay here tonight. . . What do you want to do next?"

I had hoped to spend some time gathering info from Julia, totaling up assets or surveying the property, but I only mentioned the first. Maggie said: "I have Julia doing some of that. She is utterly amazing! The printouts are probably ready. Maybe you should put the gems and money in the vault, and maybe the weapons, too. Just in case someone gets in here."

I said that no one has been in here, as far as we know, other than Scottie and us. What chance would there be that anything would be different?

"I dunno, she said, "I guess I am just extra security conscious."

I said I would do as she suggested. "What are you going to do, Mag?"

"If it's okay with you, I'd really like to look at those cars again."

I suggested that she might ask Gretchen to go with her, leashed.

It took me some time to package the greenbacks to protect them from moisture and varmints. I found some rubber-like trash bins with lids in the utility room. I was hesitant to move the weapons into the vault for fear of rust. They would likely be the first things I would dispose of. How does one get rid of weapons that are probably illegal without facing questions about how one got them?

I had no such worries about the gems, but before placing them in the vault I carefully selected four emeralds and put them in my pocket.

I was telling Julia to close the vault when I heard a roar outside. I rushed to the door. Pulling up in front was Maggie behind the wheel of the white T-Bird. Buh-Room! Buuuh-Room! Gretchen was in the seat beside her. Maggie waved and smiled, then headed out and down the gravel road.

When they returned, she still had a big smile on her face along with some grease. "It's great, Boss, take it for a spin. I had to hook up the battery and jump-start it, but it runs like new. All the batteries in all the cars are disconnected and some tires are soft. The odometer says this baby has only 7,200 miles on it. Do you think that could be true? I got the Morgan running, too, but that's in the back row."

I had known Maggie O'Connor for a little over two years and I thought I knew her pretty well. She had invited me to her home more than a few occasions and I accepted two or three times. I had met several of her family members. I had entrusted her to look after Gretchen over a couple of weekends. We had talked and kidded about different things in the office. Now I realized I was only beginning to scratch the surface. She was quite the kid.

I got behind the wheel of the T-Bird. I have to admit it felt really good.

We saw no reason to stay at the apartment, but we did return to pick up some clothes, some personal things, like my pills, some people food and Gretchen's food. I put the convertible in the driveway. We didn't run into Mrs. Dumbrille, but we both felt that eyes were on us. We decided to pick up Italian food at Morelli's. Morelli's main thing was pizza, but they also put out some decent pasta and sauce with garlic bread.

After we had eaten, Maggie settled in with Julia for a while, called her mother, and declared she was ready to try the new bed. I did some reading, walked Gretchen and finally got to see Rachel Maddow. Before Maddow finished, I learned that Maggie snored. Much like Gretchen.

Chapter Three

Happy Birthday, Maggie

I remembered to greet Maggie the first thing in the morning with a boisterous happy birthday and a terrible attempt at singing. I told her that I felt sorry about not having a present for her. I couldn't even give her the day off. Still, I said, I have something for you. I reached in my pocket and drew out the emeralds. "You will need settings. These two should make nice earrings, this one a pendant and this one a ring. We'll find a good jeweler to do the work. Do you like them?"

"Of course I do. They're beautiful, but I can't take them. Absolutely not, you're my boss. It's, it's too much."

"You can't take them because they're from me? They aren't really, you know. They are Scottie's. It's my job to find them good homes."

"They aren't puppies or kittens, Boss! They are emeralds, big, expensive emeralds! Thank you so very much, but I can't take them."

"Please, Maggie. Take them as my thank you for coming out here when I needed you. Maybe someday you will look at them and remember this crazy day. No strings attached. There's many more here to do good deeds with."

Her face showed she was beginning to yield. "Please, Maggie, please," I teased. "I never thought I'd have to beg to give a woman emeralds! Besides, I can't return them to the store."

"Some store!" she said, looking around the room. "They definitely are beautiful. Okay, I'm weak and emeralds are my favorite. Seriously, I will treasure them. Thank you, thank you, thank you! But, Boss, I haven't done anything to earn anything so special. All you had to do was ask and I would have come. You would do the same for me. We are friends, aren't we?"

Ashes to Compost

My first concern for the day was to fulfill Scottie's wish for his ashes. Pierpoint had sent them to me along with a Google map marked to indicate where I should find the gravesite of Scottie's mother. I told Maggie that Gretchen and I could do the task alone, but she said she wanted to come along for the walk in the woods.

I was never a Boy Scout. I had only two days of survival training in the service and I was no woodsman. But I had wandered about woodlands and swamps when I was a kid and I could read a map.

Maggie loaded up with water, sunscreen and a few other things and we set off. We started down a trail that began just past the barn. The woods were pretty. The sounds of the creatures were melodious and comforting.

For the most part the trail kept us in sight of the same cliff that ran behind the camp buildings. We passed three lesser trails that ran down the hillside. They were more deer runs than anything else. We had to negotiate some standing water and a couple of narrow streams that began from springs in the cliff.

Gretchen didn't know where she was going, yet she still led the way. That is until some aroma stopped her in her tracks, which was often. It could be carrion, skat, skunk cabbage or any of a number of vile things. The more odiferous the better. "We're never going to get any place if you keep sniffing everything, Bonehead."

"Oh, don't call her Bonehead," Maggie said. "She's a sweet girl and the smells are what make it fun for her."

"Haven't you noticed that knot of bone on the back of her head? That's why I call her Bonehead."

"That knot is because she is so smart her brain is too big for her head . . . . Boss, You've never told me how you came to get Gretchen."

"Maggie, don't you think it is about time you call me Chris? Everybody else does."

"Hmm, out here maybe, but not at work, not in the office. I am more comfortable calling people coach or professor or sir or ms. You know, a lot of people are going to be calling you *Mr.* St. James."

"Because of the money?"

"Yeah, you won't be able to keep it hushed up forever. Haven't you thought of how people will kiss up to you, how the women will be flocking around you? I don't want to think what they will be calling you!"

"What women?"

"The golddiggers, silly, haven't they crossed your mind? You're what? Single, 40ish, over 6 feet tall, no baggage, not a lush, not bad looking and now you're rich! You might as well put a target on your back!"

"I'm not bad looking?" I asked.

"You didn't answer me. How did you get Gretchen or vice-versa?"

"Okay. It was May 25th. I remember because I had just called my dad to wish him happy birthday. I was sitting on the steps of my place. This guy comes along driving a beat-up pickup. I pay him no mind until he stops a couple of houses down. Then I see him kick, literally kick, this pup out the door.

Well, you know that I hate abuse of animals. There is never ever any justification for it. It is just plain meanness or worse. I ran after the guy. I was thinking that if I at least got the license number I could report him, but he turned the corner and I didn't get the number. I did get a good look at him from the side.

When I turned around, I saw this scared thing cowering behind me. I knelt down beside her and talked to her. She whimpered. I asked her if she needed a friend. She put her head on my knee and I looked into those eyes. It was as if she was pleading with me to be kind to her. I hadn't been thinking about having a dog, but it never even entered my mind to take her to a shelter. I told her I could use a friend, too. I picked her up —she was all of maybe 20 pounds then— and took her home. We've been best friends ever since."

"Serendipity, right? The poor baby! You saved her life."

"Yeah," I guess so. And just maybe she saved mine, too."

"You should spend some of your money on animal welfare," said Maggie.

"It goes without saying, top of the list," I replied.

We had walked maybe half a mile when the trail turned away from the cliff, first to the northwest, then to the north. We had to be near the center of the property. We found ourselves following alongside the widest stream we had encountered. The soil was soggy and there was some standing water, despite it being late August. Maybe there was a spring nearby. The previous day's rain had added to it. The trail eventually led us into a clearing of sorts. There were ferns, reeds, cattails, milkweed, and sumac instead of tall trees.

Within the midst of it all we glimpsed a stone cross, maybe eight feet high with an altar at its front. There were three marked graves, but the inscriptions were worn beyond reading. Likely my ancestors, I explained to Maggie.

On the opposite side of the cross there was a square of gravel, the same gravel that covered the entry road to the camp. In the center was a low rock wall surrounding a grave. A wooden bench sat at its foot. A small stone marker was at its head. It said: "Molly Malloy Ferguson, 1898-1939, Mother."

I took the box containing Scottie's ashes from my backpack. I wondered how a 6'6" man of all his achievements could be reduced to less than a cubic foot of ashes. Silently, I spread Scottie's remains left to right, top to bottom across his mother's resting place. Earlier I had thought about what I might say. Maggie quietly prompted me. She was crying. She took my hand. All I could think to say was: "Rest in peace, old fellow. I will do my best to honor your wishes and your memory." Maggie began reciting an old Irish prayer:

May the raindrops fall lightly on your brow
May the soft winds freshen your spirit
May the sunshine brighten your heart
May the burdens of the day rest lightly upon you
And may God enfold you in the mantle of His love.

As she spoke she sprinkled the grave with wildflowers she had collected along the way. We sat on the bench for a few moments. Maggie said, "Listen, there's almost no sound. It's like the birds are showing their respect."

After what seemed a reasonable time, I looked at the map. "If we stay on this trail we go north, northeast. It connects with that little road that goes along the lower ridge, not far from the entrance. It might be a mile and a half altogether, counting coming up the gravel road. A little more than if we retrace our steps. Are you up for it, kid?"

"Of course I am, old man," she retorted.

A Walk on the Wild Side

We had just started out when Maggie exclaimed: "Look, balloons!" Sure enough, scattered above the valley below there were five, no six, no seven hot air balloons. The pre-festival flights had begun. "I love balloons," she said. "Did you get them for me for my birthday?"

Our trek to the lower ridge was uneventful. We were moving toward the balloons so we had a pleasant, unexpected distraction. When we reached the ridge where the road was, we rested on a fallen log. Gretchen shared our water and cookies. Maggie poked me and whispered: "Did you see that? That stick moved. There, look, it moved again!"

I looked closely: "Wow," I said, "Do you know what that is, city girl? It's a walking stick. A big insect. They are often around but hard to see." I moved closer. City girl hung back. "Come closer," I said, "You don't want to miss this."

"I don't like bugs! Especially big ones. I don't see it, only a stick."

"The stick is the insect. Let your eyes follow it. Here, I'll make it move."

"Omygawd," she said, "It is just like a stick!"

I told Maggie what little I knew about walking sticks and that led to me mentioning praying mantises. "What do they prey on? They are out here, too?"

"Yep, they are here," I said, "It is spelled with an 'a'. They look like their 'hands' are folded in prayer. Who knows what we have passed by? They are harmless and their camouflage is so good you almost never see them."

"You like seeing those things?"

"Yeah, I guess I do. The bigger ones. I don't like the ugly little ones, like earwigs and maggots. Earwigs make my skin crawl."

Maggie was looking around. "Dylan and Sean used to call me Maggot. Then I found out what they look like and I pounded both of them … Are there any dangerous things out here?"

"I guess it depends on what you mean by dangerous. Two-footed ones with guns are the most dangerous. The snakes are creepy but harmless. I doubt that a rattler has been seen in these parts in many years. Mosquitoes, poison ivy, poison sumac. Ticks. I will have to check Gretchen for ticks."

"What about bigger animals?"

"You mean lions and tigers and bears?"

"Oh, my," she finished with a giggle.

"No lions, except at Millie's on Thursday nights. I think she gets Elks, too. No tigers and there is only a very remote chance of seeing a bear. We could easily see deer at some point. If we get lucky we might see a fox. You saw a woodchuck; they are common. Gretchen chased a rabbit. You see them mostly in the evening. Most everything else is nocturnal. They are around, but we won't likely see them. Raccoons, maybe opossum. I heard an owl last night and there have been hawks overhead. Pheasants, partridge. You needn't worry about any of them unless they are rabid. Except for skunks."

"How will I know if a skunk is around?"

"It's like this. There were two brother skunks named Out and In. In went missing. Out went looking for him. When he found him and brought him back their mother asked Out: 'How did you find your brother?' 'It was easy, mom,' he said, 'Instinct.'"

"That is one terrible joke," Maggie said, but still she laughed.

"I couldn't resist."

Anti-Serendipity

The road had only a few, thick, scrubby trees along its north side. I was thinking about putting Gretchen on her leash so she wouldn't go toward the steep drop-off only a few feet away. I had peered down at the edge of the ridge. The gully below was deep on this side, then much less so on the other far side as it rose up to meet the valley floor.

Looking down had made me briefly catch my breath. I had no fear of heights per se, but I did have a fear of falling. To be up high I needed to feel secure. I had flown in helicopters with success; in fact, I toyed with learning to fly them when I was in the Air Force. But standing on the edge of a tall building or at the edge of a cliff was another thing. What if I lost my footing, or a gust of wind came along or some demented creature pushed me off? That was my fear.

Gretchen took the exact time that these thoughts surged through my head to surge ahead on her own. Something had attracted her interest off the road to the gully side. "Gretchen," I yelled. "Stop." For a few anxious moments I was filled with terror, thinking she may go over the side.

As I rushed closer, I was beating myself up for not leashing her. Phew! Gretchen was fine. She was on a little lip of dirt poking at what looked like a roll of fabric. Flying insects were circling. The area smelled of rot. I hurried to Gretchen, attached her leash and encouraged her back to the road. She resisted. "Don't mess with that," I said in my sternest voice.

"Chris! Look!" Maggie exclaimed, pointing to the pile.

"It's just gar ... " I started.

"No, it's not," she said, pointing. "Look there." "There" was where a bloody hand extended from an end of the roll.

"Move back, Maggie. Here, take Gretchen and tie her to something across the road." I moved cautiously, very much aware of how close I was to the edge of the cliff. I swatted at the flies or whatever they were and began to tug slowly at the cloth. It was soaked from the rain, and from blood. "We need to call 911," I said, "There's a dead woman here."

It took the cops some time to arrive. First, the dispatcher questioned whether we were located in the village. Maybe it was up to the sheriff to respond. As it was, the village cops on duty had to come from the airport where they were policing the balloon event. The airport is at the far north end of the village. We were beyond the south end. Their final obstacle was a large funeral contingent blocking the single-lane road along Holy Sepulchre.

The waiting gave me time to free the body from the drapery that encased it. I avoided touching it any more than I had to; nevertheless, my curiosity was aroused. She was dressed in jeans and a light fleece top. Her face, neck and upper body were badly slashed. Dried blood was everywhere, including in her hair. I looked for signs of identification but found none. I surmised that the body was likely that of the young woman assaulted in Mrs. Morgan's apartment.

Another Encounter with Broadhurst

Four cops plus Broadhurst and an EMT crew arrived almost simultaneously. Broadhurst strode briskly at the head of the pack shouting orders. No one touches the body. Put up crime tape. No one gets in here. Get ID's on those two. Etc. Etc. Curt Simmons got his ear and the two looked over at us.

Maggie, Gretchen and I watched from a dry resting spot under a tree. Curt came over and said "Wow, Chris, you guys found the body. Wow! I have to ask ya, who is this with ya."

I explained. He asked when it was we found the body. I told him. "Okay," he said, "Stay here, the Chief will want to talk with ya."

Broadhurst took his time. "St. James," he opened, " We meet again."

I nodded and said: "This is Meghan O'Connor. She works for me. And this is Gretchen. It was actually she who found the body. We were walking along and she was attracted to the odor; otherwise we might not have noticed it."

He asked what we were doing on the property. He noted that the entrance had it posted as private. I said: "Exploring it, like I said the other day. It is still private. This is the property I acquired."

"So you own it. Who owned it before you? Any buildings on it? I saw the gate."

"Angus Ferguson. He died a couple of weeks ago. There's a camp near the top of the hill. A couple of buildings."

We went back and forth. About Angus. About what brought us to be here at this time.

"Obviously you've moved the body. Did you remove anything from it or from around it?"

I didn't like the question. "Of course not, all I did was unwrap it," I said.

He turned to Maggie. "How about you, Miss O'Connor, did you touch the body or remove anything?"

She said no.

He said, "You seem nervous, Miss O'Connor. Is there something bothering you, is there something you need to tell me. Now would be the best time."

Maggie didn't like this question. "No, nothing. I have never seen a dead body, not like that. How would you feel? I just want to get away from here, from her. It was such a beautiful day. It's my birthday and we were having such a good time. And now this."

Broadhurst: "Sorry, miss, it's my job to ask questions. You understand."

Broadhurst turned back to me. "You have to admit, it is quite a coincidence. A possible murder occurs almost on your doorstep and then a few days later, miles away, you report finding a body."

I shrugged:"Yeah, I guess it is."

"You sure you didn't hear or see anything else?"

"I saw a dead woman, young, badly slashed. She's been here at least since before it stopped raining. She's wearing expensive jeans, maybe French. Her hair is colored. Dark roots are just starting to show. She is careful about her appearance —her toenails are meticulously painted. She had a good manicure, too, but she tore nails in a struggle. Probably dug them into her attacker's legs as she or he grabbed her from behind.

"She wasn't given much of a chance to fight back — there are no defensive wounds on her palms. It's not likely a sex crime. No sign her jeans had been removed. The killing was quickly done. She may have been gagged before she was killed; that's why no one heard cries for help. The murder was carefully planned and executed. In fact, it was kind of like an execution. The cut to her neck was deadly and the first. The rest of the slashes were made to cover the precision of the first one. The weapon used is probably a good-sized, very sharp knife. The wounds don't look ragged and some are quite long and deep.

"It's likely she is lefthanded. Your best chance to find prints is in the blood, but I think it will be a wasted effort. The killer is smart, and certainly wore gloves.

It wasn't a robbery gone bad. She is still wearing a nice ring —not a wedding ring and it's on her right hand— and a jeweled Bulova watch. I imagine her handbag or purse is down in the gully. Maybe the knife, too. Maybe what was used for a gag. I figure he or she tossed them over the side first, then hoisted the body and threw it toward the gully. The body probably dislodged a fallen branch or some rocks and that is what the killer heard fall to the bottom. In the dark he or she probably didn't realize the drapery snagged on those roots and against that scrub pine and stayed near the edge where we found it.

"As to tire tracks, what the rain didn't wash out of this sandy soil your vehicles have obliterated. And, oh yeah, Icky didn't do it. He doesn't drive. I can't see him bringing a body here on his bike!"

Maggie was staring at me with her jaw dropped. Broadhurst looked at me evenly and said: "What is that you do for a living, Mr. St. James? You are not some kind of *amateur* detective, are you?" He made amateur sound like a 4-letter word.

"I have a small organization that does research, mostly on matters of public policy."

"Just out of curiosity, what makes you think she is lefthanded?" asked Broadhurst.

"That's easy," I said, "Not every one, but most lefthanders wear their watches on their right hand and vice-versa. Basic Crimestoppers Textbook. She is wearing a belt with the buckle opening to her left."

"Uh, huh," said Broadhurst. "Is that everything?"

"That's all that comes to mind, Chief."

"We are going to be here for a while, Mr. St. James. You don't mind, do you?"

"Not at all, Chief, but please ask your guys to refrain from smoking. It may have rained recently, but this hillside could still go up in flames."

"Uh, huh. I will ask you for the second time, Mr. St. James, have you ever met Cassandra Cross?"

"I think that is she over there, Chief, but when we first encountered her, she was in no shape for introductions."

"You can go now," said the Chief, "We have your contact information."

Post Broadhurst

Maggie could barely wait for us to be out of earshot to pepper me with questions. "Where in the world did that all come from, Chris? You are always so laid back but you sure delivered a load on him. Do you think that was a wise move?"

"Maybe I was feeling my oats a bit too much, but wise or not, Mag, I did it. He's one of those starched, smug guys. Thinks he has some superiority over regular people. He enjoys making them feel uncomfortable. He's probably a bully. It's more his manner than any one thing he said."

"Yeah, okay, but where did you come up with all that stuff? Is there such a thing as Crime Blockers' Textbook?"

The last made me laugh. "It's Crimestoppers. My dad had a book of Dick Tracy comic strips. Dick Tracy was a fictional detective about 50-60 years ago. At the end of each strip there would be a block with some kind of crime prevention or investigation tip. That's where I got the lefthanded thing. Another tip was to check matchbooks. Most people remove matches starting from their stronger handed side. I'm lefthanded so I remember those tips."

"And the rest of the stuff?"

"I dunno. Maybe it is simply too many TV cop shows. I think that is the way I would write it up if I were writing a mystery. It more or less hangs together. There may be holes in my theories, but the onus is on Broadhurst, not me."

After Julia closed the gate behind us, a state police car came whizzing along the gravel. Before we were out of sight of the gate, a sheriff's car came into view. "The gang's all here," I said.

The climb up the roadway was a trudge. Hot, dusty and way more uphill than driving it had seemed. It had been foolish of me to come this route and I apologized to Maggie for suggesting it. But if I hadn't, Cassandra Cross's body would still be undiscovered.

We talked about the murder. We talked about spreading Angus' ashes. We talked about the beauty of the property. We talked about some of the uses I had in my head for the money. We talked less as we began to tire. We stopped twice to catch our breath. The first time it was because Gretchen came to a comfortable spot and simply stretched out. The second time it was because Maggie's knee acted up again.

I offered to continue alone and come back for her with the car. "Give me a couple of minutes," Maggie said. "It can't be much farther." It wasn't, only another ten yards and the opening in the trees to the camp came into sight.

Rest and Relaxation

The camp house provided us a cold drink and use of the bathroom. "You should get off that leg for a while, Mag. Would it help to put a cold pack on it? I think there is now some ice or bags of frozen veggies. Or could I give your knee a rubdown?"

"Thanks," she said, "I think I will just lie down for a while." I did the same thing. It was barely 2:00; still, it had already been a long day.

It was about 4:30 when I awoke to the sound of the shower. "Feel better?" I asked a few minutes later.

"Definitely. My knee is fine now."

"The offer of the rubdown still stands."

Maggie looked at me coyly. "I'll take a rain check."

I just remembered that Gretchen needs a shower," I said. "She needs to look her best for the balloon fest. We'll take one together more or less."

"I can't wait to see that," laughed Maggie.

"*You* don't get to. Owner/dog privileges. No peeking."

I gathered what I needed, then called Gretchen into the shower. She lowered her head and walked slowly as if she was walking death row. Nevertheless, she was obedient as always. I stripped to my shorts and started the process. It took two shampooings and two rinsings to rid my girl's thick coat of dirt, seeds, thistles and old hair. The water ran dark and the shower drain began to clog with thick gobs of black hair.

I was winded when we finished. I stepped out and began to wrap her in a large towel. I began to slip on the wet floor and I lost control of her. She left me holding the towel as she raced from the room. I cried out: "Look out, she's going to shake!"

I wrapped the towel around me and followed her out. Sure enough, she was chasing after Maggie. She stopped to shake water and then began her chase again. "Gimme the towel, Chris."

"Not this towel, I need it more than you do." I stepped inside the bathroom and closed the door part way. *Then* I tossed out the towel and said, "You two are on your own, now." I stepped into the shower. The rushing water drowned out the squeals from the other room.

It Gets a Bit Personal

Once Gretchen was combed out and damp dry, she inhaled her dinner. I had planned to take Maggie to the airport to see the balloons. "If people are expecting you two, we should go," she said, but she lacked her usual enthusiasm. Despite her nap and shower, she seemed tired. I know she hadn't slept as much as I had.

"We don't have real obligations until tomorrow morning. We can stay here, toast your birthday and watch the sunset."

"That sounds good to me," she said.

A little while later I mentioned to her that I had driven past the cemetery several times without stopping. I said I would stop tomorrow afternoon after she was on her way back home. "Why don't you do that now," she said, "I will come with you."

We turned into Holy Sepulchre 15 minutes later. I showed Maggie where my dad, mom, sister, grandparents, uncles and aunts rested. I pointed out a space that I said might some day be mine. And one for my brother, should he ever return.

"I didn't know you had a sister or a brother." I quietly told her that my sister, five years older than I, had died from leukemia. I never really knew her. "I guess my coming along was an accident. Mom once said I was lucky to arrive. I didn't know what she meant at the time. Later I figured out that she had considered terminating her pregnancy but Dad wouldn't agree. I guess that continued to be a sore spot between them."

"Omygawd!" she said, "Are you sure she meant that? What a terrible thing to tell a child."

"Mom had a temper and a mean streak. Dad drank a lot when I was young and they fought all the time. They had a marriage made in Hell. They made a good case for the value of divorce."

"Were you, were you abused?"

"No, not in any physical way. Oh, I got whacked a few times, but it wasn't like I was knocked around regularly. I was a latch-key kid. I was more or less ignored, neglected. Of course, I only came to know that by comparing my situation to other kids. I would get myself off to school, even when I was small, and then come home to an empty house. There was always food and clothes and such. But you won't find any pictures of me sitting on my mom's lap. And I seldom brought friends home, 'cause I never knew how they'd be."

"What about your brother? Did he look after you?"

"No," I answered, "He's ten years older than I and he left home the day he turned 18. Mom and Dad had only heard from him a few times over the years. We thought he might be somewhere in the Middle East. It was tough on them both, but especially Mom. She favored him."

"That's so sad," Maggie said. "No wonder you have the feelings you have about Cherry Ridge." Then she added quietly: "I understand about losses. My dad you know about. I lost a sister, too. Maureen. She was only five. I was eight. She would have been 25 next month. Encephalitis."

I squeezed her hand gently. "That hurt us all," she said, "but otherwise I had terrific parents and a good upbringing. Dad was a tough guy, but he really doted on me. And Mom, for the most part, is a saint. But you really had no one. Do you know why your brother left?"

"I had my grandmother for several years. She was indeed a saint. I'd go there whenever I could. As to my brother, nobody ever wanted to talk about it. What I know is sketchy things I overheard. I think he got into some trouble, maybe a girl, maybe drugs, maybe both, and took off rather than face the consequences. He had our mother's bad temper. I am sorry, Maggie, I didn't mean to be such a downer. I never talk about this stuff, but somehow I find you easy to talk to."

"I'm glad about that. I've come to think that about you, too. We have a few things in common." She silently took Gretchen's leash from my hand and walked slowly away. She was giving me a few minutes alone with my family.

We were back at the camp in time to have a couple of scotches and sit outside well beyond sunset. Our conversation was much more upbeat once we left the cemetery. Maggie called her mom and I heard her say she had never had and never will have a birthday like this one had been.

Gretchen whacked me awake about 3:00 AM. Maggie was crying out. By the time I got past the Wall of Jericho, she was just crying. I sat beside her on the bed, embraced her and said, "It's okay, you're safe here."

She clung to me, then pulled back a bit saying, "I'm alright. A bad dream. The accident. I'm sorry I woke you."

"Not a problem, not a problem at all. Do you want to talk about it? Sometimes talking helps."

"No ... Thank you. It happens. I'll be able to get back to sleep."

"Okay," I said, "I'm right over there if you need me." Gretchen climbed on the bed and settled down beside her. As I returned to my bed the memory of her warm, firm body went with me. It was simultaneously discomforting and elating.

In the morning I suggested that we'd drive to the apartment and trade the truck for the convertible. We would take it down to the airport, check out the balloons and eat junk food.

Up, Up, then Away

The discovery of the body the day earlier had rippled through most of the crowd at the airport. Fortunately, misinformation about where the body was found kept us from being connected to it. The word going around one was that someone at the funeral had stumbled upon it in Holy Sepulchre.

Maggie was impressed by the number of people on the grounds and fascinated by the balloons. She was also taken with the attention Gretchen received. We had a spot at the judging table. The mayor and the chairman of the event both noted the presence of "Cherry Ridge's Hero and #1 dog." There was clapping and cheers. As her "handler," I was required to help pass out awards for the most beautiful balloon, for the one that had come the greatest distance and so on. After the formalities, several parents brought their young ones up to pet her. A few had cameras. Gretchen loved it all.

"It would be great to go up in one of these things," Maggie said pointing upward to the balloons.

I said, "Then you should. Some of them offer rides."

"No, I can't do that, where would I come down, how would I get back?"

"You don't have to go any place. See over there? Those balloons are tethered. You can get in and they go up to the height of the ropes. C'mon, we'll get you in line."

"Really?" She said, "What if the ropes break?"

"Then we'll come get you in Oz. I've never been there."

Maggie got her ride and loved it. I'm sure she would have gone up again if she hadn't been thinking about getting home. We ate hot dogs and burgers and drank pop (not soda as I had to explain to Maggie), made conversation with whomever we encountered, and had an all-around good time.

By 2:00, Maggie was on her way home. By 4:00, I had picked up Dad's things from the apartment and was on my way, too. Once again, I was trying to get away from Cherry Ridge, but this time I knew for certain I would return.

Chapter Four

Back Home

   The Yankees had several early season rainouts. As a result they were to play a rare double-header on the last Sunday in August. I looked forward to reading the papers with the games on. After surprising myself by going to Mass, I picked up a 6-pack of Amstel—it might last me a month—and some sliced salami.
   When I returned to my bungalow outside Albany, the landline was ringing. I let it go to voice mail just as I had twice the previous night. I waited a few minutes, checked it, and learned it was Mel Reeves, the Cherry Ridge Ledger editor, still after me for more news.
   I turned the ringer off. I made a sandwich, found some pickles and stale chips and, voila, an unopened container of cashews. I love cashews, but they always made me want to sneeze. My dad would have said it was the "power of snozzative thinking." He had a penchant for making up silly words. I gathered the Sunday papers, tuned in the game and settled in for the afternoon. Gretchen was lightly snoring at my side. I was living the good life.
   My second beer made me sleepy and I found the chirping of the cell phone rousing me from my slumber. I had forgotten to turn the damn thing off. I didn't want to talk with Mel, certainly not in my foggy state. Then I realized that I hadn't given him the cell number. I managed to find the cell and flip it open before it, too, went to voice mail. I managed a dry-throated hello.
   "Boss, I mean Chris, it's me, Maggie. Are you back home? Did I catch you at a bad time?"
   "No, I mean yes, we came back last night. It's not a bad time. I must have fallen asleep watching the game."
   "Oh, sorry, I didn't mean to wake you. Do you mean the Mets or the Yankees? It has to be the Yanks; the Mets are on the coast. The game is on here. Yanks won the first game 3-2 in 10 innings. Cano homered and Mo pitched the last two. The Mets game is just starting. Should I call back later?"
   "No, it's okay. I don't remember seeing past the seventh. What's up?"
   "Well, two things. I got a call late yesterday afternoon from one of the realtors about the castle. I answered like you said. They ID'd the current owner, some XYZ kind of company. They connected with a guy and he said

he would listen to offers. They didn't say anything about an asking price. I said I would talk with you, I mean "my principal," not you by name."

"Good," I said, "We will start following up on it during the week."

"So you're still serious about it then?"

"Yeah, I think so. It might be fun to bring the old place back to life. If it's possible. We'll hire someone to look at it. What's the second thing?"

"Uh, before I get to that, you said you came back last night? I thought you were coming back today?"

"Yeah, we left two, three hours after you did. I thought we'd been there long enough."

"Oh, I wish I had known. I would have asked you to my party."

"That's okay. It was a family party, right? How'd it go? Good time?"

"Definitely. But it wasn't just family. Dylan brought his girlfriend and a couple of the neighbors came by. Mom asked a lot about Cherry Ridge and about you. Oh, guess what? I still have the car 'cause the place is closed on Sunday. My brothers wanted a ride in it and then this morning all four of us went to Mass. Mom loved it."

"That's great, maybe that is what you should get for your company car. Especially if you can get your mom in and out of it."

"Really? Shouldn't I have something more, uh, professional?"

"Nah, like I said, you look good in it. I'll help you pick one out if you want. It will be fun."

"Yeah, fun, that gets me back to the second reason I called. I wanted to tell you before work tomorrow how much I enjoyed my time with you and Gretchen. I mean, not all of it, but most of it was really great. And most of all, I want to thank you again for putting so much trust in me. I'm still in shock."

"That goes both ways, Maggie. I'll see you in the morning. I should be there by 10:00."

Cluing in Vincent

I managed to get there by 10:05. Three of the PhD candidates who worked for us were busy. Maggie and Vincent were talking by the coffee machine. Maggie made a motion asking if I wanted a cup. I nodded and waved the two of them into my office.

"Shut the door," I said. I handed six envelopes to Vincent and one to Maggie. "The top one is for you, the others are for the crew. It's a bonus, regardless of how you respond this morning."

Vincent opened the envelope and stuttered a wide-eyed thanks. "I'm in the dark, Chris. What's going on? Maggie gave me a few business cards, but she wouldn't tell me anything."

"Good," I said, "Keeping things private is the prime directive, at least for now. Let's see, where should I begin?"

I gave him an outline of some of what had occurred. I said that very unexpectedly a very rich and mysterious eccentric, a friend of my father and my grandmother, arranged to give me much of his wealth. Then he died, leaving me Auracle Media, oversight of his philanthropy, the Magnus Foundation, and his wish that I do good things with the money.

Vincent immediately wondered about the Magnus connection. He knew that our research organization had begun because I had gotten a grant from Magnus. "Ferguson must have been working on your behalf well before now. And you never knew?"

I told him I didn't know its connection to Ferguson before Scottie mentioned it in his message.

Vincent knew a little about Auracle Media. "It's not one of the really big ones, but it is substantial I think."

"According to Julia, " Maggie interjected, "Twelve TV stations, six radio stations, a bunch of mid-sized newspapers and a few magazines plus some Internet stuff."

"Who's Julia?" Vincent asked. I let Maggie explain. He said: "She sounds like my kind of female." Then he asked: "If you don't mind telling me, how much money are you talking about?"

"Maggie?" I asked.

"We don't know," she said, "It's not as much as Warren Buffet has, but it's a lot of money. Could make a *Fortune* list. It will be a while before we gather it and total it. A lot of it is in bonds. I have some samples. I'm going to check them out to make sure they are good. Today. If they are all valid, they add up to hundreds of millions. There are also some gemstones. I have a sample of them, too."

Vincent was speechless.

I picked up on where Maggie left off. "I banked about a million and a half for ready cash. There is no question there is enough that I can offer you the same deal that Maggie's accepted.

I know you've wanted to get into an academic setting, Vincent, but you can do more good and make more money with us. That should be a win-win for you. The primary goal of this venture is to distribute money wisely to bring about positive changes. I don't want to get hit from all sides like a lottery winner. I don't want to feel unsafe or have my privacy invaded. Still, any good options—big and small—will be in play. We won't be able to change the world, but we can make a little difference. The trick will be how to set it up and sort it all out.

At the same time, none of us is going to take a vow of poverty. Maybe we can indulge in some whimsical things, too. I am asking you to agree to confidentiality and commit to at least a couple of years. You get $100,000, full benefits and a company car to start. We'll arrange to pay off your school loans. After that, we see where things take us. I'm pretty sure we can all do well over time."

"You don't have to kill anybody or do anything illegal, Vincent, I already asked him that." Maggie giggled.

Vincent wanted to know what he would be doing. I told him I needed more than a right-hand man to manage all that I had begun to envision. I needed trusted people to my left and right. I needed someone willing to travel, which I knew he was. Someone to run interference for me and represent me effectively. He'd interact with Magnus, Auracle and whatever else came along. I said if you shake on it right now, we will get started.

Vincent looked at me, then at Maggie, who nodded affirmatively. He extended his right hand, the one I wanted. I held it and reached for Maggie's hand with my left. "Okay, we are a team," I said.

I jumped into it. "In no particular order, first item. We'll need more space so we need a new location. Bigger. West of here. Close to the Thruway."

"Schenectady???" Maggie asked.

"My doctor said I needed a Schenectady, but I told him my insurance wouldn't cover it," said Vincent, joking and maybe just a little giddy.

I ignored him. "Guilderland, Glenville, Niskayuna," I said, "But not Schenectady. I may have money but not for Schenectady taxes!"

"Next, we need to add players to our team. We'll need someone to take over for Maggie, to work with the crew. We will need a full-time replacement for you, Vincent. We'll need a secretary, I guess. Probably one for all three of us will do for starters.

"The first big hires will be an in-house lawyer with corporation and financial expertise and an investments expert. I am thinking a sharp, ambitious young guy or gal for the attorney. Strong ethics. Progressive. Not yet jaded. He or she will need a legal aid. I think it is required that attorneys be properly accessorized."

Vincent said: "There are all kinds of oxymorons lurking in what you just said. But, seriously, I have a college friend who works for a firm in Albany. He's really sharp, but I think he is frustrated—too many people senior to him. He'd like to set out on his own, but the financial risk is holding him back. He has a wife at home with two kids."

"Talk to him, ASAP. I want to get an LLC or whatever set up fast. Maybe we will need someone for just that. Without getting set up legally we can't do much else. What about the investments? We need someone on top of his game with high standards but practical. Someone with a wide range of experience."

They both were silent. Then Maggie said, "I can talk with one of my old profs at Siena. He knows a lot of the locals."

"Good idea, Maggie, do it. I prefer not to work with a big firm, but maybe we can steal a good person from one of them. Okay, guys, get started."

Maggie lingered. When Vincent was out of earshot, Maggie said: "You didn't tell him about finding the body or the castle or much about the camp. Was that deliberate?"

"No, not necessarily. I think I told him enough for now. The dead woman is not relevant to him. However, if he asks you anything, tell him the truth. I trust him. On the other hand, we'll get him out to Cherry Ridge soon enough. I want to see how he reacts to it, don't you?"

"Yeah, I guess. By the way we are having a simple Labor Day barbecue next weekend at our house. It's the last get-together of the summer. Burgers, salads, and stuff. I'd like you both to come. I'm going to ask Vincent to bring Melanie. Do you think the crew guys would come if I ask them?"

"I'll tell you what." I replied, "If you don't mind, let me upgrade the fare to steaks and bring beer and I bet you they will. They should be in a good frame of mind. Vincent just handed each of them $1,000."

"It's a deal," she said.

Mel Reeves Clues Me In

When I arrived home there was another message from Mel Reeves. I found a comfortable spot on the back steps and rang his number. The first words out of his mouth were "Where you been, buddy? I've been trying to reach you all weekend. You bugged out early, didn't you? I need to ask you about your finding the body. Some coincidence!"

I explained that I had finished my business in Cherry Ridge and needed to get back home. Playing dumb, I asked "What coincidence?"

"That you should come into town just before the assault in the house behind you, then find the body miles away on your newly acquired property a few days later."

"What are you implying, Mel?"

"Oh, nothing, nothing at all. It's just odd. Can you tell me how you came upon the body? Chub Simmons says you really gave Broadhurst an earful. What's that all about?"

"Well, Mel, I imagine you've read the police report. There is nothing I can add to it. No doubt you know lots more about this than I do. I was just exploring the property with Gretchen and my assistant."

"Your assistant? What's her name?"

"Mel, don't be coy. We are old friends. I'm sure her name is on the police report."

"Right. So, were you staying at your apartment or up there? There's a camp there right? I saw the gate. Pretty formidable."

"Well, I had nothing to do with the gate. It came with the property. If you must know, Maggie used the guest room. Both the motels were full up. She came out to help me decide what to do with the property. And, Mel, I will be really ticked if anything you say or write reflects badly on her."

"No, of course not. The report says that you don't know the victim, Cassandra Cross?"

I didn't answer.

Mel continued: "Apparently no one in town does. Nobody actually met her except Icky. Superintendent Kline says she was coming from England to teach languages by way of an exchange program. She lived there, but she had U. S. citizenship. Maybe dual citizenship. Young, 29, I think. He said her recommendations and experience were outstanding. Speaks, or spoke, four or five languages. He only talked with her by phone a couple of times. He helped set her up with Mrs. Morgan and she asked about the school's daycare program."

"Quite the mystery, isn't it?" I offered more evenly.

"I'll say. By the way, her blood matched with what was in the house and Mrs. Morgan confirmed that's where the drapery came from. Late Friday they found her bag in the gully. They've brought out a lot of old junk, but no weapon. Even condoms, imagine that?"

"They've been tramping all through it since Friday. The village guys, sheriff guys, and troopers. I tried to get down there, but I couldn't. 'Crime scene' restrictions. Got some pix, though. Oh, I almost forgot. Yesterday they found her rental car, abandoned behind the old foundry. Forensics is working it."

"At least I didn't stumble on it."

"What? Oh, I see what you mean."

"Who is in charge of the investigation?"

"Broadhurst, based on where the crime apparently occurred. But the others are helping out ... So, tell me about the property. How did you get it from Ferguson?"

"Simple, he gave it to me. He said that way back it was in my dad's family and he wanted to give it to Dad to get it back to where he said it belonged. They were friends. I guess he didn't get around to it before Dad died, so he gave it to me. Then he died himself."

"What's on the grounds? I'd like to see it sometime."

"Not much, Mel, not worth your time," I lied. "It's really rough terrain. Scottie was kind of eccentric and I think he just went there to get away."

"I imagine hunters go in there."

"They shouldn't. It's all posted land that's bordered by the state park, county roads and the cemetery."

"Where was Ferguson when he died? How old was he? Was he born in Cherry Ridge? I should look up his obit."

"Ninety-two. He grew up in Cherry Ridge."

"So, what plans do you have for the property?"

"None, yet, but it's good enough to stay in over night, so I am looking to sell the apartment building in case you know anyone interested."

"Speaking of selling property, there is a rumor going around that someone has put a bid in on the castle!"

Taking Care of Business

Vincent and Maggie made great progress over the next 48 hours. They had a good realtor lined up. Maggie verified that the gems and the bonds were good and had made contact with her former prof. She was aghast at the estimated value a jeweler placed on the emeralds. Vincent had an after hours drink or two with his lawyer friend who, at minimum, had agreed to get us quickly incorporated. Meeting times had been set and paperwork was in process.

For my part I called around looking for an architect or an engineer to evaluate a possible building rehab project. The first one showed disinterest when I told him where Cherry Ridge is located. The second wasn't crazy about my sense of urgency. The third, Greg Mathis, a construction engineer, was intrigued from the outset. He agreed to recruit HVAC, electrical and plumbing guys to take part if I was willing to pay the going rate. I told Maggie to call the Cherry Ridge realtor and tell him we would be sending someone out to make an assessment.

At the end of the day on Thursday, I left Gretchen at home and drove to meet with Maggie, Vincent and his friend Arnie "Sparky" Spellman. The short, red-haired, bespectacled Mr. Spellman cringed a little every time Vincent called him Sparky. He made me think of Woody Allen. He seemed interested in making a job change but hesitant about whether our rather vague venture would be to his liking.

I let the three of them banter. I learned that what Vincent had said about him appeared to be true. He was quick-witted. He had gone to the same state college two years ahead of Vincent then graduated from Cornell Law. His dad was an optician, his mom worked for the VA. He had a wife, Dottie, and two children, Delores and Dustin. He seemed confident but not cocky. I decided I liked him well enough.

Vincent made an excuse for him and me to walk to the food bar. "What do you think of him, Chris?" he asked.

"I'm okay with him. I want someone we can start at something less than you and Maggie make. Ask Maggie what she thinks and if you two agree he has the right stuff make him an offer. I think he probably will want to bargain a little. It will make him feel good. After all, he is a lawyer."

Vincent turned to the waiter refilling the buffet. Noticing his nametag he asked with a straight face: "Where's the john, Wayne?" Then he looked my way to see if I got it. Unfortunately, I did. He wanted a groan so I gave him one.

Getting an investment counselor took a couple of twists. Professor Lawrence Swann had compiled more than thirty years teaching business, finance and accounting. Maggie said that if he didn't know something about managing money, it probably didn't need to be known. He was officially retired and financially set in his own right —which I thought money managers worth their salt should be. He was only teaching as an emeritus adjunct because he enjoyed it.

By the time I met him over lunch, Maggie had outlined our goals and needs. The first thing he said was that it was too bad I hadn't seen Maggie play soccer. She could have been a pro, he said, like her heroine, Mia Hamm. I had never told Maggie that I dislike soccer, so I wasn't about to tell him.

The first twist came when, instead of providing us names to pursue, he began to interview me. I was a little flustered by it. I did not want to expose all that much information. Finally, he said, "Look, Mr. St. James, I think you are sincere and I am fascinated by your ideas. You present an opportunity to do something good in a new way, and I can see Maggie trusts you." Then came the second twist: "I want to be a part of it but if you want *me* to sign on with you, you will have to trust me. I need to know who and what I am working with."

A little while later we had an agreement in principal, as they say. Professor Swann would be our primary financial consultant. He would advise us about our choices and interact with the firms we would employ. With my concurrence, Maggie said she would give Professor Swann a copy of Julia's printout of the holdings. Later, I told her to hold back on some of the offshore accounts and the volume of gold. No point in being totally exposed from the outset.

I liked thoughtful and decisive people. We had found two of them.

The week wound down quickly. On Friday, Maggie and I visited a specialty jeweler in Saratoga Springs. It was track season, it was raining heavily and traffic was terrible, but I was insistent about making the drive. If I hadn't been, I think she would have put the emeralds in a box on her dresser. (Had I known how long the session would take, I might have let her.)

The jeweler was an artisan. He said the emeralds were first rate. The colors would bring out the green in Maggie's eyes. He said he would have to cut the small pair for earrings to make them identical. "You don't want to look lop-sided," he said. The unusual tear-dropped cut was fine for a pendant. The emerald-cut one I had chosen for a ring, was a bit large, he thought, but would make up fine.

He examined her ear lobes, asked about how she wears her hair, measured her neck, and asked about clothing she might wear with the pendant. He asked her about the length and weight of chain she might want for the pendant. He showed her sample settings for the earrings, pendant and ring. I didn't see much difference, but they did. At least I think they did; it may all have been part of a mystical game. All through the process, he was very discreet in his manner and he had no reaction when at one point Maggie called me Boss. I would not have been surprised if he had at least raised an eyebrow.

When he finished, he gave me a receipt and an estimate of his fee. Maggie's looking about the store gave me the opportunity to tell him I had several more loose stones. He said he sometimes buys them, but he has to be careful about the provenance. He said he gets his stones following visits to Europe or through the New York City exchange. He said he could give me some respected names if I wished.

Maggie found a lovely turquoise rosary. "Mom would like that. It's expensive but I think I will get it for her for her birthday. I always get her practical things. It would be nice to give her something other than clothing and kitchen things."

On Saturday, the realtor selling my building in Cherry Ridge called. So far, the only interest shown was from Mrs. Dumbrille, my tenant. The agent said the problem was the tight banking conditions. It could be difficult for Mrs. D to be approved. She didn't have any income beyond her and her husband's social security. She figured she could handle the mortgage with the rental income. I said make it happen. If necessary I would carry the mortgage myself. The agent was clearly thrilled. She said she had learned I now owned Brampton Woods, the local name for Scottie's Place. Was I interested in developing or marketing it? Once again word had sure moved fast, I thought. No, I said, not at this time.

Family Matters

The last unofficial weekend of summer started as a humid, wet washout. I did as little as possible on Saturday and tried to do less on Sunday. As the weather began to clear in the late afternoon, boding well for Labor Day, I called Maggie at home to ask how many steaks I should get. Her brother Dylan answered, checked with his mother and reported: "Mom said enough for 18-20 people. She said maybe you should get chicken instead. She said you should be here no later than 1:30. I'm supposed to start the grill by 2:00." I didn't know how much would be enough for 20 people—and one voracious dog. One each, I guess, if they were all meat eaters.

The O'Connor home was a comfortable, large, 1930's Dutch colonial with an enclosed front porch. It was in good condition, but could use some updating. The ample backyard was fenced in with 6' white pickets. I could see the driveway gate was ajar so I headed toward it with Gretchen and my box of 25 fresh-cut steaks. Six-foot-four Dylan saw me coming and met me near the gate. "C'mon in Chris,' he said, "Hi there, Gretchen. The women are inside working on the salads. Can I take that box for you?"

"I have it," I said, "But you can grab the beer and ice out of my car. I got a cold keg. I hope it is enough."

Maggie's Uncle Leo and Aunt Liz were in the kitchen with Maggie and her mother. I'd met the aunt and uncle before. Leo had a beer in his hand. It wouldn't be his last.

Most everyone invited came. The crew arrived en masse. Introductions were made. Snacks were plentiful. A game of horse started beneath the driveway hoop. The clang of horseshoes against the stakes began. The important steaks were on two grills. The croquet set was still idle.

Then Gretchen became the center of attention. She had brought her rubber ball from the car. She had shown it to Perky the Pekingese but Perky's mouth was too small to appreciate it. She took it to Maggie who gave it an upward flip. She laughed when Gretchen ran under it and caught it. She returned to Maggie, implying she wanted her to toss it again. She did. Gretchen brought it to me, I tossed it to Maggie and a spirited game of keep-away began.

Each time Gretchen would get the ball she would race in and around the crowd, effectively veering off whenever someone reached for the ball. Young Sean, thinking he could grab it on the run, took a tumble. I was on my knees on the grass when the ball came back to me. Gretchen came flying at me and knocked me on my back. These were games we routinely played alone. For the first time Gretchen got to glory in having an audience. Once she finally tired she did what she always did with me: she took the ball and hid it behind a bush. Game over.

After eating way too much food, I lost to Sean playing horseshoes. He was now taking on Ricky, one of the crew guys. Others were standing by cheering them on. Leo and Dylan were teaching a couple of the other crew how to play an Irish card game. Gretchen was in the shade of the garage with Perky so I walked toward her. I pulled a folding chair along with me so I could sit with my back against the garage wall. Perky jumped onto my lap. Gretchen, beside me, didn't seem to mind. I looked around and thought: I had forgotten that this is what it is like to have family and friends.

Aunt Liz was now playing Sean. Her first effort got a big laugh when the shoe sailed beyond the pit and landed in a rose bush. "Don't know my own strength," she said. I was so absorbed in the action and the antics that I didn't notice Maggie's mom rolling towards me until she was almost upon me. "Mind if I join you in the shade, Chris?"

"Welcome," I said, "the sun has gotten quite intense."

"None of them seem to notice," she said gesturing toward the players and watchers. "They all seem to be having a good time. How 'bout you?"

"It's been great. That potato salad of yours was outstanding. Reminded me of my mom's. She usually got just the right amount of egg, onion, mustard and, I think, Worcestershire in it."

"Really?" she said, "That's what I use, too. Your mom has passed on, hasn't she?"

"Yeah, six years ago. Dad died a while back, too."

"Sisters, brothers, aunts, uncles?"

"Deceased sister and a brother I haven't seen since I was kid."

"Oh? No close family then?"

"No, not really."

"Well, you have family here whenever you want to borrow one."

"Thank you, Mrs. O'Connor, that's nice to hear. I always feel welcome."

"Chris, didn't I ask you to call me Kay? I am not all that much older than you. I had Meghan just before I was 22 so I'm not quite 50 yet." She paused but I sensed she had more to say.

"You know, it took me nearly three years to overcome my parents' objections to Tom. I'd fallen for him when I was 18. He was this big, strapping Black Irish, ex-Marine cop whom I met when he gave me a speeding ticket. My Polish parents had no use for him and he was nearly ten years older than me. Nevertheless, I told them that when I turned 21 I was going to marry him. And I did. We got married on my birthday. My mom and dad came around and eventually appreciated Tom like a son.

Which reminds me, I want you to know I appreciate how good you are to my daughter. Not just the money. When she came back from New York she was like a wounded momma cat. Angry, defensive, yet protective. You've helped her regain her self-confidence.

It means a lot to me, to all of us. She's had a hard time, lots of pain. You know she lost her dad and came close to death herself. Her recovery was long and painful, and you know, she still has the scars from the cuts and the surgeries. And that bastard Roger—I can barely say his name—broke her heart."

"Well, Kay, you have had a lot to endure yourself. Losing your husband so young, losing a child—Maggie told me—and raising Maggie and the boys and all."

"I couldn't have done it without the Lord, without Meghan, family, friends. I may be in this wheelchair but I still feel like I have had many blessings, and maybe more to come. I miss Tom every day, but, like I said, I'm not that old and this thing isn't going to kill me. I hope to be around to see marriages and grandkids, maybe even great grandkids. Who knows? Maybe some guy in his own chair will take a fancy to me!"

"I'm sure that will all happen, Kay, the good Lord willing."

"What I don't like is being a burden on my kids. I think the boys know I want them to go out in the world. But Meghan is the oldest and takes everything on her shoulders and they let her. I guess I have let her, too. I need to get back to work.

What worries me is that she has so little life of her own. I told her I spoke to Liz and Leo about moving in with me after the boys move out, but Meghan simply does not want to hear it. She has almost no social life outside the family. I fear time is getting away from her. She rarely dates and when she does, she has no confidence. She doesn't know how pretty she is; she thinks all the guys will see are her scars."

"What scars are those, Kay? When I look at her all I see is a bright, beautiful girl devoted to her family. I sense some angst but not anger. I probably shouldn't say this but my guess is she was a gawky, tomboyish teenager who was taller than most of the guys and got teased about it. Then she matured and transformed like a butterfly into the woman she is. Any guy lucky enough to have her choose him would be moving up in class."

"Well, she definitely was a tomboy, but of course I have thought she was beautiful from the day she was born. But Meghan doesn't feel it."

"Maybe that is part of her charm. If it helps any, Kay, I kind of think these new ventures we are getting into will open up new opportunities for all of us ... By the way, where is Maggie? I haven't seen her in the yard for some time."

"Try the front porch, Chris. Gretchen can stay here with Perky and me. I think she is feeling a little moonish."

I'd been about 17 when my grandmother explained that "moonish" was short for "full moonish," something that came once a month. Maggie was on the front porch, sitting by herself on a swing. Knowing how I had quiet needs at times, I tried to silently slip away without her noticing me. A cracking sound from the wooden wheelchair ramp gave me away. "Any chance you are looking for me, Chris? You aren't leaving already are you?"

"Yes and not yet," I said. "Anything wrong? You haven't been seen for a while. Aren't you enjoying your party? I'm no expert, but I think it is going great."

"The party is great, thanks in no small part to you and Gretchen with her antics. She sure is funny. And she seems to know it. I think I was getting a little headachy from all the noise and the sun so I came in here for a few minutes. I guess I got lost in thought. Want to join me?"

"In thought? Sure, it's nice here." I joined her in the swing. "I just had a nice chat with your mom. She is some spirited lady. She's easy to like."

"Yeah, she is. Get her going, though, and she will expose all the family secrets."

"She didn't tell me any dark ones. She did talk a little about your dad. And some about her hopes and wishes for you and your brothers."

"Holidays, parties, we like them, but we always miss him. Dad could bring the best out of everyone. I have been thinking about him, too … Hey, I think I am over my little funk. Want to go back? There is supposed to be pie."

"Pie?" I said, "What kind? Never mind, it doesn't matter. I never pass up pie."

The Grind

In the office the next day Maggie was beaming. Everyone was talking about the great time they had at the O'Connor's. Although Gretchen and I had left about 7:00, the younger ones stayed until well into the darkness. I think someone made a beer run.

Nevertheless, for me at least, it was time to buckle down. It had been my practice to review the crew's output once a week and I was more than two weeks behind. The way we worked was like this:

A project would come from an entity at any level of government or from a public interest group or from an individual, perhaps a candidate for office. Our function was to research the topic's history, and seek out data and expert opinion related to it. It wasn't our goal to stake out or defend a particular position; rather it was to present the critical data neutrally, concisely and as clearly as we could. What our clients did with our reports was, of course, up to them. Sometimes the reports led to clear inferences, other times they did not.

Each of the researchers working for us was an advanced graduate student nearing completion of his or her dissertation. Each was expected to devote 20 hours per week to his or her assignments, but most invested more time. In return, each received a stipend, use of our network and growing database, and professional credits for his or her research. We had a good crew at present: a sociologist, an economist, an urban planner and two political/public policy specialists. They had young brains, but they were good ones.

It was my job, as well as part of Vincent's, to review their output as it progressed. On this day I had seven reports at various stages to review. By midday Wednesday I was caught up.

Usually when there were no pressing problems, I would spend time writing my satirical Internet column—more or less a blog—under the pen name Lance Pierce. Sometimes a more widely read site would pick it up and I would make a few bucks. But suddenly money was no longer a concern. I decided to run a piece I had on standby in order to free time for the "Scottie Matter."

While I was working, Greg Mathis, the engineer, called and asked if the following Thursday would be acceptable for his team to look at the castle. Maggie confirmed with the realtor and the date was set. She, Vincent and I made plans to go to Cherry Ridge the following Wednesday.

Before making the trip, I wanted to get Maggie and Vincent into the cars I promised. It gave me a warm feeling just thinking about it. While I had always been frugal about the things myself, I knew what the right car could mean to someone.

We went car shopping on Saturday. With Vincent up first, we arrived at the BMW dealership. He found a coupe he liked in the color he liked. The salesman noticed that Maggie was taken with a convertible; but she was still torn between practicality and my encouragement to go for a ragtop. Finally, she said she wanted to look at a Mustang, like the one she had rented a few weeks back.

Vincent thought she should go with the BMW. I said, maybe so, but that he hadn't seen her in a Mustang as I had. We were at the Ford dealership for all of five minutes when she asked: "Boss, can I have this green one?" Of course she could. It almost matched her eyes.

They both wanted to know what I was going to get. "Nothing," I said. "The last thing I need is another car. I am going to put the truck at the camp on the road. It may not be environmentally wise, but both Gretchen and I liked the one I rented."

Alexandra

I was leaving the office when Alexandra called. "Did you get my message? I was going to pop up and see you. God, did you miss out! I had really worked myself up to seeing you—and you know what that means! I can't tell you more 'cause I'm in the office. Guess where I'm going?"

She spit this all out before I could say: "Lexie! Great to hear your voice. Of course I am disappointed. I was at a funeral and had to take care of some business in Cherry Ridge. I came into a little property, by the way. Where are you going?"

"That's great, the property I mean. I'm going to London!" she said. "To work with a couple of our writers and sales people. I will be there two, maybe three months. I hope to get back for the holidays. Any chance you can get away and tag along?"

I knew she didn't really want me along. It would cramp her style. Oh, a weekend visit, maybe. That would excite her. Still, she couldn't resist teasing me. "It would be great if I could, Lexie, but you know me, always with the responsibilities."

"Well then, you will be hot for me when I get back, right? I am hoping to pop over to Paris and pick up some lingerie to model just for you." Alexandra liked to "pop" and she liked to model lingerie.

Chapter Five

Revelations All Around

Maggie, Vincent and their baggage were in her new Mustang when they arrived to pick up Gretchen and me early Wednesday. Getting everything in the trunk was tricky and Gretch and I had to share the back seat. The only time Gretchen had been in a convertible was the brief ride with Maggie at the camp. She seemed puzzled. As in, "How do I put my head out the window?"

Our plan was to reach Cherry Ridge in time to have lunch at Millie's, quickly check out the apartment and then introduce Vincent to the town, the castle, and the camp. The two of them had reservations at the Ridgeview Motor Inn. I planned to stay at the camp.

On the way out, Maggie started a game with Vincent. What should the boss buy for himself with his money? After they got by the obvious jabs—an entirely new wardrobe, a gym membership, a personality—they decided to do it alphabetically. Each would get a turn with each letter. The ones that got my approval got a point.

It went like this. Vincent: a woman named Angelina; Maggie: Australia; Me: No points.

Vincent: a woman named Bubbles; Maggie: Barbados; Me: no points.

"Try something other than women and islands," I suggested.

Vincent: "Since we know cars are out, I'll say cashews for C."

"Maggie: No fair, Vincent, that's not special."

"Have you ever seen Chris around a can of cashews? He inhales them," he retorted.

Maggie: "I can still top you, *castle*."

Me: "Point to Vincent. Cashews *are* special to me. And a point to Maggie for the obvious."

They were up to the letter "L" when they finally tired and gave up. The score was still knotted at one. "Don't you want anything?" Vincent asked.

"Remember, he's Mr. *Saint* James, Vincent," Maggie said, mocking my apparent disinterest in costly things.

Neither Maggie nor I had told Vincent about the murdered girl, so we filled him in. "How come I'm just hearing about this? You three stumble over a dead body and then go a couple of weeks without telling me?"

Maggie was flustered by his comment. She said: "We were trying to keep the lid on so many things. Chris … "

I interrupted: "Maggie was just following through to the letter on what I'd told her, Vincent. It's on me. I meant to tell you but I haven't gotten around to it. There are more surprises to come, so you can experience them in much the same way I, and then Maggie, did. You should be caught up by the end of the day."

"Okay," said Vincent.

As a start, I briefed them on some local language. "See that stream over there? It's a crick. Now, see that wider one it flows into? That's a creek." I waited until one of them asked me what the difference is. "You can jump over a crick without getting a wethopper."

"A wet hopper?"

"It's just what it sounds like. Also, some people here say warsh for wash. And woof for woof. I mean woof for wolf."

"And ground hogs are woodchucks," added Maggie, "and soda is pop or is it the other way around?"

When the castle came into view from the highway, Vincent said: "Wow, from here it is pretty impressive. It is bigger than I imagined. Is there a moat with gators?"

"Yeah," I said, "I did a little research. It's big, nearly 400' wide and about 80' deep. That's roughly 32,000 square feet per floor. It has four stories at the lowest and six stories in parts. Plus the two towers: they go to seven stories, then the turrets. It's about 180,000 square feet on about five acres. It's all brick. There are about 150 windows on the front alone, but it looks like a lot of them are boarded up."

"Can you imagine trying to heat the place?" asked Vincent.

"Actually, I kind of have."

Maggie slowed down when Vincent, surveying the streets, advised: "Watch out for Barney Fife." Then, seeing a rundown former custard stand he quipped: "Look, Custard's Last Stand." Vincent could be funny.

We soon pulled up on Ridge Street near the diner. I leashed Gretchen and let her pee on the library lawn while the others caught their bearings. "Three traffic lights," Vincent said: "How many horses, one?"

"I didn't see *any* horses when I was here before. I did see cows," countered Maggie. "There are a couple more traffic lights on the side streets. I think they just blink red and yellow."

"Maybe green hadn't been invented when they put them up. I don't think there is a problem with traffic jams," said Vincent who added, "It sure wouldn't take long to go barhopping here. One hop, no, one wet hop and you'd be done."

I tried to join in: "When I lived here we had a town drunk, but then he died. After that we had to take turns. I left town before my turn came up."

Willy and Millie were both presiding when we entered. Patronage was slow. Gretchen got her usual greeting. "We didn't expect to see you so soon again, Chris. And you brought friends."

I introduced Vincent to the two of them. "Do you mind if we sit at a table in the other room," I asked. The room was vacant.

"Not at all, Chris."

"Try the beef on Kummelweck, Vincent, if you don't mind the salt," I advised. "You might want to try the seltzer. They have cherry, grape, lemon-lime, chocolate, bromo and alka. Eat hardy, guys. The food is good and it isn't all that easy to get dinner in town."

Overhearing this, Millie volunteered: "And vanilla. By the way, Chris, the Barcelona has reopened. Dinners only at present. Nice bar. The Wallaces. Locals. Do you know them? You might want to try it. They are getting their breads and desserts from us. How about something to drink?"

Once we settled into our lunches, Millie came over to talk, as I expected she would. "Can you sit down?" I asked. She pulled up the remaining chair.

"It's all around town that you now own Brampton Woods, where they, you, found the body of that poor girl."

I summarized how I had come to acquire the property from Angus Ferguson. She said she didn't recall him at all. I described him and said he might have come in with my dad, but that would have been several years back. She asked if I had plans for the land. I told her there was a camp on the property that I would be using from time to time and that I hoped to sell the apartment building. She said she knew about the apartment.

I asked her if there was anything new on the investigation into the murder. She said not much. The cops were saying nothing and Mel Reeves reported he couldn't get anything out of them. There hadn't been any more incidents so most people thought it was an isolated event, maybe done by some itinerant. Still, it was scary.

Then she said, "I heard a couple of weeks ago that there is someone interested in the castle! Don't know who, but they will need a lot of money to fix it up. But if they did it would be somethin'."

I decided the news would be out soon enough, so I dropped the bombshell. "The rumor is true, Millie. The three of us will be looking over the castle tomorrow for a possible buyer. Just looking, mind you. Nothing more at the present."

"Omygawd, Chris. Who's the buyer?" She looked at me with a new level of respect or at least interest. I told her we were not at liberty to say.

"I have to get Willy. He will want to hear all about it. He's head of the Chamber of Commerce, you know."

Maggie volunteered to walk Gretchen while Vincent and I talked with Willy and Millie. Vincent did a good job of following my lead. He, like me, was friendly without disclosing much of anything. Willy told us that he had been in the castle many times over the years. He thought it held great possibilities, but "it's so damned big, too big for anyone to rehab. Too big for most any of the uses that have come down the road. Thank God the owners fixed the slate roof about five or six years ago. But that is as far as they got. Even if you tore it back to a manageable size, you'd have all the demo costs. The banks won't back it."

Nevertheless, he assured us that if there was anything the chamber could do, it would. Same for the town officials. "We'd all love to see the castle come back to life. It could really help the town."

I reiterated that we were simply looking, so any excitement on his part would be premature. He was excited nonetheless, and he no doubt was on the phone the moment we left.

We left the diner stuffed, although both Vincent and Maggie were still working on ice cream cones and each of us had a bag of goodies from the bakery, all courtesy of Willy. He flatly refused payment. "Make sure you stop back before you leave," was his final command.

Maggie suggested I drive and she sit with Gretchen. I wanted to go up to the castle for a brief look around before going elsewhere. I drove by my apartment building and noted a strip saying "Sale Pending" placed across the realtor's sign. Hemlock St. led up the hill and on to Erie Ave. Across Erie an uncared-for strip of blacktop wound upward to the castle. There was a worn gate across the entrance. Debris was scattered across the grounds. It appeared that there had been no attempt at upkeep. In one sense, that could be in our favor.

Standing at the base of the building made it look even more massive. Gretchen, like a Kilroy, marked her visit. We circled the building noting this and that: this was a swimming pool, that was an old tennis court. "I don't see how they can be saved," said Vincent.

When we finished encircling the place Vincent estimated: "It must be nearly a quarter mile around."

Maggie said: "I bet it is some view from up there," pointing at the highest turret. "Are we going in?"

We had seen several places where we might have entered. "I don't think it is a good idea," I said, "Tomorrow will be soon enough."

As we drove toward the motel where they would be staying, Maggie pointed out things she remembered from her previous visit. "Go past your old school, Chris, so Vincent can see it."

"That can't be of interest to … "

"Sure it is."

"Okay," I said.

It was quiet until Vincent questioned: "Is there something you two haven't told me?"

"Like what? I told you you'd learn everything before the day is out."

"It is not the business stuff, Chris, it's you two. After all this time Maggie is calling you Chris. It's none of my business, I guess, but until today I have never heard her call you anything but Boss."

Through the rearview mirror I could see Maggie wrinkle her face, but it was I who spoke: "Oh, that, Vincent. It was hard for me to get her to change, but I told her it was about time she called me Chris. She finally agreed to. But she won't in the office. What were you thinking?"

"Oh, nothing, nothing at all," he said with a sideways glance, "I just noticed the change."

We reached the motel and they checked in. "Not bad," said Vincent.

"Nice," said Maggie.

The two-story motor inn was relatively new. It had a comfortable commons area with a big screen TV, a large indoor pool and a well-equipped exercise room. The pool and exercise equipment were open to the public, thus drawing in revenue during off times for the inn. The friendly clerk encouraged the new guests to make use of the facilities. Fees for them were included with their rooms.

We made a quick stop at the grocery store for provisions. Maggie remembered seeing a grill at the camp and she cajoled Vincent into making burgers and roasting corn. I drove the rough road to the camp carefully, so as not to endanger Maggies's new Mustang. When we approached the gate she pointed to the ridge road. "It was down that road," she told Vincent, " that we found the body."

Vincent experienced the same eerie feelings Maggie and I had when he went ahead of us to "meet" Julia at the gate. I had to introduce him and he had to go through the identification recording. "This sure looks like more than just a woodsy camp," he said as the Mustang slowly reached the parking area.

Gretchen again showed her dismay with the gravel and scurried to the low deck that fronted the building.

Julia let us in. I suggested that Maggie show Vincent around. While I wanted to keep little back from Vincent, I had told her to keep the vault our secret for now. I sat down near Julia and asked her to place a call to J. Pierpoint Wadsworth.

Junior came on the phone saying he had intended to call me this week. There were some good developments and some not so good. He gave me the good news first. The care in preparing the estate was paying off. Everything was proceeding rapidly. Funds from Scottie's estate had been set aside for taxes and other expenses. The probate judge had decided some distributions from Scottie's estate could be made. As soon as the paperwork was processed, I would be able to assume ownership of Auracle Media and oversight of Magnus Foundation. He asked if I had secured an attorney and if so to have him or her contact him. I told him Arnie would do so.

On the negative side, he said they had made very little progress in locating Scottie's granddaughter. While that aspect of the estate didn't concern me, I still asked Junior to send me the names and relationships of Scottie's descendants. I said I would like to know more about the man. He said he would fax the information immediately.

I told him about the local paper editor finding two obits for Scottie, one new, one old. I asked him if he knew about the old one. "Oh, yes," he said. "Maybe eight, nine years ago. Scottie's pilot crashed and died on the way back from out there. He went into a lake. A real tragedy. Dad says the two of them were close. At first it was thought Scottie was lost, too. They searched for a second body. However, as it turned out, he was holed up out there. He didn't know about the accident until he tried to call the pilot to come and get him. A couple of weeks passed during which the news story led to a premature obituary."

Junior changed the subject. "By the way, you haven't possibly stumbled across a helicopter, a fancy one, have you? There seems to be one missing. If it's there let me know and I can check it off the list. It would be yours since everything on the property is.

Did you know Angus flew one right into his mid 80's? He held some patents on them, too. He still gets royalty checks. Frankly, he gets a lot of royalty checks. Some guy."

I chuckled and said: "No, no helicopter. I think it would stand out like an elephant wearing a propeller beanie, but anything seems possible around here."

Vincent and Maggie were up in the cupola when I finished the call. I was rooting through one of the cabinet drawers when they came down.

Vincent said: "Was your guy Ferguson a paranoid, Chris? This place looks like it was built to sustain anything short of a nuclear attack! It's totally off the grid, right? And then there is all the communications equipment, even that old style ham set over there." He was pointing to a Hallicrafters shortwave radio in the corner behind Julia.

I agreed with him and pointed out some of the more subtle aspects: "I think the walls are made of insulated panels pressed between some kind of concrete. I bet they were dropped into place—window glass and all—and then linked together. Feel here. This thin stuff covers the inside seams. It is barely visible from a few feet away. Well, this is flat wire. There is a strip every eight feet. It goes up to the overhead lights. At the bottom, it runs into this conduit that runs around the entire perimeter of the floor. The conduit is the heat run, too."

"What are you looking for?" Maggie asked.

"I dunno," I replied, "just rummaging through these papers. I don't suppose either of you read French or Russian, do you?"

"I took a little Spanish," said Maggie.

"I can read German if you run across any," said the political philosopher Ph.D., "and I know some Italian. Your super computer can translate for you."

I said: "Great idea, Vincent. Why don't you two go down to the other building? I'm sure Maggie is eager to see the cars again. I'd like to get the truck running and take it down to Ed Peck's if it needs inspection or anything else. That will give us a second vehicle. Gretchen," I called out, "Do you want to go with Maggie and Vincent or stay here with me?" It would take more to get Gretchen to move. She was well into her afternoon nap.

The Ferguson Family

I decided to begin with the letters. They would be easier to scan than anything with hard covers. I tried to start with the oldest date. That seemed to be about 17 years ago. I put it on the scanning bed and instructed Julia to scan, translate to English and print. There appeared to be about 20 letters. Some ran four pages; some were both sides of a single sheet. All were written in the same neat youthful hand.

Julia was churning out pages almost faster than I could arrange them. She (and I) were nearly finished when she said "Alert, low ink, Chris."

"Keep printing, Julia. Those sensors always lie," I said.

"Angus said 'It's how the manufacturers make their money,'" came the reply. Was it my imagination or did I detect a note of cynicism in Julia's reply?

I cursorily read a few of the translations. I was about to settle in on the couch to confirm what I had inferred when I heard an engine roar. Gretchen arose from her sleep and we both went to the doorway. The Dodge Ram, with Vincent behind the wheel, was moving from the barn toward the house. In its wake was Maggie driving the ATV. Vincent jumped out saying "It runs good. What an awesome collection you have down there! We got a couple more running, too. Maggie was a big help— or rather I helped her. She is pretty good with tools."

Maggie caught up to us and we talked a little about the cars and Vincent's reaction to the workshop. The usually articulate Vincent kept saying "Awesome, awesome." Well, that did kind of sum it up.

I told them Julia had finished translating the letters. I told them that the ones I had looked at all came from his granddaughter. Vincent shut off the truck and the two of them came in to get something to drink. Julia spoke up: "Receiving facsimile." There were several pages from Pierpoint Jr. The gist of the summary was as follows.

Angus Ferguson was born in 1919 to Andrew Ferguson and Molly Malloy Ferguson in Edinburgh, Scotland. The family immigrated to Cherry Ridge, New York in 1921. Angus enlisted in the U. S. Navy at the beginning of 1936. In 1942, the Navy listed him as MIA and presumed dead. After about 18 years, his name resurfaced when he married Irene Whiteside on August 1, 1960 in Westchester County, NY. They were divorced in 1965. The marriage produced two children, Gwendolyn Molly and Calvin Angus.

Scottie's wife, Irene Whiteside Ferguson, was born May 1, 1939 in Sodbury, England and returned to England (Bristol) in 1965. She died May 7, 1999 of natural causes.

Their daughter, Gwendolyn Molly Ferguson, was born August 14, 1960 in Westchester, NY. She married U.S. Army Pfc. Thomas Burke of Ottumwa, Iowa on June 10, 1982. They divorced in 1989. Gwendolyn then married Clive Burnwood in 1995. Gwendolyn died in a motor accident near Wembley, England on December 7, 2008. MSgt. Burke died in the Iraq War in 2004. Burnwood died in 2009.

Gwendolyn had one child, Cassandra Lee Burke, born October 5, 1982 at Fort Bragg, North Carolina.

Scottie's son, Calvin Angus Ferguson, was born June 6, 1963 in Westchester County, NY. He married Jane Schuster in 1983. They were divorced in 1985. He married Alicia Montgomery in 1985. They were divorced in 1990. He next married Bambi Winslow in 1995. They divorced in 1999. Calvin has no known children. Calvin served three years in a British penal institution (Dartmoor), 1998-2001. He served four years, four months in a Nevada State Penitentiary (2004-2008). His last known address is Las Vegas, Nevada.

Pierpoint Jr. added these notes:

"*Although both were raised primarily in England, Gwendolyn was and Calvin is a U.S. citizen. Cassandra, the benefactor of the Ferguson estate whom we are seeking, also holds U.S. citizenship. She worked as a linguist at LSE (London School of Economics) until the past January. She left no forwarding address. We have some anecdotal reasons to think she may be in the United States. An acquaintance has indicated that she had applied to a teaching exchange program. We are checking that out. Through a Las Vegas attorney, Calvin has begun a claim against the estate.*

Hope this helps,
Pierpoint"

"*Cassandra*," I thought aloud. Cassandra is the signature on the letters Julia had translated. She would be turning 28 in October. Cassandra is not a common name. What are the chances that Scottie's Cassandra could be the same young woman whose body we found on Scottie's property?

I began perusing the letters. They all started: "Dear Grandfather." They began when Cassandra was about 12. The first two were short. The later ones were longer. There was a letter every few months for a while. Then about two a year. She seemed to have written them in the language she was studying most at the time. First French, then Russian, then German, and the last ones in Italian. Which of course implied that Scottie could read each of those languages. In some she thanked her grandfather for books and recordings he had sent her. She says she keeps her mother from knowing their secret. At one point she says his encouragement to read histories and listen to music in the languages she was studying helped her increase her knowledge about more things than the languages.

When she was 17 she wrote: "I must return the generous gift you sent me for my studies. Mother found it and was absolutely livid. She said I cannot take money from you. She won't tell me why she dislikes you so much but I know she does."

Then in the next to the last letter she wrote: "Your generosity is overwhelming. I cannot express to you how grateful I am. I promise I will use the money very carefully for my studies. Thank you, thank you, thank you. I hope to come to America. When I do I will find you. I promise."

When I apprised him of what I had learned, Vincent suggested I should tell the cops. Maggie, who had met Broadhurst, was less certain. "Who knows? Maybe he would use the information as reason to search this place and you certainly don't want that."

"How about this?" offered Vincent, "Keep it simple. You tell the cop you just want to pass along what you learned about the name from the estate lawyer. I don't see how keeping the letters to yourself would impede the investigation. You can 'find' them again, later, if you need to."

Oh, Oh

I drove the truck to Ed Peck's and asked him to do a state inspection, change the oil and generally check it out ASAP. "Nice truck," he said, "Top of the line, cherry. Come back about six and it will be ready." I called Vincent and told him I would wander the streets for an hour so.

I remembered I hadn't brought along any mouthwash so I made my way to the drug store. It had still been a private operation when I was a kid. Now it looked like any other chain store. I was trying to decide if I really wanted a candy bar or not when I heard my name: "Chris, Christopher St. James."

I turned to look at the source and found myself looking into the smile of Karen Shannon. "Chris," she said, "I almost didn't recognize you with that moustache. Wow, you look great. I heard you were in town. I looked for you at the reunion last year."

I had sat behind Karen Shannon for twelve years whenever a teacher arranged seating alphabetically. I knew the shape of her neck and ears and the true color of her hair. I knew the mole she had just below her hairline. I knew the way she sometimes sighed when she breathed. I even knew her bra straps were often too tight.

She was always the girl who was a cut or two above me socially. We had hung out together a few times in our late teens, but more or less by accident. A bit of payback might be sweet. I looked at her a bit perplexed. She said: "It's me, Karen, Karen Lan. . . Karen Shannon. Don't tell me I've changed that much."

"Oh, hi Karen, it's nice to see you," I said as sweetly as I could muster.

She took a step back and lied, "Wow, it looks like you spend time in a gym."

"You look good, too, Karen." She did. A little fuller figure, but I guess the cheerleader was still in there. She could still lead us into temptation. "Like right out of the yearbook," I lied.

She said she had heard I was doing well and living, where was it, near Albany. "You're a writer, right? Is this the famous Gretchen I have heard about?" Gretchie ignored her. "I am living back here now, right next to mom and dad. Divorced by the way, but that is all behind me. Onward and upward. How long are you here? It would be great to have you come by to catch up."

She rambled on for two or three minutes and I did my best to seem interested. "Maybe we could meet for a drink, though it's hard to find a decent place here anymore. Cahoots is the best." She fetched a card from her purse. "Here's my number. Call anytime you are in town."

"Thanks, Karen, it was good to run into you. I'm sure I'll see you again."

When I was back on the street I turned and Karen's uncertain frown instantly turned into a wide smile. I waved and smiled back.

Brainstorming

We convened in Vincent's room after dinner to talk about how to spend some of Scottie's money. We snuck Gretchen in. I wasn't sure her privileges extended to the inn and her weight was over the place's posted limit on pets. Dogs could use a national bill of equal rights.

Thinking about Gretchen, the first thing I said was that I wanted to build a no-kill animal shelter in her name. That led me to thinking about homeless shelters for people, Habitat for Humanity houses and helping sick kids. I had no sense of priority, but these were the first things that came to mind and that had to count for something.

Facetiously, I suggested: "I suppose I could be like John Beresford Tipton."

"Who?" They had never heard of him.

"The TV show, "The Millionaire," back in the 50's. Each week he would have his aide give a regular person a million bucks. Anonymously. They couldn't divulge where it came from or how much they got. Then the show would depict what happened to them. Of course, it was all fantasy and drama."

Maggie asked: "How old are you? But seriously, did he pick the people? Wouldn't you want just ones in real need?"

"I don't know. I don't think that was ever disclosed. They usually had some kind of need, but not necessarily money."

There wasn't much support for that idea, so I posed another. "What if we held a national essay contest of sorts? We would have people send in their ideas for the best use of, say, a million dollars. We would guarantee we would put out the money for, say, the best ten ideas put forth in 100 words or less. And those that sent in the chosen ideas would each get maybe $100,000."

Vincent said: "You'd get swamped with entries. People would treat it like a lottery. Who would read them all? You'd have to have a very brief entry window or charge a fee or something to control the deluge. However, in theory it might work. It would be a good way to get ideas. Of course, I'd bet most of them would be self-serving. Would it be legal to charge a fee? If you charged $10 an entry and got a million entries, you'd have another $10 million! That would almost pay for the whole thing. If you charged more you'd get more and probably eliminate some frivolous entries."

Maggie said: "I kind of like the idea, and think of the benefit to the poor old post office."

We turned our attention to the castle and what it should be used for. I'd been vague about it. It was nice enough, Vincent said, to want to restore a massive old landmark and help the town out in the process, but it would largely be a waste of money if it had no real purpose.

I had eliminated its use as a health spa or rehabilitation center. Others had tried that and failed. An idea I kept was to use it as some kind of multi-purpose educational retreat, on the order of a Rensselaerville Institute, with which we were both familiar or Chautauqua. They are both kind of out of the way places, too.

I said I thought about moving the Magnus Foundation to the site. Vincent agreed and noted the staff needed wouldn't require much of the space. I mentioned our policy center, expanded, plus our new interests. He was lukewarm to this, because he recognized, without saying so, that it would mean he might have to relocate to the boonies to stay as its overseer.

Until that point, Maggie had said little. "It's such a big place, why can't you just put them all in there and add new stuff until you max out the place?"

"You mean like 'build it and they will come?' That was fantasy," said Vincent.

"Well, there is a lot of fantasy in this,' Maggie countered. "Do it in stages. Assign a floor for rooms, another floor for offices, another for meeting rooms and such and the main floor for other things. Maybe in the renovation spaces can be made to be flexible. Chris said it already has a dance floor, a dining room and a pool."

We continued in this vein until we concluded we didn't really know what we were talking about. I noticed that Maggie was looking tired. I suggested we break up until morning. Maggie did go off to her room, but Vincent and I continued to talk. I tried to flesh out the role he would be playing. The problem was I didn't know what it was, only that I wanted him and Maggie as my lieutenants.

Looking, Lurking, Lusting

Leaving his room at one end of the facility took me past the vacant exercise area and then the pool. The passageway and pool were barely lit by security lights. When I heard a splash of water I peered in toward the pool. I saw a shadowy figure gracefully and almost soundlessly making its way through the water. The figure reached the near wall and then reversed direction. My eyes lingered until the figure again reached the near wall. Then a tall, perfectly proportioned woman made her way out of the water. In the dim light I could not make out a face, but a tremor through my body gave my subconscious away. The woman moved toward a light and bent down to pick up a towel. It was Maggie. Beautiful Maggie. Once again I felt a conflict between guilt and elation.

Visiting The Erstwhile Castle

The next morning we gathered for breakfast at Millie's. Mel Reeves approached us, knowledgeable about our pending visit to the castle. He wanted to come along. I said no, but I promised him a brief interview before I left town. Reluctantly he accepted. Willy asked if we would like him to accompany us to give a town leader's perspective. Again, I said no.

The realty agency's two reps were outside the entrance when we arrived. "God Almighty!" I said. "Hold up guys. I have to think this through."

"What's wrong, Chris?" asked Vincent.

"Is that woman the agent you met with, Maggie?"

"Yeah, her name is Shannon. Karen if I remember correctly. Why? Do you know her?"

"Yeah, I do. In fact I ran into her yesterday at the drugstore. We went to school together." I pulled out the card she had given me. I had stuck it in my wallet without looking at it. Sure enough, she was in real estate.

"Whoopee!" said Vincent, "She's not bad. I feel there is some zesty history here. Don't worry, Chris, we have your back!" I hope so, I thought.

Karen was all gushy from the outset. "Chris, I didn't know you are part of this. What good luck. This is going to be such great fun." She grabbed me by the arm, trying to lead me ahead of the group. Fortunately, the engineer and his team pulled in. We went over what I was seeking out of this first visit. They explained the limits of what I could expect.

Karen's boss, Stan Williamson, told us they had a letter from the owners permitting us to enter, but they couldn't get a key to the main entrance. He gave a copy of the letter to me and I gave it to Mathis, the engineer. The electrician, Cicotti, spoke up: "I don't think we'll have any trouble finding a way in. It looks like there's power to the main box. Give me a few minutes and I'll see if I can get some lights on."

We took the time to circle the building. The engineer took some measurements and made some notes. Everybody had something to say about the condition of the exterior. Everyone agreed with me about the windows.

We decided it would be most efficient if we split up. Vincent would go with the plumbing and heating guy, Maggie would go with Cicotti and I would tag along with the engineer. Naturally, Karen had already staked out my side. The crew had extra hardhats and the engineer instructed everyone to be careful. We also had flashlights and cameras.

By 12:30 we had more or less toured the building and taken scores of pictures. Everyone was hungry so we agreed to break for lunch. Mathis took me aside and said his first impression was better than he anticipated. I had half expected to hear what Cary Grant as Mr. Blandings had been told repeatedly: "Tear it down."

Mathis suggested that our group needn't stay. What he meant was that he would like us to clear out. He said the crew would come back after lunch. I asked if I could get his opinion by the beginning of next week. He said, an opinion, yes, but with few specifics.

He wanted to know what the owners were asking for it. When I told him I didn't know, he looked at me as if I had just gotten off a banana boat. We went over to the realtors. Stan said: " The records show they paid $745,000 for it eight years ago. The slate roof cost them a bundle to repair. They said they would take $1.3 million." No doubt he was mentally calculating a commission.

Mathis countered: "Out here, in this market, I bet they would."

Stan said: "You can't build this today for $10 million."

Mathis countered: "It could take that much to put it in shape, and no bank is going to put up that kind of money."

"Well, I'm sure we could *jew* them down."

"What did you say?" I asked.

"That's just their asking price. They will come down."

"No, that's not what you said, Williamson." I was abrupt. Stan had hit a nerve at a time I was already tense: "You said you could *jew* them down. We will no longer require your services."

"What?" Stan cried, "What did I say?" He was visibly beside himself.

Karen rushed to me saying "Chris, he didn't mean anything by it. He didn't think."

"Right, Karen, he didn't think. He's done here." I quickly walked away.

I could hear Stan saying to anyone who'd listen: "I didn't know he's Jewish."

"He's not, maybe one of the contractors is," said Karen.

"Doesn't matter whether any of us is. Big mistake, buddy," said Vincent. "Take it as a life lesson."

I told Mathis he had the permission letter and that he should continue. I said I would be looking forward to getting his report. I told him the money could be arranged if we thought the project was feasible.

Karen made another effort. "I apologize for Stan. He didn't realize what he said. It's just an expression. Please don't let this affect us. Come by for dinner tonight and we will talk this out. I really would like to see you."

"Sorry, Karen, I don't have to work with the Stans of the world." The thought gave me a warm feeling. Self-righteous, too, but mostly warm.

The four of us got in the truck. Neither Vincent nor Maggie said anything, so I did. "So, guys, whaddya think?"

"He's a shithead. I'm proud to work for you," said Vincent.

"She's a piece of works," offered Maggie.

"And hot for the boss," added Vincent.

"No, guys," I said. "What do you think of the *building*?"

"Oh, I think you already made up your mind. You are going to buy this pile of bricks and fix it up like the Taj Mahal. You are going to keep us hopping until its done," said Maggie, but with a smile.

"Yep, that's what you are going to do, we'll be wet hopping," Vincent groaned. "You know the Taj Mahal is a mausoleum, don't you?"

"It will be fun," I said, "You two get to help me spend Scottie's money."

With everyone's mood lightened, we stopped at Millie's for lunch. Vincent pleased her when he said he wished the diner were near where he lived: he would eat there every day. Vincent lived to eat. He had eyed the Foosball table in the dining area since he was first in, so when Willy came over eager to hear about our morning, he asked if he could use it. He challenged Maggie.

I told Willy not to get excited about the castle. I said the engineer would be there all afternoon and it would be days before we got a preliminary report. Still, he wanted to know what I thought. I was as non-committal as I could be.

"But you think there is a chance your buyer might be interested?"

"Maybe," I said, "It will take a lot of money to fix it up. And it isn't like there is a contractor nearby who can handle it."

"You could get a lot of labor right here, Chris. A lot of people could use the work."

"Labor, yes," I said, "but it'll need some really skilled trades."

When Vincent and Maggie returned to the table (Vincent: "I crushed her Chris." Maggie: "By one whole goal.") I told them we had to get on to our real estate agent back home. Get them to pick up with the castle owners.

"I'm thinking you two could go back this afternoon if you want, or stay over until morning." Vincent said going back today worked for him. Maggie said she would like to spend the afternoon using Julia. We agreed that Vincent would drive my truck back and that Maggie and I would follow the next day in the Mustang. I didn't mention that having Maggie stay over would protect me from Karen Shannon. I wouldn't be tempted to score one for the nerdy brainiacs who drooled over her 20 years ago. It looked like it would be such an easy score, too.

We separated with Gretchen going along with Maggie. I stayed in town to first see the realtor selling the apartment and then Mel Reeves, as I had more or less promised him and, lastly, Broadhurst. I'd call Maggie when I needed to be picked up.

The realtor had the deal nearly in place. It was a good deal for the Dumbrille's. Paying about the same as their rent rate, they would own the building outright in 20 years. The agent, having heard about my role in the castle venture asked if there was some reason I had not asked them to handle the deal. I simply said that another staff person had made the arrangements. I said I would call upon them if we had future needs.

I walked up to the newspaper office, one of the oldest buildings on Ridge Street. The building also housed a dentist and a second floor containing a small watt radio station and a beauty parlor. The office was not exactly the bustling place that had fascinated me when I was a kid. Mel had one ad sales rep and two multitasking staff. Together they gathered the news, sold the ads, and did the digital layout. They transferred the digital files to a nearby city where the paper was printed. Copies were mailed out by the printer's mail house. Newsstand copies came back to Mel for distribution.

I gave Mel the interview he sought. He didn't get much out of me other than that the castle venture was a whim on the part of an anonymous eccentric investor. I told him that an engineer was evaluating the castle and would be sending a report. He wanted to know how I was involved. I said simply that the investor was someone whom I knew well. Mel prodded; I parried. He didn't bring up the murder so I asked him if there was any news.

"Nodda. Forensics turned up nothing. From what I heard, they couldn't find a record of Cassandra Cross even entering the country. No passport, not much ID. You'd think in this day and age with Homeland Security and such, it would be a snap. Maybe she came in via Canada. She was carrying a birth certificate. Says she was born in New York. They are thinking she used a different name. They sent in DNA samples and prints, but they can take a long time. They want to send the results to Scotland Yard and Interpol. Her rental car is still impounded. Quite a few different sets of prints. Some hairs. I guess they don't clean 'em up all that well. So other drivers, rental people, mechanics, who knows who?"

To change the subject, I asked him how business is. "Don't ask, Chris. I am barely paying my people. I'm down to two choices. Go under or sell out to one of the chains for a song. They'll turn it in into some kind of shopper thing. Costs are up—paper, printing, mailing, fuel— ad revenues and subscriptions are down. Too much competition. I have put out a few resumes, but the whole print business is suffering. Who's going to want a 55-year old small town editor?"

"I am sorry to hear that, Mel, a good paper is a real asset to a community." An idea began to crystallize. "I may be able to help. I can't go into it now, but don't do anything definite without talking with me first, okay?"

"Uh, okay Chris, I guess. I'm open to ideas."

I was on the street when Maggie called. "The T-Bird and the Crossfire are running and ready to be inspected. It's 3:00. If I take one of them to the shop do you think they would do it while I wait?"

I replied. "I'm three doors down from Ed's right now. Hang on the line and I'll ask."

Ed looked up with some surprise at my request, but quickly agreed to do the work. "A Crossfire, eh? Mostly a Mercedes. Change the oil and check it out, too?" I told Maggie to hang out at the diner while she waited and I would meet her there.

Tensions Heighten

I was a little anxious about seeing Broadhurst again. He was the only one visible when I entered. This time he recognized me. "Mr. St. James," he said, "What can I do for you?"

"It's about Cassandra Cross," I answered, "I have a little information that might interest you."

I handed him the fax, saying, "A while back you pointed out coincidences. Well, I think this says this is more than coincidence. Angus Ferguson's attorney is looking for Cassandra Burke, Ferguson's granddaughter. She is the only member of his family named as a beneficiary to his estate.

"You want to find out about Cassandra Cross. Same first name, same birth date, probably the same birthplace as Cassandra Burke. Both have British connections. I'd bet they are one and the same. If so, I don't think her coming here to teach was a random choice on her part. I further bet that the attorney has not learned that Burke may have married and used the name Cross to connect here. Maybe Cross is her married name, maybe it is an alias. Either way, from what I have seen, the attorney doesn't yet know that Burke/Cross has a son. I plan to tell him, but I came to you first."

Broadhurst sat back in his chair, examining the fax. "Where'd you get this?"

I told him that Ferguson's estate attorney had sent me the information.

"I want to talk with him," said the Chief.

"Sure," I replied, "The number is on the fax."

"What I want to know is where you fit into this, St. James."

Our conversation took an irritating turn: "That camp of yours, you wouldn't mind if we looked around, would you? I looked at this satellite photo and you have a couple of good-sized buildings up there." He showed me the photo as evidence.

"Look anywhere on the grounds you want, as soon as you show me a warrant," I said, "but the buildings are off limits."

"If you've nothing to hide, why wouldn't you cooperate?"

"Geez, Chief, that's dialogue straight from the cops shows. The fact is, like most people, I do have things I wish to keep private, but nothing illegal and nothing to do with your case."

"I could get that warrant."

"Not without cause and you don't have any. The buildings are nowhere near where the body was found. I have done nothing suspicious. All I have done is report finding a body and bring you useful information. If I had reason to withhold anything relevant to your investigation, why would I have brought you this fax? But if it's necessary, I will invoke my right to an attorney. I will give you his name and number now if you wish."

Broadhurst sighed. "I guess we are through here. I don't like you St. James, but I guess I should say thanks for this. I have a feeling we will be talking again, soon."

Checking in with Pierpoint

I reached the diner ahead of Maggie. I sat near the front where I could see her pull up at Ed's. I called Pierpoint. I wanted to tell him about the connection I suspected. This time I got Senior. He already knew. Broadhurst had wasted no time. "I just got off the phone with Chief Broadhurst. He's coming here tomorrow to look at our reports. What a tragedy. Here we've been searching high and low for Cassandra and suddenly we learn she was killed out there in Cherry Ridge no less. And then learning she left a son behind. I have never experienced anything like this … He becomes the heir. We have a lot of work ahead of us."

I asked about the boy. Senior said: "Broadhurst says child services has him under care and supervision. Now we have to try and find the father and see if we can reunite them."

"What about the uncle, uh, … "

"Well, he's a nefarious piece of works. I think we told you he put a claim in on the estate. If we can't find the father he would be the boy's next of kin. What you saw was just the tip of the iceberg. He's been in and out of trouble most of his adult life. He's a scammer with an ugly streak. No judge in his right mind would award him custody of the boy. But he may try and we will prevent it."

"What's the boy's name? What will happen to him?" I asked.

"Broadhurst said it is Colon. It depends. If we can't find a suitable relative, then a court would probably assign an administrative guardian and try to place him with a reputable family. His inheritance would go into a trust. It's a rare situation and I'm not clear on the law. We'll do the research. We will probably petition the court to represent him. After all, he is our client's, Scottie's, grandson.

"By the way, I set Broadhurst straight. He seemed to imply you might have some link to what happened to Cassandra. He said it took place near your apartment, you found the body on Scottie's—your—property, and then you brought him our fax to you. He thought that was too many incidences to be simple coincidence. But I explained to him that you had nothing to gain through the girl's death. That the property and all were given to you prior to Scottie's passing and that the bequests to you were separated from the rest of the estate."

As I was finishing up with Pierpoint, Maggie came across the street. "Ooh, that looks good," she said admiring my banana split, "but didn't your grandma ever tell you about snacks before dinner?"

I couldn't convince her to have a split, but she did order a single dip cone. I brought her up to speed about what I had been doing. She took it all in and wondered if Broadhurst was going to be persistent about seeing inside the buildings. I told her I had tried to bluff him and he might call me on it. Then again, what Pierpoint told him might have cooled his jets. We would have to wait and see.

Maggie reported that all the cars were running except the TR-7. I wasn't surprised. She said Ed told her he was open in the evening. She said that if we wanted to, we could still get the T-Bird in before we left the next day.

I grinned: "Did Ed hit on you?"

"No. Why, was he supposed to?"

"He has a reputation," I explained. "He's like his father. Well, he used to be anyway. Maybe he learned his lesson. About eight to ten years ago he got caught by an angry husband who busted him up pretty good with a baseball bat."

"Wow. A baseball bat. Is that Cherry Ridge justice?"

"It can be effective and usually no one dies. I'll tell you about the Pecks. Ed is the third generation that I know of who has had that station. Back in my dad's day, before OTB and the lottery, it was the place to bet on horses or numbers. They had punchboards and there might have been poker games after hours. You could buy girlie magazines and calendars and condoms. Ed's dad got pretty rich but he blew most of it away."

"*Girlie* magazines? That sounds old-fashioned. Condoms? Why not just go to the drugstore?

"Different times, Maggie."

"By the way, what are punchboards?"

"They're boards with lots of small holes in them. The holes are filled with rolled-up paper. You would pay a dime —maybe more— to punch out a hole with something like a swizzle stick. The paper would tell you what you won, if anything."

"So it was a way to gamble?"

"Yeah, a pretty popular one. At one time they were in drugstores, bars, social clubs and other places. I haven't seen one in years, and that was in an antique shop. But I bet they are still made and used."

"I learn the damnedest things from you."

"I guess I have a head for useless information."

"Not useless, interesting."

It was too late for normally frugal Maggie to check out without paying for a second day. Besides, she said, she wanted to use the pool. We bought subs and drinks. We drove the short distance to the state park so she could see it and so Gretchen could pee on new ground. It was still light when I dropped her back at the motel.

Thirty minutes later I was settled into the camp, trying fruitlessly to organize my thoughts. I had one irrational fantasy where I drove down to the old Warren house and presented myself to Karen Shannon who took me into the old bomb shelter. Then my cell phone rang. It was Maggie. We talked until midnight when the cell ran out of juice. I never once thought of Karen Shannon. Not then and, for all intents and mal-purposes, never again.

Rook or Castle?

The report from the engineer was mixed, as I expected. We would need a whole new complex heating system. To make it effective we needed to invest in insulation. The electrical system was a hodgepodge of knob and tube dating to the 1930's or earlier combined with more modern wiring. Code would require that the knob and tube be replaced if we were to do any insulation work. The new load requirements necessitated a complete replacement.

The plumber said there was virtually nothing about the pipes that was worth saving. That is, where there were pipes. Most of the accessible copper had been stripped and stolen. Fortunately, he said, modern tubing was relatively inexpensive and easier to install. His biggest concerns were the faulty iron and tile drainage pipes, and the lack of an adequate number of bathrooms, assuming we would want one per sleeping room.

In a nutshell, we needed all new mechanicals, plumbing and insulation.

There were pluses. First, Mathis had concluded that the structure had been built on a solid ledge of rock with solid brick and mortar lally columns. Consequently, there had been little movement over the years.

The oversized wood beams, some exposed, were mostly sound, although he expected some would need reinforcing.

There were a couple of springs in the basement, but they were under control. The slate roof, according to Mathis who ventured out on to it, was in outstanding condition. We had seen no broken slates on the ground when we toured and he found only a few that were cracked.

The quality of the skeleton, the brick and slate was what made the place salvageable. They had provided protection from the elements. There was a little water damage inside. Most of it was from around chimneys and near windows. The dance floor looked somewhat worn but it would respond to sanding and refinishing. The same could be said for most of the public room floors. The walnut and mahogany bar and comparable wood cabinets and trim were all in good to excellent condition for their age and lack of care.

Mathis's overall verdict: Reclamation would be feasible. Estimated price of reclamation: to be determined following design work and specifications.

Maybe I had heard only what I wanted to in the report; nevertheless, I concluded we would bring the old place back to life. During the first week in October we made the deal. By the end of October we were looking at rough sketches. Vincent had taken day trips to have various architects and builders look over the place.

Everyone cautioned that this size project would take a long time, but my response was always the same: They produced design drawings for the Empire State Building in two weeks and built the whole damn thing in 410 days. That was in 1930-31. Renovating this place with all the modern tools and materials available shouldn't take that long. Of all the pros I talked with, I liked Greg Mathis the best. Maybe it was because he liked old buildings. Maybe it was because he was willing to fast track the project. Whatever the reasons, I hired him to run the project.

I made a quick trip to Cherry Ridge to gather up the old bonds. We cashed them in and Swann oversaw investing them. We transferred a couple of the numbered accounts and invested them. We had learned how to liquidate the gems, so I gathered most of them, too. As I drove back home I tried not to think of what I had with me. I was beginning to get some insight into the paranoia that wealthy people can experience.

Town Meeting

By mid November we had enough information to quell the rumor mill and go public. I contacted Willy Logan and asked him to organize a town meeting at the largest venue in the town, the high school gymnasium. The bleachers were full and additional seating had been set up on the wooden floor. Cameras were in front of the makeshift dais under one basketball hoop. It was intimidating. Willy introduced me.

"Good evening," I began. "Thank you, Willy, for the kind words on behalf of both Gretchen and myself. She can't be here tonight because it would keep her up past her bedtime." A bit of laughter rippled through the crowd. This was a serious time for them and they were attentive.

"Many of you know me or knew my father and uncles, and some of you may remember my grandmother. Some of you may be shirtsleeve cousins. I see faces out there familiar to me from school days. They are all a little older, but then aren't we all?

You may not know that my grandmother's ancestors were among the first settlers here. At one time they owned, farmed and logged a portion of South Ridge, which some of you call Brampton Woods. Some of those same ancestors are buried there; others are buried in Holy Sepulchre. In more recent years, Angus Ferguson owned the ridge. Not many of you knew him but he, too, was raised here.

I mention Angus because it was from him that Serendipity Ltd. acquired the ridge. And it is through his inspiration that we decided to acquire the castle. I am here tonight with my colleagues to describe to you the plans we have for the castle. Let me introduce them to you." I introduced Vincent, Maggie, Arnie and Mathis.

"Now to get right to the point, I am pleased to formally announce that the long dormancy of the Hillside Castle will soon be over."

There was tentative applause. Someone called out, "We've been hearing that for as long as I can remember."

I went on: "It will not be torn down, as some rumors may have suggested. It will be fully renovated over the next year or so and then, as The Serendipity Manor, it will become a vital contributor to Cherry Ridge." This time the applause, led by Willy, was much more enthusiastic.

"Whaddya gonna do with it?" sang out the same voice. "Give Chris a chance," a woman said.

"At present our plans are incomplete," I answered. "We will soon be going out for bids for the extensive work. There will be provisions in the contracts that will require the successful bidders to hire from the local region. So, there should be many jobs for those qualified." This was met with real cheers. "There will be money spent in town." More cheers. "And eventually, there will be some long-term jobs and new people coming to work there."

Mel Reeves, standing front and center, asked: "What's your time frame, what's your cost estimate?" I turned to Mathis as if I needed him to respond.

"Our preliminary budget for making the building weather tight and bringing it up to code is $5.2 million," he said. "While we will save what we can, we have to replace nearly everything inside because it is damaged beyond repair, worn out, doesn't meet requirements or has been stolen. The cost will go beyond that as we make enhancements. As to the time frame, we are on a fast track. We hope to begin deconstruction as soon as all approvals are in place. If all goes well, we will have a partial re-opening by this time next year."

"You didn't answer me," said the loudmouth, "Whaddya gonna use it for? A rehab center, a halfway house?"

"Shut up, Charlie," said the woman, "If it is, you should be the first patient!" The audience roared.

"All I can tell you now," I responded, "is that it will be run by Serendipity. It will have educational, philanthropic and recreational orientations."

Mel Reeves again: "Who do you people work for? Who is Serendipity?"

Another person chimed in: "It sounds like it's Chinese. I bet it's a front for the Chinese or one those Asian religions. They are buying up everything."

I noticed that Karen Shannon had worked her way close to the front. I motioned Vincent to come to the microphone. I whispered to him: "It's time to let another cat out of the bag. Tell them who owns Serendipity. Make it simple."

"Serendipity Limited," he said, "is solely owned by Christopher S. St. James. He is not Chinese. He's a Cherry Ridge Roman. Roman Catholic that is." Leave it Vincent to get off a quip.

Two guys caught Karen Shannon before she hit the floor.

I left the podium saying my colleagues would answer further questions. I motioned to Maggie to come with me. As I worked my way through the crowd, hands were extended to shake or to pat me on the back. I now knew what it had been like for Gretchen. I tried to be courteous without slowing down.

Alexandra II

E-mail provides an impersonal way to be personal. I don't use it much. I fear it will encourage people to use it to contact me. And then I would feel an obligation to respond and an unending cycle could result. Hell, I don't like using a phone. Nevertheless, I found the following in my in-basket:

"Christopher! Command appearance. Friday. At the Marriott. Dinner there at 7:00 sharp. I arranged to come up there for a signing. I can only stay the one night so be prepared. Take that great pill! I have to go to NYC for Saturday and Sunday signings. One of our Brit authors. You'd like his work. Don't keep me waiting. I'm bringing the lingerie I got in Paris. Am I talking like I have been in London for ten weeks? E-mail me back. Luv ya, Alexandra."

Well, one night. At least I wouldn't have to make arrangements for Gretchen. She could use the doggie door if she needed to.

I was on time Friday. Alexandra greeted me at the bar with a kiss and a hug. She was wearing a navy blue suit over a white blouse with one more open button than necessary. She had had a drink or two. "The signing ran late so I came straight here. I didn't get a chance to change. Do I look alright?" "You look wonderful. That's some London tan you're sporting." She got the joke.

Midway through dinner she seemed a bit fidgety and her talk became a bit coy. "Oops," she said, "I dropped my napkin. Can you reach it for me?" I slid my chair back from the small table. I couldn't quite reach the napkin so I dropped to one knee.

Alex spread her legs, reached for my hand and put it on her thigh. "See anything interesting down there?" she cooed. I certainly could.

As I settled back in my seat, I said: "Where's the Paris lingerie?"

"That's what I am not wearing," she said breathily. "It's all the rage in Paris. Ready to see more … or less?"

The waiter couldn't come fast enough to process my card. The elevator couldn't move fast enough. Fortunately we had the car alone because she had her hands all over me once the door had closed, as if closing was needed. "Room 342" she whispered.

Only seconds had passed when she began showing me her "Paris lingerie." It consisted of a necklace and nothing more. "Undress me," she said. I unclasped the necklace and let it drop to the floor. She was as ravishing as usual. Maybe more so.

There was little opportunity to sleep. I had taken one blue pill before coming to the hotel. I took a second in the wee hours of the morning. When I did awake it was dawn. I knew it wasn't Gretchen in bed with me. "I so do like it in the morning," Alexandra said. A little later she said: "That was wonderful. You remembered what you've been missing, didn't you?"

We showered and she began to dress. "If you get a move on we have time for breakfast. Then you can drive me to the airport."

Over breakfast we talked like old friends. She told me about her work and particularly her stay in London. She only cursorily mentioned another editor she had taken a fancy to. I told her I had inherited a little money and things were going well. Suddenly she asked: "Who's Aggie or is it Maggie? Not that it matters. I've had it happen before, but not with you, so I'm curious."

"Maggie?" I asked. "There is a girl who works with me, for me, her name's Maggie … What's happened before?"

"Last night you called out her name. I didn't mind."

"I don't remember doing that," I said defensively.

"Well, you did, but like I said, it's no biggie. Besides, you got better and better." Leave it to Alexandra to get the most out of my embarrassing utterance.

We parted outside the airport. "No need to park and come in with me. Here's a little something to remember me by." I expected a deep kiss, which I got. I did not expect her to grab me quite so personally at the same time. And then, she was gone.

Chapter Six

An O'Connor Christmas

On the Monday before Thanksgiving I announced to the staff that I wanted them to come up with a list of donations we could make for Christmas or, in the case of Arnie Spellman and one of the crew, Hanukkah. Gifts for poor kids, shut-ins, homeless. An arbitrary million dollars worth. Then I tasked a couple of the staff to set up the distribution as quietly and anonymously as possible.

The O'Connors invited me to spend Thanksgiving with them. I declined but said I might stop for pie after I did a shift at the homeless center. It was the one selfless thing I did each year. Then again it wasn't so selfless because it made me feel I was contributing something.

I was tired and feeling depressed when I finished, so I spent the evening home alone with Gretchen. The conundrum I had been wrestling with since gaining Scottie's wealth weighed particularly heavy on me that day. I saw so many people who had so little. I saw how uplifting, albeit temporary, a good meal could be. I saw the generosity of those helping at the center. Charity was present; faith and hope not so much.

My conundrum was the feed a man a fish, teach a man to fish parable. At one end of the spectrum I could use the money to feed people, shelter them, and clothe them until it was gone. But that would only be temporary on a large scale. At the extreme I could try to follow some grandiose utopian plan to make some massive change in the human condition. Not likely.

What could I do that would be both manageable and effective? I was smart enough to know the questions, but too dumb to know the answers.

In contrast, Christmas Eve was another matter. When the O'Connors asked me to share it with them I eagerly accepted. Maggie had asked me to come around the year before. I had made excuses. This time I said I would drop by for a while. I realized I had missed being with them at Thanksgiving.

Sean greeted me at the door when I arrived. He took the packages I was carrying and called out "Chris Kringle and Gretchen St. James are here bearing gifts."

Uncle Leo, Aunt Liz and Kay were in the living room where there was a blazing log fire. "We don't need Santa Claus, we need Smokey the Bear," said Liz.

"Come in," welcomed Kay, "There was no need for you to bring presents."

"I couldn't come empty-handed," I replied.

I had tried to be thoughtful in choosing the gifts without going overboard. I gave each of the boys pairs of season ski passes. That took care of Dylan and his girlfriend Luanne and Sean and whomever he might invite along. I gave Leo and Liz a weekend at a Vermont lodge. They had talked about going there but never had. I gave Kay a shawl hand-knit or purled or something by my grandmother, one of three in my dad's stash. She loved it. Choosing something for Maggie had been my problem. I went through a very convoluted and arduous thought process. It went like this:

Having nothing special to do, let alone a date, on New Year's Eve meant little to me. In fact, I hated New Year's. If anything bad happened in my life, there was a good chance it would be at New Year's. My marriage ended. A car accident. My favorite great uncle hanged himself. The list went on. If there wasn't an incident, I was sure to be in a deep New Year's depression. Doctors call it Seasonal Affective Disorder. We call it SAD. How apt.

Still, I thought, Maggie might feel bad if she didn't have a New Year's date. I thought: she may be one of those pretty girls that everyone assumes is dated up well in advance so she doesn't get asked at all. If she does, it's probably by some creep. Consequently, I had thought about saying to her: if we are both without anything special to do New Year's Eve, we could spend it together. Then I realized that that sounds like a pity date. I did not want to embarrass her by suggesting it. Do I sound like I over think things? Besides, I had made it known I was driving to Cherry Ridge for the holiday. Like I had some reason to be there. But then, running out of time to find the right gift for Maggie, I re-thought my decision. So...

Maggie opened the small box I handed to her. "It's from Gretchen," I said. A black onyx charm of a Labrador Retriever. "Oh, it's so cute. Thank you, Gretchie. It looks just like you. Come here so I can give you a hug."

She shook the second box. It was lightweight and it didn't rattle. Inside was my hand-written invitation to dinner along with buttons for the Saratoga Springs First Night Event. My handwriting is terrible and it had taken me numerous tries to get the invitation to look presentable. I said: "I hope I am not being presumptuous."

"What is it, Meghan? What does it say?" her mother asked. Maggie read the invitation.

"Maggiepie has a date for New Year's, Maggiepie has a date for New Year's," chanted Sean.

"Stop it, Sean," said Kay. I guess little brothers never change no matter how old they get.

Maggie gave me a sheepish smile. I wasn't sure if she was pleased. "Is it okay?" I asked. She nodded a soft yes. "You can dress up or down, whichever you like. But tell me ahead of time so I won't do the wrong thing." I still wondered if I already had.

In the background, Kay was saying: "Of course she will dress up, won't you, dear? We'll go dress shopping, Meghan. You should get something new for New Year's Eve."

The O'Connors had a gift for me, too. Maggie handed me a carefully wrapped narrow box about three feet long. I could not guess what it was. "It was Tom's," Kay explained, "He treasured this but we're all Mets fans. Do you like it?"

I was beaming from ear to ear. The box held a Mickey Mantle Louisville Slugger game bat signed by the great Mick himself. I could not have been more surprised or pleased. "This should be a family heirloom!" I exclaimed.

"Don't move Chris," Kay said, "It looks like Maggie has another gift for you. You two are under the mistletoe."

"You have to kiss her, Chris," prompted Sean, "though I don't know why anyone would kiss the Magpie. Oh, I get it, it's the Gift of the Magpie." We all groaned.

"Yeah, kiss her," laughed Dylan, "It's the rule. Make it a good sloppy one."

Maggie was blushing. She whispered: "It's okay, you don't have to."

I took her by the shoulders and gave her a little peck on her lips. "That doesn't count," said Kay, "Make it a good kiss or neither of you get pie."

I shrugged. Maggie shrugged. "It's for pie," I said. I took her in my arms and felt hers tentatively surround me. She closed her eyes and we exchanged a long dramatic kiss—maybe too long, especially in front of her family. So long it made me tremble. Midway I sensed a camera flash.

"Got it!" shouted Sean.

"Now *that* was a real kiss!" sighed Luanne, Dylan's girlfriend, staring him in the eye. The room became embarrassingly quiet for a few seconds.

Maggie broke the silence: "We did it, now where's the pie?"

Kay called out: "Let's see that picture, Sean. We all want copies." I was beginning to feel like I was in a sappy Hallmark Christmas movie. If you watch one too many of them you can get diabetes.

We had a great evening filled with laughter. Everyone seemed very willing to make Maggie the butt of their jokes. When I took my leave, Maggie showed me to the door. We were out of earshot of the others. She handed me three wrapped packages. "This one is for Gretchen, this one is for you, Chris, and this one is sorta for both of you. I wanted to give them to you privately. I know you only have that little tabletop tree, but you can put these under it. Then you will have something to open in the morning."

She went on: "Chris, I have something to ask you. Mom's noticed that we have been spending time together—not that she objects or anything, she doesn't, she likes you— but she finally came out and asked if we are *dating*. I told her we are just hangin' out. That is right, isn't? Now we are going out New Year's Eve. Pals spending time together, right?"

I was caught off guard. We'd used tickets we had received to see a play, we had seen a movie, we had played scrabble and we had frequent lunches together. "Uh, yeah, the best of pals. What do the texters call it? BFF? But am I keeping you from things you want to do? Did you have other plans for New Year's? I mean I don't want you to think you're obligated to do things with me. Sometimes I don't see the implications of my impulses."

"No, it will be fun. I am looking forward to it. I just wanted to give you a heads-up in case Mom says something to you. You've seen how she can be. How she reads what she wants into things. We're good, right?"

"Of course we're good, Maggie."

When I got home I looked for a favored book of quotations. I quickly found the one I was looking for. It was attributed to Emil Ludwig.

Die Entscheidung, zum ersten Mal küssen ist das wichtigste in einer Liebesgeschichte. Es ändert sich die Beziehung zweier Menschen viel stärker als noch die endgültige Kapitulation, weil dieser Kuss bereits darin, dass Kapitulation.

In English it read: "The decision to kiss for the first time is the most crucial in any love story. It changes the relationship of two people much more strongly than even the final surrender; because this kiss already has within it that surrender."

I didn't wait until morning to open the presents. They were thoughtful on all accounts. Maggie had given Gretchen a cute stuffed pink bunny to add to her collection. It was similar to her slippers. My present was a beautiful watch. On the back it said: "You never know what time it is." The flat package contained a framed photo of Gretchen and me. It was a candid shot of a happy moment at the camp. I didn't remember Maggie taking it. I wondered if she knew I had taken a few of her with my camera phone? I wondered if I would ever figure out how to get them off the phone and into prints?

I thought about calling her and asking if I could attend Christmas Mass with her family. I was sure she would say yes, but then I thought it could be interpreted that I might be more than Maggie's "pal." Her church friends might just start asking: "who is that old guy with Maggie O'Connor?" Like I have said, I can over-think things. Then the landline rang. It was Maggie.

When I answered, she said, "Good, you are still up. Mom said I should have asked you to go to Christmas Mass with us. Would you want to? We are going to the 10:30, but we will be leaving about 10:00 so we can hear the choir. You could bring Gretchen and she could hang with Perky. We'll have brunch afterward. Can you come?"

I answered, "Sure, we'll be there by ten. Merry Christmas, Sweetie." Now why did I call her that?

New Year's Gone Awry

The office was closed until after the first, although we had a crew moving our stuff to new digs in a bigger, nicer building the realtor had found for us. I did some writing, reviewed plans for the manor and took Gretchen on long cold walks. The only time I spoke with Maggie was when I called to say when I would come for her New Year's Eve. I understood she was going skiing with Dylan and Sean.

When I arrived at the O'Connors on New Year's Eve I felt like a teenager going picking up his first prom date.

"Maggie is still getting ready," Kay said when I arrived. The house was unusually quiet.

"You aren't going to be alone tonight are you, Kay?" I asked.

"No, Leo and Liz and Frank from down the street are due later. We are going to play pinochle. Frank is an old fart, but I will make some pin money and we will watch the ball fall," she laughed.

I caught sight of Maggie's long legs coming down the stairs. They are so long and she came down so shyly that it was like slow motion. She was wearing a knee-length golden dress, hosiery and high heels. "Doesn't she look beautiful, Chris? Those gorgeous earrings you gave her really go with the dress, don't you think?" All I could do was gulp and hope my eyes weren't bulging out.

I said, "It's the woman who makes the dress and the earrings look good." It is then when I wondered why she hadn't put on the pendant and ring.

"How *gallant*," said Kay, stretching the word to its fullest. I had gotten something out right.

Moments later, seated in the car I joked, "Maybe we should go some place really dark. Otherwise, the way you look I might have to fight guys off. I'm getting too old for that."

"No way!" She said, "It took me two hours to look like this and I want to show this rig off. But thanks for the compliment, old man."

It was a 30-minute drive to the restaurant. We began chattering. Light talk, fun talk. There was a brief pause, then Maggie said:

"I ran into Roger the other night." I said nothing. "You remember Daphne? I've talked about her and you've met her when she came by the office." I said of course I did. Daphne is Maggie's friend from high school and college, her closest friend. I waited.

"Well, as you know, most Monday nights we meet up at the fitness center. Sometimes she comes by for dinner first, but usually we meet after dinnertime; but the other night she wanted me to come straight from the office, so I did. We did our routines and we were on our way to the women's locker room when she said 'Don't turn around, Roger's here.' He called out to me really loud so I couldn't ignore him or escape into the locker room.

"He said he had tried calling me several times, but I was always out. I guess my family has been screening his calls and not telling me. He was like, apologetic. He said he knew he had been a fool and a bastard and he wanted to make it up to me. I said something like 'It's all history now, Roger, I've moved on.' He begged me for just a few minutes, over a drink, to give him a chance to explain. He is so manipulative!

When I said no, he said 'Let me take you out New Year's Eve. We'll do it up like we used to.' That infuriated me. Who was he thinking about? Like we ever did it up! Like he could just drop back into my life and think I would be waiting for him! I told him 'I have plans, Roger, and they don't include you.' That's when Daphne said something like: 'Yeah, she has a New Year's date with a great guy. He's classy and handsome, and treats Maggie with respect.'

"Roger got really angry—I'd forgotten how spoiled he was and what a temper he could have when he didn't get his own way. He grabbed me by the arm. When Daphne came forward he pushed her and called her a Lesbo bitch. That was a mistake. Daphne kicked him square in the balls. He dropped to his knees. He called us both bitches. That's when I hit him with all I had. My hand still hurts. I don't know what I ever saw in that guy."

At that point she stopped. I said, "That tells me never to cross you or Daphne. You feel okay about it now?"

"Well, yes, and no. It felt really good to punch him, but I shouldn't have done it. You know what?" She started to giggle. "I think I broke his nose! There was a lot blood flowing but I didn't care. The people watching clapped their hands, even the guys. One of the women said 'You go girls.'"

"Was that the end of it? Are you worried that he might show up again?"

"That was the end of it then. He was gone when we came out of the locker rooms. But Daph and I are going to change gyms. She thinks he may have stalked me from work. She said she saw a circle on his left hand ring finger, like it hadn't been long since he'd removed a ring. She thinks he is on the rebound."

While I checked our coats, Maggie went to the ladies room. When she returned, heads swiveled, a major accomplishment in an upscale Spa establishment on New Year's Eve. She had added the pendant and the ring. I flushed with pride as we strode toward our table. As soon as I could, I asked: "Is there something you want to tell me, Maggie?"

She blushed: "Mom doesn't know about the pendant and the ring. I don't think she even knows the earrings are real. She'd think they were too much and I shouldn't have accepted them. But I do love them." Sometimes this woman was far more mature than me; sometimes she was still a little girl.

We finished our small salads. I was eager to get my twin lobster tails. Maggie had ordered something very French. I hoped she knew what she was doing. She checked the evening's events schedule while we waited. She seemed to want to take them all in. "You have us on this end of Broadway," I said, " and then way down at the other end. Remember, it's cold out there."

"Yes, but . . .wait, I think my phone is ringing."

She took her phone from her purse. Her face grew ashen. She gasped. "Yes, which hospital? We are leaving now. Call me as soon as you know anything more. Dylan, Sean? Okay, I'll call him." She got up quickly, "Chris, it's my mother. We have to go. She's had a heart attack or a stroke."

I pulled two hundreds from my wallet and hastily paid the waiter. "That should be enough." I said, without waiting for a reply. Maggie was pulling on her coat as we flew out the door. "Hurry, Chris, hurry!"

I tried to calm her and learn more about the call at the same time. Her words came out in a rush: "I have to call Dylan. Liz said he didn't answer his cell. Why didn't she call me first? Liz said Mom felt pain in her leg—she barely feels anything—then got dizzy and collapsed. They called 911 and an ambulance is taking her to the hospital."

"Which hospital, Maggie?"

"St. Peter's," she said.

"It would be," I said, "That's about the farthest from where we are now."

She grew angry with Dylan for not answering. "Damnit, Dylan, answer your phone!" She was angry with Liz for not calling her first. She was angry with herself for not being there.

We were doing 75 down the Northway and yet she was encouraging me to drive faster. I said, "Easy, Maggie, she will be okay when we get there. Remember, it's New Year's Eve. There are a lot of drunks out. Lots of troopers patrolling. It won't help us get there if we have an accident or get pulled over."

The thought of a drunken driver on the road hit home. "I'm sorry, Chris, but I need to be there." She was on the verge of tears.

I pulled in front of the ER entrance: "Go on ahead, I'll park the car and find you." I watched her push through the revolving door. She tossed aside her high heels and sprinted out of sight.

I collected Maggie's shoes on the way in. There were three people ahead of me at the front desk. No doubt it was a busy night in the ER. I asked for Kay O'Connor. The tired receptionist asked if I was family. I explained and she directed me to a waiting area. I had been in ER's a few times. No matter what the staff does, it is never enough. The calmer the staff is, a necessary and desired trait, the more agitated some family members can be. It is as if they want the staff to be as frantic as they are. I heard one woman scream out: "What if it was your child?"

It was a long twenty minutes or so before Liz came out searching for me. "How is she?" I asked.

"She's more or less stable. Blood clot. She got treatment in time and she is going to make it, but they don't yet know if there will be any permanent effects. Come with me." I said something about rules limiting visitors to family. Liz said, "Forget that, you are family."

At a second waiting area, right outside the busy ER, Sean and his date for the night were sitting with Leo. They looked worried. Leo was telling him he should take Bunny—or was it Bonnie—home. He was reluctant but finally agreed to with the assurance that if there were any change Leo would call him.

I followed Liz into one of the back corners of the cross-shaped ER. Liz pulled open a curtain to reveal Kay with Maggie at her side. I was heartened when I saw Kay was conscious. She was hooked up to monitors and an IV. Maggie was smiling at her mother and holding her hand, but her look turned to deep concern when she turned toward me. "Mom's going to be okay," she said.

"Of course she is, she has pies to bake." I said.

"She wants you to come closer, Chris," Maggie said. I moved to her side as Maggie slipped her hand into mine.

"I'm sorry I ruined your evening, Chris. You had such a beautiful girl with you."

"I know, Kay, I know." I sensed she wanted me to move still closer. I did.

She whispered: "If I don't make it, will you take care of my girl?"

"I won't have to Kay, you are going to be fine."

"Promise me Chris."

"I promise, Kay."

The nurse came in, checked one or two things and spoke with Kay in a soft tone. "We are going to move you now, Mrs. O'Connor, to a room where you will be more comfortable." Liz, Maggie and I took that as a good sign.

Kay was going to be in ICU at least for the night. Maggie insisted on being the only one to stay. Dylan would be showing up. I offered to stay, too, but Maggie said she would call me if she needed me.

I went home, let Gretchen out to pee, changed my clothes, found a book and a couple of magazines. I was back at the hospital not long after the ball had come down in Times Square. Once again, I thought, some New Year's. I was in the waiting room when Dylan arrived in a panic. He was a bit drunk. I caught him up the best I could and directed him to his mother.

Several minutes later, Maggie came to where I was sitting. "You came back?" she asked.

"I did," I said, "I thought I should be here." I handed her a bag. "This is the best I could do, a sweat shirt and shrunken sweat pants that I can't get into and sweat socks. I thought you might like to change. How about getting a sandwich and some coffee? Dylan's with your mother and all you had was salad."

"Thanks," she answered, "I guess I could use a cup of coffee."

I convinced Maggie to eat a piece of pie with her coffee. She picked at it and asked: "Tell me what Mom said to you."

I lied: "She wanted to know where the pendant and ring came from." She looked down as if it was the first time she remembered she was wearing them. She wanted to get back to her mother's side. I told her I would be nearby if she needed anything.

I felt a nudge. I opened my eyes. It was Maggie: "You've been here all night, haven't you? Sean's back, Mom's alert, and they are taking her down for some tests. She may have some effects from the stroke. Will you take me home so I can shower and get some breakfast?"

Dylan had come home a few hours earlier and was sleeping it off. Maggie let Perky out and then fed him. I helped Maggie make some scrambled eggs and toast, all the while reassuring her that her mom would be fine. We sat on the couch to eat. I encouraged her to sleep a few hours before going back to the hospital. I was sure she had not slept at all during the night. She was contrary.

We talked softly for a few minutes. When she grew silent I looked over. Her eyes were shut, her mouth was open and she began to snore.

Good for you, girl, I thought. I lifted those long legs, sweatpants and all, onto the couch. I grabbed Kay's shawl from the back of a chair and put it over her. I put the keys to the Mustang on the coffee table where she could find them. Finally, I crept silently to the door and let myself out.

Recovery and a New Year

Later that day Maggie called. "Mom's doing well. They are keeping her here to run more tests. She will probably go to the rehab center for a week or so. She is going to have a tough time for a few days, but they think she can make a full recovery."

"That's great news, Mag. Anything I can do to help?"

"I don't think so. Sean and Dylan have jobs until school starts again, but Liz will help. You've been great. I'm sorry the O'Connors messed up your New Year's."

"That's not important. What is important is that Kay is okay. Call me if you need anything. Call me anyway to keep me posted."

I phoned Vincent to give him the news and tell him we would be without Maggie for a few days. He said he would call Maggie. Did I think flowers might be in order? It would be nice of you, I said. Vincent said, "That sure puts a damper on things. I was going to come in tomorrow with my news, but I will tell you now: Melanie and I are getting married!"

I congratulated him and said it was about time. He told me Melanie wanted a traditional church wedding in June. He said, "You are responsible. We had been holding off until we could afford it, and now we can. You ought to think about getting married yourself." The newly converted often tended to proselytize.

I said, "Not likely, I'd have to find someone and the thought of that makes me tired."

"Maybe if you got out there more, Chris, you might find it not so tiring, and just maybe you wouldn't have to look very far. That new girl in the crew is really cute even if she is a sociologist," he teased, "and I have seen the way she looks at you."

"She's just a kid. Besides, Maggie already warned me about golddiggers."

"Did she now?"

I went to visit Kay the next day carrying flowers. Maggie, as I expected, was at her side. Vincent had acted promptly and there was already a bouquet there from him. "Meghan says he called her and he is getting married at Corpus Christi," Kay said, " They make a nice couple."

She was sitting up. She had some paralysis on her left side and her speech was labored. She looked tired. She repeated what she had said earlier: "I'm sorry I spoiled you and Maggie's New Year's, Chris. Worst of all," she tried to laugh, "I was ahead $18 playing pinochle but I will never collect."

I asked if she needed anything, if there was anything I could do for her. "Yes, there definitely is. Tell my daughter you need her at work. There is no reason she has to sit here all day long. The staff can take care of me just fine."

"So, she's using you as an excuse to loaf, is she? Should I threaten to dock her pay?"

Maggie walked outside the room with me. "I really don't want her to be here alone, Chris, you understand don't you?"

"Certainly I do. Take all the time you need. Once she is home you can get an aide for her. I will help you with that if you want."

On Friday Kay called me at the office. "Chris, I am trying to get checked out of here. You know I am a nurse and I don't think I need to be here. They ran all the tests and I am going to be fine. I simply need to take my meds and do my therapy. I can do most of that at home. Meghan wants me to stay. She is overreacting. She is driving me nuts. She's hovering over everything."

"What can I do, Kay?"

"Talk to her, Chris. I think Meghan fears I will have another attack."

"Well, I can try, but I don't know if I can make a difference. What about Liz?"

"Liz was here last night and told Meghan she thought I would be more comfortable at home but that didn't sway her."

That night I went to the rehab center. Kay immediately brought up her desire to go home. Meghan interrupted her saying: "Mom, we have been all through that. You need to rest and get your strength back."

"Chris," Kay said, "Will you come and get me tomorrow and take me home? My daughter won't do it." There I was, right in the middle of two strong-minded women.

"I could ... " I said meekly.

Maggie interrupted, looking at me with daggers in her eyes. "Don't *you* encourage her!"

"Well, I, I ... "

It took some time but we finally worked out a compromise. If her doctor agreed, Kay would stay through Sunday. We'd get a health care aide in as soon as possible and Maggie would come back to work where, as Kay said "she is really needed and doesn't get to run everything."

Within a few days Kay was settled in back home. She needed extra help with her daily routine. Maggie reluctantly let the aide do her job. The aide was capable and efficient. Kay liked her well enough.

At work I noticed Maggie was a bit cool to me. I didn't understand why. Maybe she was just preoccupied. I took her to lunch on Friday to see if I could determine what was bothering her. I failed to draw her out. So I asked her if it would be okay for Gretchen and me to stop by to see Kay that evening. She said okay, Gretchen always makes her mom smile. Still, her agreement wasn't all that enthusiastic.

Gretchen and I brought Kay some locally made jams from the organic food store she favors. She was pleased. Gretchen sat next to her where she could smile up at Kay and get pets in return. I could tell Kay's spirits were on the rise. We chatted while Maggie seemed busy elsewhere in the house.

Kay told me she could feel her strength returning. She admitted that before the attack she had gotten careless about her exercise routine. "I have to get my legs up more often. I have to have someone move my legs every day to prevent atrophy. That helps prevent clotting. I hope I can keep having someone come in every day."

I was concerned about Maggie's absence. When she came in with her mother's pills, she said, "Mom, do you want to start for bed? It's about 9:00." I took that as a signal to leave.

"No," Kay said, "It's still early for you two. I can start getting ready, Meghan. I'll call you when I need you."

Maggie's side of our conversation was strained. She talked about how good Perky was for her mom and about how well Perky and Gretchen got along. It seemed like a gap had developed between Maggie and me. A gap I did not understand.

When Kay called for Maggie's help I again took it as signal to leave, but she jumped up so quickly I had no chance to say anything. Shortly I heard the TV come on in Kay's room. Perky left to join her. Soon Maggie returned.

"I didn't want to leave without saying good night," I said.

"I'm glad you didn't. Mom said I should apologize to you. She said I was rude by not coming out and not offering you something to eat or drink. So I apologize." It was a flat statement.

"Maggie, what's wrong? Have I done something to offend you? We have become close over these last few months. Please tell me what's bothering you."

"Oh, it's nothing."

"Maggie, please."

"It's not you, although I was ticked at you for taking Mom's side in the hospital. You don't know her needs like I do."

"I'm sorry, Maggie. I felt caught between the two of you. I didn't mean to take sides. I'm not family."

"You are, too, as far as Mom and Liz and Leo are concerned. And I think Dylan thinks the same, too and Sean would, too, if he ever thinks." She half smiled as she referred to the free-spirited, nothing-ever-troubles-me Sean.

"What about you, Maggie?"

"You know."

"No, I don't, not really. But what I meant to ask was, what about *your* needs?"

"My needs? I don't have any. I can't complain. My life's better than most people's. It is good. I have my family, a good job and income, thanks to you."

"That's fine ... for now. But what about your future? Are you leading the life you want?"

"I can't think about that now. Sure, I had dreams. Once I thought I might be a pro soccer player. Then when I realized I probably wasn't good enough, I thought I would be teaching math and coaching by now. With a husband and kids. But that's not the way things worked out. First there was the accident, then mom. There's a reason for everything. I just don't know what it is. Sometimes I just feel a little sad. It's nothing, it will pass."

I knew about feeling sad, more than I would let on to Maggie or anyone. She was always so upbeat; I had never seen her express sadness.

I said: "You know your mom is doing fine. Psychologically, she seems to be her old self and she is physically much improved."

I took a risk: "Maybe you should lighten the burden on yourself. The insurance covers the aide coming in and your mom likes her, so why not take advantage?"

She shrugged. "Maybe I can. She sure has been on my case a lot more lately. She does like Lillian."

Pleased with having made an inroad, I said: "You know what makes me sad?"

"What?" she asked.

She couldn't know what an admission I was about to make, or what I knew I was opening myself up to. "I can't dance a lick. Your mom says she was a good dancer and that you are, too."

"Sure you can dance, everyone can. You must have been dancing."

"Not me. Not a step. Oh, I tried. Like the cow that backed into the propeller, utter disaster. I move like a penguin on drugs. It's embarrassing to watch."

She didn't laugh. "I guess I could teach you … if you are willing."

I wasn't all that willing, yet I said: "You will? I think I would like that."

Her mood had softened. We put on the news and our conversation was once again comfortable and easy. We talked into the wee hours of the morning.

We discussed music. Her tastes were eclectic: the Celtic Singers, Stevie Wonder and the Black-eyed Peas. She hated rap. She quit the flute in junior high, could play a few chords on her brother's guitar, and she has recently wished she could play piano, like her brother Sean.

It wasn't original, but I told her the only thing I could play was the radio. My parents had never encouraged musical lessons. She knew I liked jazz, but I hastened to say I knew little about it. I told her I discovered the storyteller-singer Harry Chapin and that I liked the early, less complicated Beatles songs. When she asked me to pick a singer, I said Groucho Marx doing "Lydia the Tattooed Lady." She giggled her magnetic giggle, then pressed me for a better answer. So I said I loved hearing Sarah Vaughan do "Broken Hearted Melody." Again, I was a generation or more behind my age.

We talked about books we had read and books we wanted to read. I knew she liked Stephen King because she often had his latest nearby. I was surprised to learn she loved reading histories and biographies about people from the distant past to the present.

I leaned toward British mysteries and Vonnegut and Grisham. In the past I had been drawn to the classics in general and classy science fiction from H.G. Wells through Asimov and Heilbroner in particular. Very little of the newer stuff. I had read Nevil Shute and Philip Wylie—I might have once considered "The End of the Dream" my favorite—but now I couldn't tolerate the doom and gloom. And I despised anything to do with vampires or monsters.

She asked me that if I were to write a book what kind would it be? Probably a political thriller, I said. "I don't think I could do sci fi, or a mystery and certainly not romance."

"I would want to write about some strong woman who made a real impact on things," she said.

We exchanged our thoughts on old movies. She was consistent saying her favorite is "An Affair to Remember." Her favorite old time actors were Cary Grant and Greer Garson. I liked *film noire* and most anything with Jimmy Stewart or Robert Mitchum. We both liked madcap comedies, Steve Martin, and Mel Brooks. We split on Woody Allen. Somehow it didn't seem like our 12-year difference in age was quite so great.

As I was leaving I said: "Okay, you are going to lighten up with your mom and I am going to learn to dance. One more thing: how about if I ask you to go out on an honest-to-goodness date? Not just two pals hanging out, but a real date-date. Me man, you woman? Me Hercules, you Xena? Tomorrow night. We'll have dinner and maybe we can score tickets for the show at Proctor's. If not, we can take in some jazz or something else. Your mom said Liz and Leo are coming over, and maybe Gretchen can hang out here, too. What do you think? Will you go out with me, Meghan O'Connor?"

"Gee, Chris, if you put it like that," she giggled, "A real, official date-date? Wow. I'll have to check my schedule." She turned away walked two steps and turned around, "It looks like you are in luck. I am free tomorrow night. What time will you pick me up? And make sure you come to the door. My mom will want to check you out."

Chapter Seven

Pilot Study

On the first Monday of the new year the demolition contractor held the first job call for the castle project. We didn't have all the bids in, but we could do the prep work.

Vincent attended and reported it had gone well. All the needs were filled. Vincent was enjoying his role in the project. It was very different work for him, but he had good instincts and, I thought, better personal and personnel leadership qualities than I. Besides, we were learning that our engineer, Greg Mathis, really knew how to push: Want a chance at the job at a fair price? Then respond on our schedule, not yours. He reasoned that there were more competent subcontractors available than work available.

It had taken a bit longer for the court to act on the Magnus Foundation. The auditor Swann hired for us, an expert on non-profits, concluded that the staff was bloated and expenses were excessively high. When the court gave us a green light to take control, Vincent and I talked it over. We decided that he, Arnie and I would make a surprise visit the following week. It was only a couple hours drive to the office, only a few miles from the Ferguson labs and headquarters.

The next day I accepted a surprising, yet timely phone call.

"Christopher St. James?" The caller asked.

"Yes, who is asking?" I replied.

"Paul, Paul Randolph, sir. I got your number from the lawyer handling Angus Ferguson's estate. You were a friend of Ferguson, right?"

"Not exactly. My father was. I barely knew Ferguson. What can I do for you, Mr. Randolph?"

"I see. I didn't know your relationship with him. I would like to tell a story if you are willing to listen to it."

I said I was. His story went like this:

Paul Randolph's father was Miles Randolph, Scottie's pilot, the one killed when his helicopter went down about ten years ago. Although the authorities called it an accident with the probable cause of pilot error, Paul thought it was murder. He said his dad was among the best chopper pilots in the world. There was no sign in the autopsy that he had a health problem. The weather was clear. He said that both Ferguson and his dad were meticulous about maintenance and knew the chopper inside out. They had virtually hand-built it in Scottie's facilities.

"Well, we all make mistakes," I said, "Sometimes things just happen."

"Not to my dad. Not when he flew. He flew under all kinds of conditions. In war zones, during black ops. Dad worked around the world for intelligence networks, both foreign and domestic. That is how he had come to know Ferguson."

"What? Are you are telling me that Ferguson was mixed up in espionage?"

"Espionage and a whole lot of other things. Black ops, rescues, gunrunning, extortion, probably smuggling. I don't know what else. I guess you might call him an opportunist. Dad was recruited out of the Navy and worked under Scottie for a few years. Then Ferguson managed to get out of the business. He was rich by then, and got richer. When Dad wanted out, Ferguson gave him a job as his corporate pilot."

I was gaining some insight into how Scottie started on his road to riches. I said, "Are you suggesting that one of them or both of them had an enemy who wanted them dead?"

"Maybe a lot of enemies. You have to understand: I didn't know anything about this until close to the time of my dad's death. When I was a kid, I thought he was just a freelance pilot. He would go off for a time, like a traveling salesman, and then he would come home. He talked about flying in general, but never about what he exactly did. I overheard a few things he said to my mom, but I just thought dad had an exciting career going on. I wanted to be like him. I went to engineering school and then joined the Air Force.

Once I was on my own, I didn't see much of him for several years. When I did, everything seemed okay. He liked working for Ferguson. Then he called me a few weeks before the crash. He seemed almost paranoid. He started saying that someone had tried to kill Ferguson, maybe more than once. Dad was about 60 then so some kind of dementia was possible, but he was sharp as a tack about everything else.

He said Ferguson had built some kind of refuge out in the boondocks. He had taken to routinely carrying weapons. Dad said that he might be on the hit list, too. After he was killed, Mom told me some things and it all added up. I wanted to tell the authorities. Mom convinced me that there was no real evidence and no one would believe me; but I could not let go of it. I spend a lot of time on the Internet and I came across Ferguson's obit. Eventually that led me to reaching you."

I was stunned. In five minutes or less, layers of mystery had been unraveled. "Why do you think I should know this?" I asked.

"Well, Dad had been flying from Cherry Ridge when he went down and he had mentioned Cherry Ridge before. I surmised that the refuge might be there. When I called Wadsworth to see if the estate had anything connected to my dad or Cherry Ridge, Wadsworth gave me your name. I figured it was a long shot, but maybe you might know something."

"Well, he shouldn't have given you my name, but that's water over the bridge or under the dam. What is it you want from me?"

"I figure that Ferguson maybe had records or something at that place in Cherry Ridge. Maybe you've found something? Maybe you can look for anything that would lead me to my dad's killer?"

"Well, I can tell you I haven't." However, I thought, that does not mean there isn't something there.

"Mr. St. James, if my dad was murdered, and attempts were made on Ferguson, then maybe there is a connection with Cherry Ridge or maybe you. Maybe you could be in danger, too."

"Well, like I said, I haven't discovered anything that would suggest a connection. Still, where are you?"

"I'm in Westchester at my mom's with my family. It's not far from Ferguson's plant and offices. I finished my 20 years with the Air Force a couple months ago. I'm taking some time before going back to work. Did I say? I'm a pilot like my dad."

"Westchester, eh?" I looked at my calendar. "I'll be in your area next week. I would like to talk with you further in person."

"Sure," he said," Where and when?"

Randolph's tale confused me. I had already determined my prime suspect in the killing of Cassandra Burke-Cross. Obviously, I had neither evidence to prove nor any way to prove anyone's guilt. Moreover, it was not on me to do so. Now Randolph had presented a scenario that offered a valid alternative. A professional hit on Scottie's granddaughter could have been an act of revenge by an old enemy, especially if that enemy had not learned of Scottie's demise. Maybe someone of that ilk might also be interested in Ferguson's fortune.

Magnus Visited

Vincent, Arnie and I left early, at least for me, to visit Magnus. Maggie wasn't needed. She was going to stop by my place during the day and check on Gretchen for me.

When we entered the Magnus building, Arnie approached the receptionist who was preoccupied with her manicure. "Mr. St. James and associates to see John Slocum."

"Do you have an appointment?" came the reply.

"No," said Arnie, "But Slocum will see us."

"I'm sorry, Mr. Slocum is away on vacation. In the Bahamas, I think. I can see if Ms. Hoskins is available. She is his secretary."

Ms. Miriam Hoskins took some time to get to the front desk. She had a troubled look on her face. Maybe it was permanent. She looked over her glasses and asked: "How can I help you, gentlemen?"

"You can tell us who is in charge here."

"That would be Mr. Slocum, our Chief Operating Officer, but he is away at present."

"So we have been told. And in his absence?" Arnie probed.

"That would be Mr. Sanders, but I think he has gone to lunch."

"At 10:15 in the morning?" Arnie exclaimed. "Look, Ms. Hoskins, this is Christopher St. James. Does his name mean anything to you? He is the new president of the Magnus Foundation. In other words, he's your boss. Where's your conference room? You have exactly 15 minutes to get Mr. Sanders and all senior staff into that room."

Arnie was rough on her, but we had decided to start out with an air of authority. I felt glad I had someone to play the pit bull. Left to myself I would have been inclined to say, okay, I'll come back another time.

Sanders didn't make it in the time Arnie had allotted. It seemed the senior administrator present was the controller. Only five of 18 with management titles were in the building. A very loose ship.

Arnie and Vincent established the basis for the change in leadership and summarized the findings of the court review and audit. I whispered to Vincent to have the entire staff convene at 1:00 in whatever space would hold everyone. Just before noon I excused myself and left the building. I walked a full block to a Starbucks—there wasn't one closer—to meet Paul Randolph.

Retired Lt. Colonel Randolph was sitting in a back corner from where he could see the entrance. When he stood up I could see he had the military bearing I expected. Six feet tall, trim, with buzz cut hair. He was wearing a crisp suit and tie with a flag pin.

I had him clarify a point or two about he had told me over the phone; otherwise, he had no information to add. I told him I had gone through most of the paper records in the residence and had found nothing of relevance. I told him I would be visiting Cherry Ridge. I said that perhaps there might be something on the computer or in a workshop Ferguson had on the site. I told him I would contact him if anything pertinent turned up.

I asked a little about his family and his plans. He said that, unlike fixed-wing pilots, chopper pilots were in high demand. He said he no longer wanted to be deployed for lengthy periods. He wanted a solid home base where his family could settle in. I told him I knew little about helicopters and regretted not learning more during my own service time. I even asked him if a man of my age could learn to safely handle one. He told me a little about the training required.

He thanked me and I thanked him and we parted ways. I had wanted to meet him to size him up. He seemed sincere. More importantly, I tended to believe there might be something to his story. He seemed to have no agenda beyond resolving his dilemma surrounding his father's death. I thought I would likely feel the same way if I were in his position, but I wondered if I would act on those feelings as strongly as he. I decided to make my next trip to Cherry Ridge sooner rather than later.

I returned to the Magnus building. I had mixed feelings about the action I was about to take. At the same time, my reluctance had been lessened by what we had encountered earlier in the day.

When I entered, maybe half the employees on the payroll were present. A table had been set up near the entrance from which Arnie, Vincent and I would address the group. At 1:05 I asked Vincent to lock the entrance.

The controller introduced us. She got the names right. Arnie noted that the court had reviewed the operations and financial status of the foundation. He said the findings of our auditors put the effectiveness and some of the fiscal practices of the foundation in question. At 1:15 I sighed and stood up to speak. The entrance door rattled. Someone was trying to get in. Someone said "It's Mr. Sanders." Another asked if the door should be opened. I said, "No, he will learn soon enough that he doesn't work here anymore." I saw mixed expressions cross several faces. Smiles and angst.

My words were simple. "Mr. Angus Ferguson, the benefactor of this foundation, left me a mandate to fulfill. One part of that mandate is to have this foundation achieve its stated goals more effectively than the evidence shows it is presently doing. Therefore, as Mr. Spellman stated, there will be changes. There will be staff changes. Operations at this building will be transferred to Cherry Ridge, New York where a suitable building is being prepared." There were gasps and groans.

I expect the transfer to take place no sooner than September and no later than the end of the year.

I do not take your possible job loss lightly. I know personally what it is like to lose a job when you are not at fault. No doubt some of you are doing your best, doing good work. All of you will have the opportunity to submit applications and resumes with the possibility of relocating to Cherry Ridge. All of you who remain through the closing of this facility will have any and all agreements fulfilled and receive a severance package. For the present and until an interim administrator is in place, activities will be suspended."

Anguish and dismay were obvious. Vincent whispered in my ear and then stood to modify my last statement. "A skeleton staff will remain pending the arrival of the administrator to attend to immediate needs. Those names will be posted prior to our departure. No one is to remove anything other than personal property from the building. There will be a 24-hour security presence." As he began to take questions, Sanders came in via the back door. "What the hell is going on?" he shouted. He soon knew.

We had not come as unprepared as it might have seemed. Arnie had hired a security team and it was outside awaiting his orders. Moreover, Arnie's father-in-law, a recently retired school superintendent, lived within commuting distance. His only obligation was as an adjunct professor at a nearby college. Arnie was confident he could do the job and would take it. Based on the lack of leadership we had just experienced, I told him to complete the arrangements. Consequently, I was back home in time for Gretchen's dinner and a brisk, cold walk.

We still had to deal with Auracle Media. None of us knew much—make that anything—about the business so we struggled over what to do. Someone suggested hiring an independent consultant. Not yet, I decided. Swann and the auditors were digging into records. No one seemed to think it would be wise to move its center to Cherry Ridge. I had to agree. It was the part of Scottie's largesse that I truly did want to get my hands on. It was also one that would likely require travel. I hated traveling.

We learned the company held an annual corporate leadership conference in Florida in mid-February. They usually scheduled it after the Super Bowl. A corporate paid vacation and a suitable trip for spouses, I thought. No way was I going to Florida. Simple solution. They would move the conference to

Saratoga Springs. The suits and their spouses or whatevers wouldn't like it, but it would be less costly and I could easily attend.

Back to Cherry Ridge

I wanted to get to Cherry Ridge before the conference. The first week in February might be the worst week to travel in upstate New York. Only the winter sports enthusiasts and snow plowers liked it. The days are still short, it is usually bitter cold and the chance of heavy snow is always present. I do not do many winter "s's": no skiing, skating, snowboarding or snow plowing. I do as little shoveling as possible. Moreover, I am usually in the depths of my SAD state. My skin breaks out and itches from dry air and I often have a case of the sniffles if not worse. I eat comfort food and put on weight. If it were not for Gretchen's great tolerance for cold and even greater desire to play in snow, I would never willingly venture outside.

Nevertheless, I checked the forecast and decided Gretchen and I would go out to Cherry Ridge. I had the 4-wheel drive truck so I was confident I could get there. Whether or not the camp was snowbound remained to be seen.

We arrived in Cherry Ridge without incident. I drove straight to the castle, soon to be Serendipity Manor. There was a temporary gate near the entrance. I stopped the truck and let Gretchen out to relieve her self.

A young man approached me saying: "You can't enter without one of these and a hardhat." He pointed to an ID card pinned to his heavy coat. I told him my name. "Mr. St. James," he said, "I'm Howie Miller. My dad, Ron, knows you from school. Nice dog you have there. We have a German Shepherd."

I told him I remembered his dad, about two years ahead of me in school. "Give me a sec to call my foreman. He'll get you a pass and a hardhat."

While we were waiting he let a truck exit. It was loaded with old toilets. "That should be the last of them. I think nearly everything is out now."

I engaged the boy in conversation. "How do you like working here?" I asked.

"I like it well enough when I am not out here in the cold for too long. The money's good. The foreman is a good guy. I'm hoping I can catch on as a helper for the next phase."

I asked him if he knew how many locals were working there. He said, "I dunno, maybe 20 to 25. Some truckers and most of the laborers."

"Anyone with complaints, anyone gotten hurt?" I asked.

"Oh, a few guys quit the first week, but they didn't want to work so hard, or it was too cooold," he mocked. "One guy got a broken hand when something fell on it. Maybe a few cuts or bruises. Otherwise, I haven't heard of anything bad."

The foreman arrived and ushered me to the demo supervisor. The supervisor said they were done with all the heavy work. They were a day ahead of schedule. The next day they would be going through floor-by-floor, room-by-room sweeping and vacuuming. Mathis was expected to come by and sign off on the work. I looked in a few of the rooms. I was pleased. Things seemed to be going well.

Upon leaving the castle, I decided to bypass Ridge St. and Millie's and went straight to the camp. I drove slowly but steadily. The truck handled the 6 to 8 inches of the virgin snow on the "tunnel" road with no trouble. I wondered if it would be as easy in the more open, twisting road to the top. When I reached the gate I asked Julia what the temperature was inside. She said 55°. I told her to turn it up to 68°.

It was warm when we arrived. I asked Julia to multi-task. I gave her what I knew about Cassandra Burke/Cross and told her to do a complete search. "Boolean or something?" I suggested. "I can go beyond Boolean," she said. This time I got to say: "Fine."

Then I said I wanted her to do a similar search on Angus Ferguson. She balked. "That task violates the prime directive. It could endanger Angus Ferguson. It could endanger the system," she said. It can't hurt Angus, I thought, but maybe a deep probe into his background could put the system at risk. I was not willing to take that gamble. So I said: "Do a search of resources that will not endanger Angus Ferguson or the system." She complied. I think that if she could have, she would have shrugged.

I had another task for Julia. There was something bothering me about the satellite image that Broadhurst had. Something that was not in the frame of the map I had used to find the graves. I told Julia to bring up a photo of the property. She brought up a recent one. The roof of a building I had seen in Broadhurst's photo was now absent. It should have appeared in the open area on the hillcrest. However, Broadhurst's photo had been taken when the foliage was green. Julia's was snow covered.

I told Julia to find me a similar photo without snow cover. She did and this time the rectangular white space appeared. I thought: it must be something at ground level. Maybe a concrete slab for a building never finished. Or maybe a pad for a helicopter?

I asked Julia: "Where is the helicopter?" She showed me the same photo with a marker on the "slab."

"Julia," I said, "There is no helicopter in the photo."

"It is there," she replied, "Below the surface."

I heated some canned soup and ate it with crackers. I gave Gretchen a little food from the supply we had laid in the last time we were there. I bundled up and headed out to the road and across to the path on its other side. I assumed the path led to the clearing.

Not in the best of shape, I struggled to make my way. I was glad I had left Gretchen behind. She could handle the snow, but the climbing in some places would have been a challenge she need not face. The height I was climbing was not great, but the path at first paralleled the ridge before it began to rise. In all, I probably traveled 200 yards to rise less than 150 feet.

Typical of the worn hills in the area, the crest itself was quite flat. If anything it sloped toward the south, away from me. I suspected that it had been cleared generations ago to be tilled, maybe by my ancestors. In looking outward upon it, I could see a rectangle of snow that was a few inches higher than the snow around it. It must be the slab, I thought. In walking toward it, I nearly missed seeing a little kiosk of sorts just inside the tree line to my left. I went over to it and found a small version of Julia's gatekeeper device. It was shuttered. I released the clasp and, before she could take the initiative asked: "Julia, are you there?"

"I am here, Christopher."

In short order, Julia had exposed the opening. She slid its lid along tracks on either side. I made my way to the opening already wary of falling in while trying to see inside. My worry was unwarranted. I didn't have to get very close before I could see the rotors of a helicopter a few feet below the surface. I got down on all fours when I reached the edge. By my uneducated standards it was a large chopper. Maybe not a military Huey, but something much more than a little sporting craft.

Despite the fact that a ladder ran down one side of the pit, I had no desire to risk an entry. On my command, Julia returned the lid with most of its snow cover intact.

After I returned to the warmth of the camp, I called Pierpoint and left a simple voice mail: "I found the missing helicopter."

I checked in at the office. Vincent, Arnie and Maggie listened together using the speakerphone option. I told them about finding the hidden chopper and that I had no idea what to do with it. I told them that I thought the work was going well at the manor. I told them to make a note to tell Mathis to see that a kid working on the place, Howie Miller, be retained in some capacity. Finally, I told them we were going to stay over a day or two. They said that was just as well, a nor'easter had turned their way and a previous forecast of 4 to 6 inches had changed to 12-16. It was prudent that we stay where we were.

It was still only mid-afternoon and I wondered if I could attach the snowplow to the truck. I had driven small plows when I was young, but that was 20 years ago. Those plows were already on the trucks. The one thing this place seemed to be missing was a large snowblower. I thought that if Maggie were here, she would have one delivered by Sears!

I considered driving to Millie's or getting in some fresh groceries. Instead, I scanned through what Julia printed out, and I pulled out Scottie's journals and such that were still in the drawer. The next thing I knew it was dark and Gretchen was prodding me to let her out to pee. We ate what I could find and I looked forward to what Rachel Maddow had to say.

Brrrrrr!

"Julia, what is the outside temperature?" She replied, "-2° Fahrenheit," she replied. The wind was gusting to 30 mph. It was colder than a bitch's wit. It was colder than Anniston to Jolie. It was colder than Hillary (the mountain climber, not the Clinton.)

I wondered if the truck would start. I should have put it in the barn. Fortunately, it had a remote starter. After showering and taking my meds, I pushed the button. I couldn't hear it running. I moved closer to the door and Julia opened it. I pushed the button again and the truck started. I finished dressing and prepared for the cold. "Pee quickly, Gretchen, or you will be making a yellow icicle." The cold air enervated her and she wanted to romp in the snow. "No play now," I said, "We are going to Millie's."

We were able to park in front of the Cherry Ridge Inn. You could have rolled a bowling ball down Ridge Street without hitting a car. Only three patrons, the grill cook and Willy Logan occupied Millie's.

Willy was seated at the counter. I had never seen him look so glum. Connecting his expression with his tall baker's hat I asked, "Why such a long fez, Abdul?" He didn't get it, but he did brighten when he saw Gretchen trailing behind me. He brought me coffee and took our order: turkey sausage for Gretchen (along with her personal bowl of water) and a Western omelette, rye toast and OJ for me. While the cook was working on it, Willy sat down across from me.

"You looked pretty down when I first walked in, Willy. Anything wrong?"

"Just the usual this time of year. Plus Millie is home with the flu. She almost never takes time off, so ya know she's really sick."

"Oh, I'm sorry to hear that, please give her my best wishes," I replied.

"And look around you, it doesn't pay to open this time of year."

I looked up at the old clock. "It's still early, Willy, people tend to start slowly when it gets this cold."

"It's not just today, Chris, it's been this way for a couple of weeks and it gets worse every year. We are getting a little boost from your workers, but it isn't offsetting the downturn. Those who can afford it are down south; those who can't, stay home. I hate laying off my people but I might have to. It's not that Millie and I are hurting mind you, but every winter I have to dip into the reserve a little deeper to keep them on."

"I'm sorry to hear that, too, but the winter won't be with us that much longer and the people will be coming in. Besides, we will have a lot of hungry, thirsty people working up there soon, and they will move around more when it is warmer."

"I hope so," he said. "How's it going up there? I hear they have taken tons of stuff out."

"Yeah, the demo and clean out is supposed to be done this week. They had to knock out quite a few walls to turn the single rooms and old group baths into modern spaces. Some of that 1800's stuff had to go."

"Somebody said you are calling it, what, Serendipity Manor. Where'd you get that from? People are still going to call it the castle."

"From Ferguson in a way," I said, "Maybe they will, but a new beginning deserves a new name. It wasn't always called the Hillside Castle."

"That's true. It's gone through a few name changes. So, you really think you can make a go of it?"

"I do. This will be different, Willy. We aren't depending on the trains to bring in people as they did half a century ago. There will be visitors, some for a day, some for a week or more, and there will be people working there all the time. Those people will be buying houses, sending kids to the schools, and spending money in town."

"What about you, are you gonna move back here?"

"I don't know, but I have the place out in the woods. It was cozy there last night."

"You have always been evasive about how this all came about. How you got into it."

"Well, Willy, I'd tell you but then I'd have to kill you," I joked. "I will tell you this much. I am just the instrument, if you will, of old Scottie Ferguson. It's his money that is behind this. He felt he had a responsibility and he gave it to me to carry out."

"I vaguely remember Ferguson. He was the old guy who came in here with your dad a few times, right? I can't quite picture him. Tall, right? I guess I knew he owned Brampton Woods, but I have never been beyond the cemetery. So why his interest in Cherry Ridge, Chris?"

"Other than that he grew up here, I can't say . . .. Keep your chin up, Willy. You will start seeing positive results."

Media Mogul

From Millie's we trekked over to the newspaper office. There were a few more cars on the street and a few more people out. I looked toward the bank's thermometer. It was a balmy three degrees.

Only Patti, Mel Reeves' long-time assistant, was in the office. She said Mel should be in shortly. She asked if I wanted to wait. I accepted her offer of a cup of coffee. "Quiet, here," I said.

"Yes," she said, "Deadly quiet sometimes and I don't mean the obits."

Mel came in and invited me into his crammed office. "Just toss that stuff on the floor," he said, meaning the stack of files and magazines on the only chair other than his own. "I just came from a car wreck down by the airport. A mess, some injuries but the EMT's said they'd make it. Took three of them to the ER. Not locals. Got a couple of good pix. When did you get into town?"

"Yesterday. I stopped up at the project, then stayed the night at the camp."

"Was it tough getting up there? The camp I mean? We haven't had a lotta snow, but it piles up in the woods."

"I took it slow. The 4-wheel drive helps."

"Do you have some news for me or this just a friendly visit?"

"I hope it's both, Mel. The last time we talked you said the paper is in trouble."

"Yes. It is just Patti and I, and Marvin part-time. I was thinking about calling you like you said but ... "

"But what? I meant it."

"Okay, I'm sure you did, but unless you want to buy the paper or you have a job for an old news dog, I don't see how you can help."

"Well, you sure are an old news dog. I'm here to talk about both those things."

"You are?"

"Tell me about the purchase offer you got. Is it still on the table?"

"I guess so, Greenfield Publications has offered me enough to clear my debt and pocket a few thousand dollars. If I don't take it, they will expand in here one way or another and I might get nothing. Buying me out gives them a foothold and speeds the process."

"Who's Greenfield?"

"They are a chain of mostly weeklies. Most of their papers are not much more than shoppers, glorified old pennysavers. My guess is that all they will have here is an ad rep. They will likely assign a news compiler—that's what I call them—from a nearby town to cover Cherry Ridge."

"Have you ever heard of Auracle Media, Mel?"

"Hmm, don't think so. Who are they?"

"That's okay. They own some TV and radio stations and a few newspapers."

"Oh, I see. You think they might make me a better offer?"

"Probably not. Actually, I have a better idea. How would you like to sell me, say, 80% of the paper and you stay on as managing editor?"

Five minutes later we had a handshake deal. I would clear his debts and provide some working capital to get his staff back. "You're crazy, Chris," he said, "You'll lose money, but I guess I would be crazier not to take your offer. I will sleep better tonight than I have in a long time. The bars aren't open or I'd buy you a drink. Will you accept one of Willy's apple fritters and coffee?"

I told him I would, but I needed one more thing from him before that. I needed him to go with me to the radio station upstairs. He said, "The radio station? Are you going to buy that, too?"

It took a while longer than buying the paper, but that is what I did.

The radio station was owned by a young couple who lived in a sparse apartment in the rear. Their toddler took to Gretchen and she to him. Todd Burnett had grown up with a love for radio. "Love him, love radio," his high school sweetheart and wife Joanne said, "As long as I can remember, all Todd wanted to do was run a radio station."

They had acquired the AM license and set up the station five years earlier. They had chosen Cherry Ridge because there was no local competition. It had taken all they could raise to get going. I admired their initiative, but it was obvious success was eluding them.

"We have 5,000 watts," said Todd Burnett, " but we can't get out of the valley. If we could afford to get a tower on one of the hills we could have a greater reach."

I was candid with him. I had never listened to the station except maybe if it was in the background at a Cherry Ridge shop. I learned it was mostly music geared toward the younger set, from the Burnetts themselves on down. I didn't see how that would fly in an aging town where the youngsters were occupied with IPods and the like.

Todd said they aired a few canned shows and couple of religious hours because "they fill time and come to us free or nearly so." They also tried to keep up a steady stream of announcements about community activities, the time and temperature. They subscribed to a national news headlines service but had no local coverage.

It took me some time to convince the Burnetts that selling their station would be in their best interest. They would stay on as the general managers and on-air personalities. They would retain 20% ownership. However, they would have to change the way they sold airtime and they would have to re-program. For instance, I wanted them to cross over with Mel's paper in selling advertising. I wanted them to set aside a daily time for Mel to do the local news. I wanted conversation, maybe a daily interview show with locals. If the interviews generated call-ins, all the better.

I would like to hear a good after-school program for kids, something parents and teachers might support and listen to as well. Overall, however, I wanted them to gear older, toward more old-fashioned radio listeners. I wanted variety scheduled toward different demographics. What I wanted was an entertaining, informative, community-oriented radio station. I even wanted them to dig into the vast supply of old radio dramas and comedies and air them. It is hard to stay depressed when listening to The Great Gildersleeve or Fibber McGee and Molly.

The format change was a tough swallow for the Burnetts. Nevertheless, fulfilling their needs for a steady, livable income, a nicer place to live and a broadcast tower on the hill sold them. My wants, their needs. They knew Mel and he vouched for me.

I was now a "media mogul." Oh, that's right, I already was.

Mel, Gretchen and I went into Millie's for our celebratory apple fritters. Well, to be precise, Mel had apricot and Gretchen had an oatmeal cookie. For a moment, Mel grew serious. "You are really bailing me out, Chris. And I don't think the Burnetts could hang on much longer without your help. I don't really understand why you are doing this, or bringing back the castle. I don't see where you are going to make any money so I figure you have other reasons.

There are more things going on in your head than you are letting on. You are your dad's son, that's for sure. He was always quietly doing good things with limited means. This town has been stagnant for a long time, but there are good people in it. Maybe what you are doing will be the thing to get them out of their malaise. I hope so. You can rely on me to help you whatever way I can."

His words gave me a warm feeling, one I was beginning to like. He called his wife with the news. There were just enough people in Millie's to ensure that that same news would be all over town before Mel could print it.

Before I left Millie's I asked the counterman to package up a pint of soup, a loaf of fresh bread and several slices of the ham he had taken out of the oven. As an after thought I asked for a dozen oatmeal cookies—half plain, half Scotchies. As usual, I had to discreetly leave cash behind. I went across to the convenience store next to Ed Peck's and bought milk, a wedge of New York cheddar and a can of cashews. From there we drove back to the camp.

I called the office to report in. I was telling Arnie about my pending purchases when I heard Maggie in the background say, "We need to put him on a leash." Then, "Tell him we need him back here to prep for Auracle. I responded: "Don't worry. We will be back tomorrow. I'm looking forward to the Auracle meeting."

Chapter Eight

Panic, Crash Landing and Exposure

I had indeed been looking forward to the Auracle meeting. Of all the things that had come via Scottie, the prospect of leading a communications media company was the most intriguing. Media is the key player in a democracy, the best means to rapidly inform and educate.

I viewed the Auracle meeting as an opportunity to learn, particularly about the decision-making process. But, the first thing I learned was that the corporate leaders were used to having a hands-off, absentee owner. My mandate that the meeting be held in Saratoga Springs was not well received. When faced with going to upstate New York in February—and not even to a ski lodge—they arbitrarily shortened the event to a couple of mid-week days from the five weekdays (plus two possible weekends) that they could have spent in Florida. They cited cost-savings as the reason.

The organizers delivered some pro forma messages following Tuesday's kickoff breakfast. It was not well attended. Apparently, prima donnas saw the luncheon meeting to be the real deadline. The suits needed to be seen when the CEO delivered his keynote speech.

Vincent, Arnie, Maggie, and newer staff members were to visit as many of the sessions as they could. To get further off-the-record insights, some were willing to "sacrifice" and do some barhopping with whomever they could tie in to.

I had credentials, too, but I had them under an assumed name. I suppose that I was carrying the clandestine scenario too far, but I thought it might be in my interest to move about anonymously and not be manipulated.

In doing this the first day, I learned there were jobseekers, show pushers and ad reps in the hotel trying to make sales. I also learned that the prime movers were meeting separately off site.

Whatever my perception, I was way out of my element and I wasn't tuned in. My interest waned. I lacked concentration. I lacked desire. All were negative harbingers of something unrelated to the event.

The conference was to end with a formal dinner complete with entertainment and announcement of some personnel shifts, new hires and promotions. Over lunch at a nearby deli, Vincent told me the conference coordinator had asked him if I was attending. Vincent said he had been non-committal.

I guess I was not giving him my full attention because he said I seemed detached. He asked if I was feeling all right. I evaded a direct answer. I told him I was going home early to change and check on Gretchen. An all too familiar feeling was creeping over me.

Despondency or feeling blue or whatever you wish to call it is a state of mind. Clinical depression is more. It is a state of mind and body. For no apparent reason, my spirits had been sinking over several days. The conference was at first a distraction, but not a solution. I was having trouble getting out of bed in the morning. I was having trouble getting to sleep at night and I was feeling fatigued all day. I was doubtful and indecisive even about the simplest matters. I could read the signs. I did not know where they came from, but I knew where they could lead me. I had not had a real bout in nearly a year, but I feared a big one was coming on.

When I was a kid, I had a chronic stomach disorder that was never really diagnosed. I took little pink pills. It didn't matter what I ate or what I didn't eat. When I was in my late teens, the condition disappeared spontaneously, never to return. It took hindsight to realize it was gone.

Then for several years I had recurring migraine headaches. They followed me through my service years, college and graduate school. I tried pills and shots. I tried to link them to changes in the barometer and stress levels. What I could link them to were periods of depression.

Then the headaches ended abruptly, never to return. But the depression remained and sometimes deepened. Anxiety and panic attacks began to be its sidekicks. It was as if some transient demon, maybe a product of angst or stress, whatever that is, would attack me.

I was never flighty. I was never visibly nervous. No stammering, no tics, no fingernail biting. I had always been low-key and largely undemonstrative, misleadingly so. I suppose others read that as timidity, calmness or lack of emotion.

My erstwhile wife had sometimes joked—or so I thought at the time— that she had to take my pulse every so often to see that I was alive. Initially, she seemed to like me for my apparent steadiness, but then in the end she found it intolerable. "I would rather take some lows to have more highs," she had said. She didn't see and I didn't admit that the lows were depression.

I don't remember much about the drive home. I was trying desperately to ward off the anxiety that was enveloping me. I knew I had to forestall it before it became a full-blown panic attack. I only remember telling myself to focus, focus, focus. I wanted to get off the Northway. The speed, the openness was my enemy. At the same time my brain told me it was the fastest way to get home.

I finally pulled into the driveway. I sat there a minute shaking. I gained some control, entered the house and mechanically let Gretchen out to pee. It was a bright, sunny day but I felt enshrouded in darkness. Once inside I took a Paxil, stripped off my clothes and stood under the shower. I took an Ambien, went into the bedroom, pulled down the shades and crawled under the covers with Gretchen alongside me. I hugged her to me.

My mind was racing. Thoughts of how I had failed over these last several months mingled with thoughts of my shortfalls during my more distant past, both small and large. I thought about how silly acting on my whims must seem: the attempts to be secretive, the castle, buying the paper and radio station, my pompous actions at Magnus and on and on. Finally the sleeping pill gratefully kicked in.

It was truly dark when, nearly 9:00, Gretchen managed to paw me awake. She was hungry. I could have been, but I was not. My sleep had been fitful but it had brought some relief. Greater relief came when I realized it was too late to make the Auracle Media dinner. I put in a call to Vincent hoping it would go to voice mail and it did. I said, "Vincent, I won't be there. If anyone asks, say I was taken sick and can't make it. Say something nice to the gathering. You can handle it. Have a good time."

While Gretchen was making yellow snow, I thought about having a stiff drink. Instead, I found a box of crackers and a bottle of Arizona. I was cold so I put on flannel PJ's and my robe and crawled on to the couch.

I fell into that uncomfortable state between full consciousness and sleep. Not as bad as a nightmare, it is the place where repetitive thoughts reside. Some task, some worry, be it large or small, would take over my thinking. I would try to work through it, only to have it start all over again. It was hard to break free. Often some external distraction was needed to break the pattern. Even when I was adequately handling the depression I could find myself in this semi-conscious state. The sleep disorder doc I had consulted did not know what to make of it, thus the reason I had the Ambien.

This time my release came when I heard someone open the front door. The figure walked past me toward the bedroom. "Chris, are you in there?" came the soft voice. "Are you awake, are you okay?"

"I'm here, Maggie. On the couch. I'm okay, you needn't have come."

"Vincent said you are sick. Did I wake you? What's wrong? Can I turn on the light?"

"Please leave it off. I don't want you to see me like this."

"Like what? Are you hurt? Have you been drinking? Taking pills?" She turned on the light anyway. She cast aside her coat and gloves and sat down beside me. "If you aren't sick and you aren't hurt, what's wrong? Tell me, please, you're scaring me."

I didn't want to say anything. She gently prodded. Reluctantly, and at first awkwardly and slowly, I told her I was having an anxiety attack. I tried to explain what it was like. The surge grew and the floodgates opened. I rambled and went off on tangents but it all poured out, most of it anyway. Few secrets remained, from my childhood to the present. I had never felt so exposed, so vulnerable. I expected her to back away at any time, to run away from the shambles that I felt I was. But she didn't. She began stroking my forehead, then rubbing my back. I had barely moved. She said little. Her gentleness was calm and comforting. Nurturing. I began to feel the tension in my body subside.

I had not looked at her. I was embarrassed to show such weakness in her presence. I feared seeing her eyes. When finally I did, I said: "I guess that's all of it. Now you can see why I didn't want you to see me this way."

"Chris," she said, "There is one thing I am not clear about. Obviously you were neglected and lacked love. Were you abused?"

"I guess it depends on how you look at it. In the context at that time. Yeah, neglect. Like I said, I was left alone a lot when I was little. I was verbally abused. I got spanked and hit with switches and a yardstick. But it wasn't frequent and I didn't go to school with bruises and welts."

"Both your parents did this?"

"Mostly just one. I don't think she could help herself. She couldn't control her anger."

Her face was wet with tears. "It is okay, Chris. You have turned out just fine despite the past. And now all this responsibility fell on you all at once. Who could be prepared for that? Sure, it's been weird, but you *have* been doing wonderful things—everyone who knows thinks so —but you mustn't be impatient. You can't change the world or even your own world in just a few months. It is going to take time.

You are straightening out Magnus, you have gotten people jobs and we can see what you are trying to do, doing for Cherry Ridge. You are just beginning. With time you will do great things for many people in many places. I am sure of it. Vincent, Arnie, the others, they are, too. They all think the world of you. You can count on them. My family, too."

"They don't think I'm screwing up?"

"No, of course not. We like and respect that you have your own way of doing things. If it is a little different, it is what makes you you—a smart, gentle, sensitive man. The man we all care about. Somehow that crazy Scottie Ferguson saw that in you, and chose you."

"Meghan, even if you are lying, you're an angel."

"I am neither a liar nor an angel, Christopher. Take a breather, trust your instincts and trust me like I trust in you."

She then said: "When's the last time you ate anything other than those crackers? You have crumbs all over the place. I'm going to make you something and then you are going to bed. Tomorrow will be a better day. You will see. We'll get you in to see your doctor. You need an exam and you need to get your meds checked."

When I awoke early in the morning I was on the very edge of the bed. I could hear Gretchen snoring. I also thought she was taking up too much space. "Gretchie," I said, "Move over. I am going to fall off."

"Sorry," came the reply, "I am used to sleeping alone." It wasn't Gretchen beside me.

Before she left Maggie fed Gretchen and took her outside. She encouraged me to stay away from the office. She said she would tell everyone I had stomach flu. Her final instructions to me were to put on some of my old radio shows, sit at my laptop and write something. She said I always seem content when I am putting my thoughts on paper.

Getting My Act Back Together

All day long I listened to recordings of radio programs originally aired more than sixty years earlier: *Burns and Allen, The Shadow, and The Whistler.* I keyed in the first words "The Diner" and went with the flow. If it hadn't been for seeing to Gretchen's needs and a call from Maggie, there would have been no interruptions.

Maggie said her reason for calling was to tell me she had told the staff I would be absent for a few days. Her real reasons for calling were to see if I was okay and had made an appointment with my doctor. I realized she wouldn't let me be so I made the call. She called again in the evening to confirm that I had, to ask if I had eaten and to see if I wanted her to come by. I told her yes, yes and no, I was going to turn in early.

I didn't want to leave the house but I went out the next afternoon to have the vampires do their vial bloodletting. Three vials. The tech asked me if I was likely to faint. I said no. She said more men than women do, so she usually asks. "The bigger they are the harder they fall. We don't want you to get hurt," she said.

The cold fresh air was bracing, so when I returned home I took Gretchen on a long walk. The exercise was good for both of us. I told her I had been neglecting her need to walk, run and play. Mostly I had been letting her out on her own in the backyard. She looked at me as if to say, "It's about time!"

When we returned there was a message from Maggie on my voice mail. Her mom was having the card players over and she wanted to get out of the house. She was bringing dinner and some dance CD's. I was going to get a lesson.

She brought shrimp, haddock, chips, coleslaw and a whole bottle of Balsamic vinegar. "Got any beer?" she asked.

She wanted to see what I had been writing. I told her it was all still pretty rough. Still, I opened the file so she could see I had keyed in several pages. She noticed the CD's of the radio programs. She wanted to know what I had been listening to. "I know about George and Gracie and I know 'The Shadow' from a movie, but what's 'The Whistler'? Is it a music program?"

I told her and she asked if I had any comedies. I said sure, hundreds, maybe thousands. She said pick one that we can listen to while we eat. I couldn't think of one that she might like. Finally, I pulled out *My Favorite Husband* with Lucille Ball. It was not a show I favored, but I knew she had seen Lucille Ball on television and maybe in movies. Who hasn't? She was surprised to learn that Lucy had been on the radio. I guess she liked it well enough; she laughed a few times. However, she did not encourage me to play another. Instead, she put in a CD and began to clear floor space. The music was a very slow waltz.

The dance lesson could have been absolutely painful: "Stand up straight. Relax. Not that much. Put your hands like so. No, up here. Start on your left foot. Forward, to the side, back, now back where you started. Count: one, two, three four, one two, three, four. Glide and guide; don't stride and push. We aren't marching. Closer. I don't smell. That's too close. Relax. You are too stiff. *Feel* the music but *listen* to me. Ouch!"

Gretchen thought the scene was amusing. "Look at me, Gretchen," I said, "I'm dancing with a Pole dancer!"

Meghan groaned: "I get it, but I don't like it."

At first Gretchen thought she should get in on it. Maggie cautioned her: "It's your papa's turn now; you have to wait."

We kept doing the same steps to the point I was getting vertigo. She showed me how to turn and move around the floor using those same steps. I did not think I was getting any place, but she claimed I was. "You are starting to relax more. That's good. Once you have it on autopilot you will start to enjoy it. Let's take a short break."

I went to get a drink of water. I noticed her checking her right foot with a grimace. I had barely sat down when she said, "Ready to go again?" This time the music was a little quicker.

After the third go-round, she said I was improving. She said I would never be a threat on "Dancing with the Stars," but I could be a decent dancer once I had more confidence. "When can I learn to dip?" I asked. Maybe next time, she said. Then she volunteered: "I am enjoying this. It is nice to have partner tall enough for me."

More than an hour had passed so I asked her if she wanted to watch a movie on TV. She said sure, so I tossed her the guide. "Oh, 'An Affair to Remember.' It's just starting. I love this movie." I figured I must love this girl because I patiently sat through the whole thing without making one wry comment.

When the movie ended, she said wistfully, "Isn't that a beautiful movie?" and then, "I should be getting home." Neither of us had referred to my bad night. I thanked her for the lesson and admitted that I, too, had enjoyed it. Then I started to thank her for the other night.

She interrupted me. "If you ever think that is starting to happen again, you tell me. Don't wait until you are all messed up. And keep your doctor's appointment."

"Yes, ma'am," I said, "I'll dance you to the door." She giggled as I glided and guided. Her coat was on a hook behind the door. When she reached for it I took her in my arms and kissed her warmly.

"Where did that come from?" she asked softly.

"From my heart, Maggie."

"You might want to do that more often," she said.

I was about to act on her encouragement when she turned the doorknob, grabbed her coat and fled into the night. She called out "Good night, Gretchen, good night Chrissy, sleep well."

Chrissy? I turned to Gretchen. "I think something important just happened." I'd known Maggie for nearly three years, but I had only really come to know her since last August. We shared unusual events together and a memorable Christmas kiss. We shared nights together under unusual circumstances. We shared laughter, worry and sadness. Always with mutual respect, caring and affection. We had come to know each other in unique, special ways.

Sure, I had had thoughts about her as a glowing vibrant, sensual woman. That was the biology, the chemistry. I had resisted those thoughts and she had not encouraged me. "Lead us not into temptation." I was always going to be nearly 12 years older than she. It was likely I was always going to have some emotional baggage, and I was saddled further by the responsibilities that had befallen me. Still, my feelings for Maggie were deeper and different from any I had ever had for anyone. Maybe at nearly 40 years of age I was experiencing true first love.

Things Take Off

The Auracle Media conference had not caused my anxiety and panic. Nevertheless, I did not want to again approach the company so unprepared. Consequently, I asked the office to gather volumes of information about it and find a consultant to advise us. Which is what I should have done when the idea was first presented. One of the crew members suggested the Newhouse School or Columbia's School of Journalism as a resource.

I spent parts of nearly every day over the next weeks going through the materials and reading the web sites of each Auracle entity. I was willing to let the money people tell me how it stood financially, but I wanted to know directly how it stood editorially. The latter was fully within my comprehension. When next we held a meeting, I would work from strength not weakness.

In the meantime, Mathis was providing us with a steady stream of bids, contracts and reports for Serendipity Manor. He reported in on a weekly basis. He brought along or sent a steady stream of documents, renderings and photographs.

Despite the cold, snow and wind, the windows were all in place. Mathis and company was on track to meet the ambitious schedule. Three to fourth months of preparation and then six to seven months of section by section renewal. It was not the pace of the Empire State Building, but it was a highly satisfactory one.

As to budget, we were on track. While I was not happy to learn that the two Cherry Ridge motels had raised their winter rates to accommodate the foreman and skilled workers who were staying over, I put the blame on us.

We should have negotiated and bought out the rooms in advance. I asked Vincent to have someone look into doing that for the next six months.

I was so occupied that I thought little about the camp or the Cross murder until Paul Randolph reached me at the office. I had let him know that I had found numerous references to his father on the camp computer but that they were routine. They were about technical issues related to the helicopters or travel plans. I had also found drawings and schematics in the workshop that bore his Father's name. I had offered to share the latter with him at a later time. I guess the later time was about to arrive.

I asked Paul if he had decided on his work plans. He said he was weighing offers but he and his wife were undecided about where they wanted to live. Given that it was winter in New York, warmer climates had their appeal. On the other hand, both Randolphs had most of their family in the north.

So, I once again acted on impulse. "It seems I have a helicopter, Paul. A pretty big one. It is in Cherry Ridge. I have been thinking about putting it to use, but for that I would need someone to fly it. How would you like to go out to Cherry Ridge and see it? Maybe you would like the town. It has a little airport. Maybe you would like to work for my company. You could transport our staff and maybe provide the hospital with airlift service. Things like that. And while you are there you could review the papers I found in the shop."

The final thing I mentioned may have been all that interested him. If it was, it was enough for him to agree to a visit to Cherry Ridge. I told him I would call him as soon as I knew when I would next be making the trip.

My doctor's appointment went well. The receptionist remarked that I hadn't been in since June. They needed me to update my personal record. It was needed: my dad was still listed as next of kin. Dr. "O" always ran late—I think he started each day behind—so I had ample time to fill out the questionnaire. I put in the new employer, changed the phone number and address, and changed the insurance carrier. I put in "None" for next of kin. I guess I would have to get used to that. For "person to contact" I hesitated, and then I wrote in "Meghan O'Connor."

The lab work showed no problems. My liver was tolerating my usual meds, my total cholesterol count was down and the "good" cholesterol was up. My blood pressure was a little high. The doc seemed to listen carefully as I told him, superficially, about my life changes and, more particularly, about my anxiety attack.

One option he posed was to increase the Paxil, another was to try a new med. "But I don't want to do either, Chris. You were doing well. Then you took on new stressors and once winter set in you seemed to have stopped getting exercise. You need it. Your weight is up some and, clearly, your spirits are down. I promise you, exercise and a better diet will help."

Then he asked, "How's your social life?" Doc "O" was a practical man. I figured he was asking me delicately about something more specific. I grasped for straws. "Quiet," I said, "I am sort of seeing someone. Nothing serious. She's teaching me to dance."

"Good," he said. "We've talked about the effect of the Paxil, right? Did I prescribe anything to counteract it? The blue pills? It works good for me."

They Look After My Well-Being

Arnie Spellman had shown us what he could do. Serendipity Ltd. was now a Limited Liability Company solely owned by me. It had divisions for Auracle Media, St. James Policy Research Center, and Serendipity Development Co. I was President and CEO, Vincent was COO, Maggie was CFO and Arnie was something listed as "Of Counsel." Nothing of administrative significance went through without Vincent's approval. Nothing of financial significance went through without Maggie's signed approval. I think I was left with approving the new coffeemaker. I found a really cool one on the Internet.

We were growing organizationally. Vincent had three aides and a secretary. He had hired one of our early crew members, with his Ph.D. in hand, to take on his role as the crew's overseer. Maggie had an administrative assistant and a bookkeeper. Arnie had a paralegal whom he had brought along from his previous employer and a secretary. There were a few others in the office whose jobs I knew little about. Along with Swann, the team had established a board of directors for Magnus, which of course, had members from Serendipity. We were reviewing resumes and interviewing for Magnus jobs, but we would not hire until just before the move to Cherry Ridge.

Eight, nine months ago I knew the few people around me. Now, much of the time I was learning new names and wondering what in hell everyone was doing. For example, one morning I went into our building to find a woman stationed at a desk outside my office. Previously there had been neither a young woman nor a desk. She was petite with blondish hair. She looked very young. I didn't recall anyone telling me about a pending new hire or a visiting relative. I approached her to introduce myself.

"Good morning, Mr. St. James, I am Lynn Valente, your new assistant. Good morning, Gretchen. Is there anything I can do for you, sir? Can I get you coffee? One cream, no sugar is that correct?"

"Thank you, but I can get my own," I said. She looked disappointed, so I said, "Check that, one cream, no sugar is right. None of that hazelnut stuff. And maybe a plain donut."

"I will bring it right in, Boss."

She did. "Anything else I can do for you, Boss?"

"Yes," I said, "Sit down." She did. "First off, my name is Chris. If you are going to work here, you call me Chris. Who hired you, Ms. Valente? Did someone tell you to call me Boss?"

"Mr. DeSantis and Ms. O'Connor hired me. It was Mr. DeSantis who told me to call you Boss. He said you liked that."

I chuckled. "Mr. DeSantis was having a little inside joke with me, Ms. Valente. You can refer to me as Mr. St. James to others, but you call me Chris, even if you hear Ms. O'Connor call me Boss. Okay?"

"Yes, sir, Chris."

"Good, now tell me what your duties are?"

"I'm supposed to be your receptionist/secretary."

"Uh, huh. And as my secretary what are you expected to do?"

"Whatever you need me for. Type, file, take notes, photocopy, run errands, walk Gretchen if you're busy —I like dogs. Ms. O'Connor said that was required. I am supposed to screen your calls. They gave me a list. A few names get through right away. Others I am supposed to ask you about first, and then some are to be routed to others in the office. If someone not on the list calls, I am supposed to check to see if you are "in." I have it right, don't I?"

"I guess so. Has anyone told you I don't keep regular hours?"

"Yes, sir, but the phone still rings and there are other things I can do. I have been busy."

"How long have you been here? Is it going okay?"

"I started Monday. Everyone has been so nice. The ladies took me out to lunch yesterday."

Miss Valente left. Arnie came in. He was direct: "We have been talking amongst ourselves, Chris. We are a little worried about your safety."

"My safety? Why? Did I tick off somebody?"

"Not that I know of. It is many things, but foremost is it is where you live. It's not safe."

"What's wrong with where I live? I know it isn't much of a place but it is all I need and the neighborhood is okay. Gretchen and I walk around all the time."

"That's what I mean. You walk around all the time. Have you ever thought what might happen if someone tried to kidnap you or maybe just Gretchen?"

"Nobody does that stuff anymore, do they? I mean, I know kids are vulnerable, but I can't remember the last time I read about a real kidnapping of a grown-up in this country."

"That doesn't mean it doesn't happen, couldn't happen. And your house, it has no security system. You have that pet door that's big enough for a small person to enter. It would not take much to break in. What if someone came by and grabbed Gretchen and held her for ransom?"

"Well, first off, where I live doesn't exactly tell anybody I have money."

"Maybe it doesn't, but what if someone did trace you there? You would have little or no defense."

"Look, Arnie, I appreciate your concern, but I don't want to live in fear."

"I understand, and that isn't what I mean. It is just the opposite. Look, I have a security system and it helps me feel a little more comfortable, especially when my family is there without me. I'm just saying a little precaution could go a long way."

"What do you have in mind?"

"Well, we'd like you to move to a more secure location but until you do, we will like have a system installed at your place."

"If Gretch will be safer with a security system then I guess it is okay. But I will have to think about making a move."

"Do you mind if we look into a new place for you?"

"I guess not, go ahead."

"How about a driver?"

"I haven't played golf in years."

"Seriously, Chris. The right driver could also be a bodyguard."

"No, no driver. I'm not going to sit in the back like some coddled VIP. Maybe for a long car trip, but I have you guys for that."

"Okay, for the moment no driver. One more thing, Chris. I bet you don't have a will, do you?"

"Well, yeah, I do, sort of, somewhere. I wrote something up."

"How long ago?"

I thought back. I made out a will after my divorce so my ex wouldn't have any claims on what little I owned. "Maybe ten years ago. Everything goes to my dad. Oh, I see where you are going."

"I could do it, but it will be time consuming and it really should be done by someone outside the office, someone who knows how to handle large estates. There are enormous tax implications. A lot of what you want to do could fall apart not only without a will but also without a good succession plan. New York taxes would eat up your estate. If you don't want someone local, I would call upon the Wadsworths. They are familiar with some of your assets."

More complications with having money. I sighed: "You make good arguments, Arnie. It's not something I like to think about. Who does? Will you call Pierpoint and see what they can do? In the meantime, I'll give some serious thought to the consequences of my departure, short- and long-term." It went unsaid that I had no viable heirs.

Chapter Nine

Icky Stone

March brought unseasonably warm weather that exposed the dinginess of the accumulated snow. During my fourth or fifth dance lesson—it was at the O'Connors with an audience of Kay, Gretchen and Perky—I told Maggie I was going to Cherry Ridge to meet with Paul Randolph. Paul said he would drive out with his wife. He wanted Dawn to see the town and the school. Cherry Ridge would not show off well with all the brownish slush and dirty water. Still, we had rooms at the Ridgeview, so I could tell him we had a nice place for them to stay for a night or two.

I asked Maggie if she wanted to go with me and meet Paul and Dawn. It was a test of sorts, because she had only spent one night away from home—the night she comforted me—since Kay had her attack. Kay was quick to encourage her. She felt she was better than ever. She said that between Lillian—who had become Kay's daily companion as much as her aide—and Liz, she would be fine and that we should go for as long as we wished.

Our plan was to leave following lunch on Friday. We were to courier some paperwork to Greg Mathis on behalf of Arnie, so we stopped by the office en route. Lynn Valente called out to me as we exited: "It's Mel Reeves from the 'Cherry Ridge Citizen Ledger.' He says it is important."

"Chris," Mel said, "I only have a moment. Broadhurst is about to start a press conference. The city papers and TV are here. He's about to announce he has the Cassandra Cross killer in custody. Icky Stone!"

"What!" I roared, "That's insane!"

"I know, but there is some circumstantial evidence and get this: Chub told me Icky confessed. I gotta go. I'll call you when I can."

"Mel, we are just leaving to come out there. Do you have my cell number? Call me as soon as you know more."

We were half an hour out of Cherry Ridge when Mel called again. Maggie put the phone on speaker. Mel said: "It was a real circus. They had three TV news cameras there plus the papers. Word got out and about a hundred people showed up outside the Town Hall. Broadhurst said, and I quote: 'Our town can rest quietly tonight. We have taken a predator off the streets.' He has Icky already tried and convicted."

"That's crazy, Mel. Icky doesn't even drive. How was he supposed to get a body into the woods?"

"He might not drive, but he can drive. That's what turned on him. Two days ago Icky's mom had a seizure. He was in a panic. Instead of calling 911 for help, he put his mom in her old car and drove her to the ER. Somebody took note that Icky had driven there and reported it to Broadhurst. They are still checking the car to see if they can find anything connected to Cassandra Cross.

That's not all. When they did the search along the ridge they found a campsite with items they traced to Icky. Apparently he sometimes hung out there, so he knew the area. They already had his prints in the house and on Cross's rental car. When they searched his house, they found a knife. The M.E. says it could be the murder weapon."

"That's all questionable or explainable. Why in the world would he confess? I can't believe he did it. I can't believe Broadhurst thinks he did."

"Under duress is my guess. Myrna Stone died. They took him in minutes after she passed. Icky's been accused of all kinds of things over the years. She was always there for him. Without her he was putty in the cops' hands. Icky didn't care. I think he would have confessed to anything. They say they have his confession on tape."

"Myrna died? I knew Myrna. What Icky must be going through! I don't think he has anyone else. What about a lawyer? I bet none was present when this all went down. Find out for sure, will you? We will be at the town hall in less than 30 minutes. Meet us there."

"Call Arnie?" Maggie asked. "He's probably still at the office."

"Yes. Put him on speaker."

Arnie came on. "Arnie, it's Chris. A young guy was picked up for the murder in Cherry Ridge. I am 99% sure he is being railroaded for something he didn't do. He's just lost his mother and he is slow-witted. He's really vulnerable. I need a topnotch criminal lawyer in Cherry Ridge as soon as possible. Tonight. Whatever it costs. Tell me what we can do in the meantime."

Mel was sitting in his car when we arrived outside the town hall. After a few words, the three of us entered the police station. I didn't know the cop at the front desk. When he looked up his eyes went to Mel. I said: "I'm Chris St. James. We are here to see Gerald Stone."

"He can't have visitors. Chief's orders."

"Okay, then, I'll see the Chief."

"The Chief's not in. I'll take a message."

I saw the back of Broadhurst in his office. "If the Chief isn't in, then who is that in his office?"

Hearing the voices, Broadhurst came to the door and said to the officer, "It's okay, Royston. I'll take it from here." Then he turned toward me and said: "*Mister* St. James, what can we do for you?" It was not a friendly question.

"We would like to speak with Gerald Stone."

"Sorry. He's being held for a heinous murder of a defenseless young woman. No visitors."

A couple of other officers came into the room, Curt Simmons being one of them.

"Look, Broadhurst, someone needs to talk with Icky about his mother's funeral arrangements. I am willing to make them and I want to know if he knows her final wishes."

"I'm sure that will all be taken care of, St. James. You needn't go to any trouble. Like I said, no visitors. It's for his own protection."

I was getting angry. "His protection? Who protected him from false arrest, Broadhurst? You can't possibly believe he is guilty of being anything other than slow-witted."

"That will be for a court to decide, but the evidence and his confession say we have the guilty party."

"Who is his attorney?"

"The court will appoint one for him."

"So you have been questioning him without his having legal counsel?"

"We go by the book, St. James. He was Mirandized. He didn't ask for a lawyer. Now, if that is all, I have work to do."

"It's not all. I'm telling you in front of these witnesses that if anything happens to that man-boy, I'll have your badge."

"Are you threatening me, St. James?"

"I am not threatening, Broadhurst. I am making you a guarantee. If Icky doesn't get every legal right he is entitled to I will use every resource at my command to make you wish you had never heard of Cherry Ridge."

As I turned away I saw Chub with his head down. "Curtis," I said, "I am disappointed in you. You have known Icky since he was a kid. He followed you around when you delivered newspapers. He's your friend. You know he didn't, couldn't do this thing."

As we reached the fresh air Mel said, "I'm with you, Chris. Broadhurst's always been an arrogant son of a bitch. Maybe he has gone too far this time. Most of the force doesn't like him, but his wife's father, Chet Lemmon, is the council loudmouth and the council thinks Broadhurst's effective."

When we reached our cars I heard Chub's voice call out. "Wait up, Chris, I need to talk with ya." I waited. "You're right, I shoulda stuck up for Icky. The Chief is like Coach Dilbert. Always raggin' on us. All he cared about was if he got a win. Remember, Chris?"

I remembered. "Chub, I'm sorry I called you out. You didn't deserve that."

"Oh, but I had it comin'. You woke me up. Me and the guys have been puttin' up with a lot of shit. Excuse me, Ms. O'Connor. It's not the Cherry Ridge we knew, Chris. Marnie is gonna kill me, but I turned in my badge and walked out."

"You quit your job? It shouldn't have come to that."

"Yeah, I had to man up. I'll manage, but it will be tough to tell Marnie especially now that she's having another one. Maybe I could catch a construction job at the castle? Maybe if you. . ."

"You've got a job at the castle, but not construction. You can work security, hell you can be security chief, and with a few bucks more in your paycheck."

"God, Chris, security? Thanks! God, I can handle that. I feel better already. I can't wait to tell Marnie."

"Maggie," I said, "Do you mind walking Mr. Simmons to his car? Give him a card so he knows whom to call."

Mel started to speak but I hushed him. I wanted to eavesdrop on Chub and Maggie. She said: "Call the number on this card on Monday afternoon. They will be expecting you. Okay?"

He said, "Chris sure is a great guy, but then I guess you know that, don't you? Are you his girl? Ya know, he was a good ballplayer. Not real fast, but he had a helluva curve. And smart, too. I could tell you stories, Ms. O'Connor."

The last thing I could hear was: "Oh, really? I would love to hear them."

Maggie, Gretchen and I went to the camp. I was eager to hear something from Arnie. Maggie made a couple of calls. I called Jim Blackstone, a local funeral director. He said it was sad to hear about Myrna and Icky. He had occasionally hired him to do some cleaning and yard work. He didn't know who was handling the arrangements, if anyone. It wasn't as if Icky was in any position to do anything.

I told Blackie that under the circumstances he could probably get past Broadhurst and see Icky. I told him to tell whomever he had to that the funeral was pre-paid. He would not have to lie; he could come by the Barcelona about 7:30 and he would get a check. The Barcelona is where Mel and his wife were to meet Maggie and me for dinner. We could do nothing more for Icky until we heard from Arnie.

It was almost 8:00 when Arnie called. "Where are you guys?" he asked.

"In Cherry Ridge," I said.

He said, "Yeah, I know. I mean, where are you in Cherry Ridge?"

"We are having dinner at the Barcelona. It's on Ridge Street."

"Oh, okay, now I see your truck. I'll be right in. What's good on the menu? I'm famished. Order me an Old Fashioned, will you?"

Arnie sauntered in with a big smile and handshakes all around. He seemed pleased with himself, and he had reason to be. He had already met with Icky Stone, introducing himself to the cops on duty as Icky's lawyer. He was able to ascertain that Icky was somber, but physically all right. There was no indication he had been knocked around. Icky was reluctant to talk. Arnie told him he had been hired to represent him by friends of his mother. Icky didn't ask for names. When Arnie asked him if he had made a phone call, Icky said he had called his pastor but she hadn't come around. Icky was more concerned about his mother than he was about being jailed. He was worried she was alone and he didn't know if anything was being done for her.

"I assured him that his mother would have a proper funeral," Arnie said, "I assumed we would be taking care of that if need be, right? I also told him he would be at the funeral."

I interrupted him: "How could you say he could go to the funeral?"

"Easy Chris, I'll get him out in time. The confession won't hold up. I don't think he knew what he was confessing to. From what I gather he was agreeing to anything in hopes he could tend to his mom. I advised him not speak to anyone without me present. Everything else they have is shaky and circumstantial. Icky is unaware of any warrant for the search of his home, and there may not have been one for your property. They weren't very forthcoming at your local cop shop.

Is there a place to stay here? I may be here a few days."

Maggie started to say he could get a room at the Ridgeview when Mel interrupted: "You are welcome to stay with us. We have an extra room and Ella loves to have guests." Arnie said the motel would be fine.

"I won't hear of it," said Ella. "You drove all this way to help one of ours; the least we can do is give you a comfortable bed and a good breakfast." It was settled.

I said: "I didn't expect you to drive out, Arnie. I thought you were going to call in a criminal lawyer."

"You got one. Me. I'm all-purpose, remember? Seriously, I talked to Bill Holliday and he briefed me on what I needed to do. I could act quicker, so I packed a bag and here I am. I think Holliday's team will take the case if we need that kind of firepower, but I can handle it at this stage.

The thing I can't understand—even if Stone is guilty —is why they pushed so hard for a confession when they did. He wasn't going anywhere. They could have waited a week or two and have less risk of public opinion being against them. Now they need a hard-ass judge to let the confession stand under the circumstances. Under duress, no lawyer. They would eventually lose on review."

"Well," I said raising my glass, "Here's to you Arnie, your efforts are greatly appreciated."

The dinner was good. The desserts from Willy's bakery were outstanding, as expected. The prices were fair and the service was friendly. No one questioned my bringing Gretchen inside—her status was still preceding us. One of the owners, Lew Wallace, was tending the bar. He came over to say hello to Mel and Ella. Mel introduced us. It was good to know that Cherry Ridge again had something more than a good diner and fast food places.

It was late when Maggie, Gretchen and I arrived at the camp. We were eager to get some sleep. Fortunately, my growing concupiscence for Maggie did not keep me awake.

We spent Saturday morning futzing around the camp. Maggie worked with Julia; I watched TV news and read online newspapers. Same old, same old: another uprising in the Middle East, a coup in South America, global warming and the ever-present presidential politics. Gretchen was in and out half a dozen times.

Arnie called about eleven. He had arisen early and visited Icky. He had calls in to the county D. A., the county sheriff and others. Blackstone called about the funeral arrangements. He had met up with Arnie, spoken to Icky and his pastor who had come to see him. She hadn't neglected Icky. She had been out of town. Myrna's funeral would be at 11:00 on Tuesday.

The Randolphs met us outside Millie's for lunch. We arrived just as they were getting out of their car. After introductions, we started toward the door. Dawn Randolph asked: "Your dog gets to come in?"

Maggie answered: "Gretchen has special privileges in this town. You'll see."

She did. Millie had seen us coming. I couldn't tell whom she fawned over more, Gretchen, Maggie or Dawn. She escorted us all with a flourish to the dining room where Arnie and Mel already were seated. "Paul and Dawn Randolph, meet two more valued members of the Serendipity team."

After lunch we all drove up to see the progress at Serendipity Manor. We had to take care because, even though it was Saturday, it was a full-out workday. Mathis had devised a scheme whereby he divided the castle into six almost distinct buildings. Each had its own heating, electrical and plumbing systems. Mathis had a project supervisor under his supervision working in each section. At times crews were working from the top down and the bottom up. They were, as one worker put it, "smokin'."

From the castle we drove in three cars to the camp. Maggie noted to me that I was being much more open about it. "They are all on the team or I think they will be. I have to extend the trust." She nodded her assent.

When we waited at the gate, I pointed down the logging road and told them that we had found Cassandra Cross's body along it. That sobering thought subsided when they heard Julia's voice at the gate.

Once inside "Fort Ferguson," as Mel dubbed it, I served up beer and soda and found an Arizona green tea with honey for me. Good stuff. We ventured down to see the shop and cars. Paul Randolph, educated as a mechanical engineer, was stunned by the construction, by Julia, well, by just about everything. Mel said, "I thought you told me there was little to see here; but I can see why you didn't want to advertise it. Imagine, this has been here right along and no one knew it."

I gave Paul the stack of documents that in some cases bore his father's name. I could see he was impatient to review them so we left the Randolphs in the care of Uncle Andy. I instructed Julia to let them into the camp house should they want to enter. For the second time I was going to leave Gretchen alone in the house. She needed to get used to being there on her own from time to time. Then again, the Randolphs were close by.

Arnie took pencil and paper—Icky liked to draw—as well as some reassurances to Icky. Mel headed home to help his wife prepare for dinner guests: our crew.

Maggie and I went off to a Saturday vigil Mass. During the drive, I told Maggie a few things about the church. After the service she said, "It's a beautiful old church. I can almost picture you being up there as an altar boy. ... Are you okay? You suddenly seem quiet."

"It's disturbing to see what's become of the parish. Once there were two thriving parishes in town, three priests and two separate grammar schools staffed with nuns. Two or three Masses on weekdays and five or six between the two of them on Sunday. Now there is but one church open and it has to share its priest with other towns. There hasn't been more than one or two nuns since before my time and they finally closed the school a couple of years ago."

"That's happening all over, Chris," she said, "Too few priests and fewer committed Catholics. The schools got costly to operate without the nuns. The people show up for Christmas, Easter, Baptisms, weddings, funerals, and not much else. There are not as many with strong faith. Our pastor calls them 'event Catholics'."

"Why do you think that is, Mag? It should be easier now to be Catholic. The prejudice and hatred aren't what they once were. Fewer barriers and we don't have to defend being Catholic."

"Yeah, but there are so many choices and options out there. The kids hear things that draw them away. And if they hear things from the church that they don't like, they go elsewhere to find something more comfortable. Or they go no place at all. And their permissive parents let them. They want the path to heaven to be the path of least resistance."

"You mostly mean things having do with sex, don't you?"

"I'd say sex is a large part of it. I don't think it is all that philosophical. They don't want to be told what is right and wrong. They want to act on their feelings and make their own choices."

"Choices."

"Personally, I think safe sex practices are a good thing and the church is going against nature when it discourages them. Millions die from STD's and AIDS and that shouldn't be. And if God wants a child born, He will find another way."

"What do you mean by find another way?"

"I mean that I believe that God deals in souls. If He wants that soul to be a part of life, He will place it somewhere."

"That's an interesting take. I can't really disagree with it. Birth control practices prevent unwanted children, but birth control doesn't kill an unborn child."

"How do you feel about choice, Chris?"

"Like you, I guess. I think adult women make their choice about control over their own bodies once they agree to have sex. They didn't have that choice before modern technology. It was a matter of yes or no, and in male-dominated societies it almost had to be yes. Now, if they use no protection they have rolled the dice, so to speak. I think when they make that choice they still have another one: to bear a child for nine months, then give it up for adoption if they don't want it.

"It isn't that much to pay in return for the life of another person. People pay much more for bad decisions in other situations. Of course, the burden of responsibility falls disproportionately on women. I don't know a good way to make men truly and fully accountable."

"So, you have thought about it. Hypothetically, if someone like you and me were not married but had sex together, it should be protected sex? And if I was to get pregnant anyway you would want the child?"

Maggie had gone from our philosophical discussion to our 'hypothetical' personal relationship. I knew the issue was of utmost importance to her. I immediately said: "Certainly. Absolutely."

There was a long pause. Then she said: "Hmm. We are lucky that our parish is still doing well."

Expounding at the Reeves Home

Gretchen was pleased with our visit to the Reeves mainly because they had a motley standard poodle that she quickly befriended. Ella Reeves made a warm spot in everyone's heart by putting on a terrific home-style dinner: roast beef with mushrooms and onions, mashed potatoes with homemade gravy, fresh rolls, two side vegetables and her special cheesecake with raspberries for dessert. Mel and Ella talked proudly about their three grown children and two grandchildren. They both answered questions posed by Arnie and the Randolphs about the town and its history. Dawn Randolph especially wanted to know about the school.

Paul was quieter. He hadn't found anything in the papers that helped with his quest. On the other hand, he had gained some insight into projects and inventions his father had worked on with Scottie. That prompted me to ask: "How was your dad fixed when he died, Paul? I am wondering if Scottie shared financial gains with him?"

"He did, Chris, at least some. I know they shared some patents. Dad left mom everything and she is quite well off. No worries there. I guess my sisters and I will benefit when the time comes."

"Well," I said, "If you find anything in the documents that proves profitable you are entitled to your share." Arnie, taking up my interests, said he would like to get copies and have them evaluated. Paul and I agreed that would be a wise move.

I had already decided to share my thoughts with them about the Cassandra Cross murder. In the comfort of the Reeves' living room after dinner seemed like the time and place to do it.

"I think we all agree that Icky is innocent. Mel, Ella, you know his history and you've met him, Arnie. He has been haunted by accusations of perversion, but nothing has ever been proved. Nothing has pointed to his being dishonest or violent. He doesn't have the wherewithal to commit a calculated murder. And the Cross murder was clearly calculated. Her throat had been precisely slit; the rest of the slashings and stabbings were window dressing.

It is coincidence that he was the last one known to have seen Cassandra alive. His prints in the house and on her car are easily explained. Mrs. Morgan had asked him to help Cassandra move in.

His camping out in the woods some way from where Gretchen found the body makes him no more a suspect than it does me. In my day, we kids roamed around up there. As I recall, there was an old sugar shack off the road a bit where we would hang out. I think that is where they found signs of Icky. Furthermore, Maggie and I saw debris that suggested the logging road might have been a lover's lane, so he wasn't the only one who had been along there.

As to the confession, I don't give any credence to it. I don't know why Broadhurst focused on him, other than that Icky presented an easy target. I think he is blinded by his own compulsion to clear a prominent murder case.

Arnie is certain the charges will be dropped. However, there is more to this. To some extent it connects back to Paul and me. You see, I don't think Cassandra Cross's reason for being in Cherry Ridge was simply to be an exchange teacher. I think she saw an opportunity to come to a town she knew was associated with Angus Ferguson, her grandfather."

Mel gasped: "Her grandfather? How do you know that? Does Broadhurst know?"

Paul immediately exclaimed: "So you think her murder has something to do with my dad's?"

"First things first, Mel. I didn't say that, Paul. I really don't know one way or another, but there could be a connection."

I asked Paul to tell the others about his questions about his father's death.

When he finished, Arnie said, "I understand your feelings, Paul, but a lot of what you say is speculation. There's no hard proof."

I went on: "Well, Cassandra's relationship to Scottie is pretty clear. A DNA test can confirm that.

On another evidentiary level, I found letters to him from a teenage girl named Cassandra who was clearly living in England. She calls him grandfather. The timeline with Cassandra Cross's age matches up. In the letters she say she wants to come and find him someday. That implies to me that she didn't know exactly where he lived—there is no evidence of how he got her letters—but if he posted his letters to her from Cherry Ridge, she would have a lead. The biggest coincidence in all this is that she came across the teacher exchange program and seized upon it.

Cassandra Cross may be her married name. Pierpoint has found no record of her marriage in England, but Julia found a domestic violence report that involved Cassandra and a Randall Cross. Randall Cross also had other run-ins with the police. Maybe her desire to leave England was hastened by an abusive spouse or lover. In fact, it is not impossible that he followed her here and murdered her."

Everyone wanted to ask questions but I had more to say: "Now, Mel, Broadhurst doesn't know about the letters. I didn't volunteer them because he was going on about somehow linking me to the incident. Broadhurst has known for some time that Pierpoint Wadsworth has been searching for Cassandra Burke as she is the sole family beneficiary of Scottie's estate. He knows because I gave him a copy of a fax I received from Pierpoint. Her relationship to Ferguson is documented. The two Cassandras have the same birthdate, etc., so I'm 99.9% sure they are one and the same."

"So, Chris, you are saying it was no crime of passion, that someone came here to deliberately to kill Cassandra?"

"Well, I can't rule out passion being part of it, but I am quite certain it was calculated."

Arnie asked: "Do you think there is one killer or two separate killers out there? One who killed Paul's father and maybe tried to kill Ferguson and another one who killed his granddaughter?"

"I don't know, folks, but I do feel that whoever is responsible for Cassandra's murder would love to see Icky swing for it. The cops would stop looking for the real murderer. Then again, we may not have heard the last of him, her or them."

On the way back to the camp, Maggie and I were still talking about the murder scenarios. She seemed to think that the Randolph helicopter accident/murder was unrelated to the Cross killing. She said that from what she knew about abusive relationships, it would not be that farfetched for a spurned abuser to follow and kill his victim. "I'd never want to be in that kind of relationship and now I kind of feel I might have avoided one with Roger."

I suggested we change the subject to other things, so she turned back toward Gretchen and asked her if she enjoyed her new friend, the Reeves' poodle. Then she told me she took an instant liking to the Randolphs. "Good people, good values. She's really sweet. Pretty, don't you think? Like what's-her-name in that TV show. You know the one I mean. Do you think they will move out here? It would be a big change for them. I would like her for a friend."

"I think Paul will want to once he sees the chopper. I think they both have had enough of moving around. She grew up in a small town. If it was a good experience for her, she might like the move to Cherry Ridge. Her folks and sisters all live near Syracuse, so she would be closer to them. Maybe we will find out tomorrow."

"You know Chris, you have really softened on this town. Used to be you didn't want to talk about growing up here and when you did you could never say anything good about it. Now you have gotten really attached to it. And what you are doing for that old dump on the hill. No one in their right mind other than you would be doing it. Are you thinking of moving back here?"

"Yeah, I guess I have softened, in an odd way. There are some good things to say about small towns in general. They are safer, the pace is slower, and you don't have to battle crowds and traffic. And today's communications have them connected to the outer world. I did hate this place for a long time. There were many negatives, many bad memories—some I told you about—and there still are. However, it is one thing to bitch about them, another to try to change things for the better.

You know, I have come to think of the castle—the way we found it—as a metaphor for the town. Tired, old, rundown and with little reason to hope for the future. Just maybe the metaphor will hold and a rejuvenated castle will mean a rejuvenated town. I don't know if I could ever move back here, but the fates have conspired so I can't seem to stay away."

We managed to conclude the evening without further deep discussions. The Walls of Jericho went up and soon I heard both my girls snoring.

The Randolphs Visit

Julia let us know of the Randolphs arrival late Sunday morning. They kindly brought along the Sunday newspaper. The ladies stayed behind as Paul and I made our way around the ledge and then up the hill to see the helicopter. There were still several inches of slushy snow and each of us slipped more than once. This time we could see the top of the silo, as Paul tended to call it. I spoke to Julia. Paul was peering in before she had the lid entirely off. "It's a Sikorsky twin turbine, heavily modified. Big sucker."

He saw the ladder and before I could say be careful, he was on his way down. I thought I saw water on the floor. "It isn't much," he said, "just a small puddle." Using a flashlight, he made his way to an opening in the sidewall. "The controls are here," he said. He flipped a switch and recessed lights came on all around the pit. "C'mon down." he urged, "It's safe." I gingerly made my way down, almost toppling when my coat got entangled on a rung of the ladder.

Paul took in the machine from every angle. He opened the door and encouraged me to get in. "I'd say it is about 10-12 years old with every advancement they had then, with some added avionics and electronics I have never seen. It looks like a lot of effort has gone into reducing the noise level. I guess it is the kind of thing a couple of old spies might do."

Most of what Paul said was lost on me but I did filter out: 130 to 135 knots, 550 to 600 miles or more range, big payload and expensive to operate. And "a dream machine."

"Can you try and start it?" I asked naively.

"Not down here. Not now. The batteries are no doubt dead and I need to drain the lines and replace the fluids. I'll probably have to replace lines and fittings, too. We don't know how long it has been down here. Rust, corrosion. It looks like it has been sealed up pretty tight but you can still smell the mustiness. Some of these parts might be one of a kind. Maybe dad and Ferguson made them right here in the shop. It might take a month or more to get it flight ready. Once we get it topside I'll know better."

Paul went on to explain to me that the control room had switches to operate the lift beneath the chopper. "Maybe your Julia can operate it, too."

"Let's be careful about what we touch," I said. "I don't want to get stuck in the control room with that thing above us. Let's go up and ask Julia. Do you really want to bring it up now?"

"Sure," he said, "Let's see it in the full light of day."

Julia complied with my request. It took 30 seconds for the chopper to rise out of the ground. It was like a scene from a movie. I wasn't sure I wanted to even stand on the top of the lift. My hesitation made Paul laugh. "It's holding this baby," he said, "I think it can handle your 200 pounds." His eyes glowed: "It's a real beauty. Do you mind if I take pictures?"

"Go ahead," I said. "Just make sure I'm not in any of them."

Back with the ladies, Paul rambled on about working on and piloting the chopper. He said some of the drawings he had reviewed applied to the chopper.

Seeing her husband's enthusiasm, Dawn asked about homes in the area. I told her there was nothing very new, but the market prices were quite low. They could get much more house for the money than they could where they were. She said she'd seen some big, beautiful homes as they drove on Ridge Street not far from the business section. "It would be fun to renovate one of them, Paul," she said.

I told her that they sometimes do come on the market and it wasn't impossible to tender an offer on one that wasn't actually up for sale.

The Randolphs openly discussed moving after school ended in June. Paul said he could come out as soon as the weather warmed and begin working on the helicopter and looking at houses. We hadn't talked about money. I looked at Maggie who nodded and smiled as I said, "Paul, whatever your best offer is I will better it."

I was fairly certain, Mrs. Randolph willing, that not only did I have a helicopter, I had a new pilot and engineer, and new friends.

Late that evening a storm began to make its way up from Pennsylvania. It would make Monday a trial. It started okay as I led the Randolphs to and then left them at the office of the realtor who had sold my apartment house. The Randolphs were going to make the contact and then hastily depart to the east in an effort to get beyond the storm.

The trial began when I got back to Scottie's Place about 10:30. The snow was coming down heavily and Maggie had it in her head we were going cross-country skiing. She thought the camp trails would be a great place to ski. I was, to say the least, less than enthused about it.

The whole skiing thing had started around Valentine's Day when she convinced me to be outfitted with boots and all the paraphernalia. I envisioned it as future garage sale stuff. I had managed to keep off the damn skis except for a couple of awkward outings in a local park. When we had come out this time, she insisted on bringing along the gear, despite the mild, slushy conditions. My luck had run out or Maggie had an in with the snow gods: the fluffy snow was coming down at the rate of one to two inches an hour.

I had been gone less than 45 minutes, but that was enough time for Maggie to have gotten the snowmobile out. Gretchen was sitting on the deck watching her drive between the entrance and the woods beyond the barn. The snow was coming down so heavily I nearly lost of sight of her. She turned around, came back, pulled to a stop and shut the machine down. "It's fun, wanna try it?"

"Are you crazy?" I said, "If the wind picks up a little, this will be a blizzard!" There was already about eight inches of new snow.

"Your loss," she said. I drove the truck slowly behind her and we garaged both vehicles. As I trudged back to the house she caught up with me: "The forecasters say there is supposed to be a lull this afternoon. So we are in luck. It will give us a chance to ski." Yeah, some luck, I thought.

I tried to weasel out: "I should go see Mathis. We have that paperwork to pass along."

"Nice try," said Maggie, "Mathis won't be there. The roads are getting bad. No one is supposed to travel. It's a snow day. Remember? I love this weather! Like when we were kids. We are *supposed to* play in the snow."

So, once the lull came, play in the snow we did. It wasn't too bad, unless you count the times I fell and the time I couldn't stop and crashed into a Scotch pine. Or the time I was on my back like a turtle with Gretchen licking my snow-covered face. Or the time ... Well, Maggie and Gretchen had fun.

It might have been nicer when we got back inside and I showed Maggie my bruised elbow. I thought I'd get some sympathy. "How did you do that?" she asked, as she put her hand on my elbow.

"Ouch, that hurts! You mean you didn't see me fall? You didn't hear me yelp when I hit rock instead of snow?"

"Poor baby," she mocked.

Arnie called to say he was outside the County D.A.'s office. The D.A. had political leanings different from Broadhurst's and they had locked horns in the past. He had reviewed the matter and referred to it as "a rush to judgment." He said the evidence was inadequate. Icky hadn't been properly arraigned. It was a fiasco. The D.A. said Icky should be released pending further investigation.

Arnie had learned that, despite the weather, Icky's aunt and two grown cousins had arrived from Buffalo. They would be at his home when he got there. Arnie was trying to get there, too, before heading back home. I told him he had done great work.

RIP Myrna Stone

It would have been a struggle to attend the funeral the following day had Paul not helped me get the plow on the truck. Even after we got down off the ridge, the roads were nearly impassable. The funeral was at the First Reformed Church, Reverend Ellen Dutcher presiding. She delayed the start time because people had to fight the road conditions to arrive.

I had wondered aloud that there might only be a handful of people. Instead, it looked like the whole congregation had turned out, along with other friends of Myrna Stone. The Reeves and the Logans were present. Mr. and Mrs. Dumbrille, Mrs. Morgan and others from the neighborhood attended. The small, unembellished concrete block church was packed. If anyone did mention Icky's trouble, they did so in hushed words. Maggie and I overheard nothing about it.

The service was simple: some traditional music, a Bible reading, some traditional prayers. Reverend Dutcher's words were comforting. She asked if anyone cared to share with the congregation.

At first no one moved. Then, to my surprise, Curt, nudged by his wife, rose from his seat behind Icky and his three family members. Despite his garbled grammar, his words verged on eloquence. Tears ran down the big man's face as he spoke of Myrna's kindness to him as a child and to her love for her son.

His few words inspired others to rise and speak. Church members noted her devotion to God and to Gerald. Red Cross and hospital workers remembered her volunteer work. A neighbor spoke about how she would visit her when she was sick and send Gerald over when she needed help.

There was another reading and a prayer, then a final hymn. It was in three words, a moving experience. At the end I said to Maggie: "Anyone should be so fortunate to be remembered like this when the end comes."

Outside, Chub caught my eye and briefly left Icky's side. "The word's out that you were behind gettin' Icky released. Thanks for gettin' him out, Chris. It's a good thing you done. Miz O'Connor told me it would take a couple of weeks before my job would be ready, so me and Marnie can look after Icky."

Maggie told him he was officially on the payroll but it would take some time to get his identification, insurance and other papers processed. He would get a voucher to pay for uniforms and equipment he would need. She also said he would be getting a vehicle. That is the first time I had heard about it, but it made sense. For my part, I told him he spoke well.

We picked up Gretchen after the service and headed to Millie's for a late lunch. The Logans had returned from the after-funeral reception. They, too, noted that it had been good of me to help Icky. "The sentiment in the town has turned toward Icky," said Millie, "Something has to be done about Broadhurst. He's gotten too big for his britches."

"Now, Millie, don't go starting something," said Willy, "There are those who think he brought order here."

"Maybe so," she countered, "but some people, decent law-abiding people, are scared of him and that shouldn't be. You've heard the stories, just as I have."

"What stories?" I asked.

They both hesitated, then Willy said: "There's rumors about him roughing up some people, mostly teenagers."

"Him personally?"

"Not necessarily. A couple of the newer officers seem to follow his lead."

"And there's that thing with Watson," Millie offered. "It's said Perkins has pictures of the two of them and that's why Perkins beat that DWI a few months back. And he's up for the second sergeant's job when Smitty retires."

"I know Officer Perkins on sight. Who is Watson?" I asked.

"You haven't met her, Chris? You must have seen her. The only woman on the force. He promoted her over others to sergeant after only three years. She's a shift leader. The word is Perkins has pictures of the two of 'em. He took it with his phone camera through the one-way mirror in the interview room. Apparently they thought they were alone and the thing was blacked out."

"So what do the pictures show?" I asked, as if I couldn't guess.

"You know, what a woman can do with a man and vice-versa."

"Is she married?"

"Yep, Fred Watson. He's an electrician at the college. He did some work for us on the side. Nice guy. Coaches Little League. They have two, no, three kids. They are not from here. They are from out by Batavia, I think."

From Millie's we planned to go to the supermarket. We needed some supplies and something for dinner. The street took us past a car dealership. "Pull in," Maggie said, "I want to look at that Jeep for Chub." A few minutes later she asked, "Can't you just see that with amethyst lettering saying 'Serendipity Manor Security?'"

"Amethyst? You mean purple, don't you?" The world of women, or at least Maggie's world, is much more colorful than mine.

I thought Maggie would go inside the camp while I garaged the truck, but she came with me. She went over to the snowmobile and began to fuel it. I said: "You're still in your good clothes!"

She replied: "Hurry up, then, we still have plenty of light. We'll change and go for a ride ... that is, unless you'd prefer to ski."

I have to admit the ride was fun. The machine carried two easily, so I rode behind her. It would have been cozy if I hadn't been so damn cold. After about 20 minutes we were deep in the woods, close to where months ago we had turned to go to the gravesite. Maggie stopped and switched places with me. She showed me how to handle the controls. Her only caution was that I should go slowly until I got a feel for it. I thought, she needn't have cautioned me. Going slowly is what I had been doing all along —in more ways than one! It took us 30 minutes to retrace our path. Despite my heavy coat, I liked knowing she was holding me by the waist.

Once back inside she said with authority, "We need three things for next year: a big snowblower, a real fireplace and a cozy trailer so Gretchen can ride, too. Do you think she would like it?" I answered:

"Maybe, if we can get the noise down." What I was thinking was that she said "next year." Other than those three "needs," I wondered if she was comfortable with things just the way they are.

After an excellent dinner, I did the clean up. Maggie called Kay. She had checked on Kay each day, but this was the first time she settled in to talk at length. She stretched out upside down on her bed, like a teenager talking to a friend. Gretchen snored beside me on the couch as I listened to Maggie recap nearly every detail of the past four days. I heard her say: "I don't know, maybe tomorrow. I wish we could stay all week, the snow is nice and Chris is finally taking to it. We haven't come close to really exploring the woods. But he will get antsy and we do have some work to do. I will let you know."

When she finished, she made tea and offered me some brownies she'd gotten at Willy's Bakery. We sat on the couch and watched TV much like an old married couple, the kind that are warm and fuzzy with each other. The kind who are intimate yet not *intimate*. I wondered if that would ever change.

Before I turned in I asked Maggie if she felt a need to go home. I told her we could stay a couple more days if she wanted to. She said she would like that. I told her I didn't mind leaning on Vincent because he would be off for nearly a month for his wedding and honeymoon. Still, we should call him in the morning, bring him up to date and ask if he needed anything from us.

Wednesday morning was bright and sunny. The temperature rose. It might make the upper 30's by afternoon. We skied. A few times Maggie would surge ahead, then wait for me. She was such a natural athlete.

Gretchen tagged along. Heavy snow could bog her down, but the new fallen snow was light and fluffy. She enjoyed cantering along our broken trail. Maggie wanted to extend ourselves beyond our last point so we could see more of the woods. We followed the meandering trail along the ledge. We passed some side trails as we kept to a westerly tack. Eventually we reached the end of the property. A marker showed where the state park began.

Gretchen was tired; I was exhausted. I asked Maggie if her knee was giving her any trouble. She said no, that skiing seemed to be good exercise for it. We rested on a downed log, drank tea from a thermos and ate some crackers. Maggie offered me part of some kind of power bar, but I declined. After sniffing it, so did Gretchen.

I fell asleep after lunch. Maggie had been on the phone for an hour with Vincent, her assistant and my secretary/receptionist/phone-call-screener. She had also talked briefly with Swann. When I awoke she was on the Internet. "We have gas here, right? They have these fireplaces that look like real wood fires without the smell or mess. Can I get one?"

I told her it was late in the season for it to do us any good. "Yeah, but it's probably the best time to buy. I found some trailers for Gretchen to ride in. I like this one with the sides high enough so she can't fall out but still see. I also picked out this big snowblower thing. See it? It costs damn near as much as a car, though. And here is the Jeep I want to get for Chub. Like it? I found an aftermarket shop not far away where they outfit trucks and vans. They do lettering and they can put a yellow light on it. Well, not just yellow, almost any color you want. Do you think he should have a siren? That would be too cool. I'll check with him, he should have say about what will work for him."

I tried to be as enthusiastic as she was. Still, I said wryly, "You sure like to shop don't you, sweetie?"

"I am woman, see me shop," she laughed. After a few seconds she said: "That is the second time you have called me sweetie." I said I guess I did. "That's nice. I have only heard you call Gretchen that."

The afternoon went swiftly. We stopped in to the radio station so Maggie could meet the Burnetts. She fell in love with their toddler. I told the Burnetts I liked the changes they had already made and asked if they had specifications for the tower. We'd get them checked out and get some bids so we could erect it in the spring.

We went up to the castle. They had lost time the last two days because of the weather, but progress continued. Maggie brought up the decorating. I told her we hadn't thought much about it, but I wanted to keep it simple. She asked if she could be involved. I said: "Don't you have plenty to do as it is?"

She made a face. "It wouldn't be work, it would be fun. You know, more shopping with your money!"

She said she had seen work done by a design firm in Saratoga Springs that she really liked. "I think it's called Scarlet and Plum. Are those names or colors? Wouldn't that be a great color scheme?"

It wasn't what I meant by simple, but what could I say? I found it hard to ever say no to her.

Thursday the melting snow made for poor snowmobiling and worse skiing. So Maggie's reason to get outside was to see the chopper. We took the long way around so Gretchen could go with us. I leashed Gretchen before I had Julia open the lid. Maggie's reaction surprised me: "It looks scary. I couldn't go up in that thing."

"What do you mean? Last summer you were up in a balloon."

"This thing is different. It's got those big whirring things and I don't see how it stays up."

"Well, how about that? *I* can't wait to go up in it. Do you think they make doggie earplugs so Gretchen can go?"

We had a light lunch before spending the afternoon riding around Cherry Ridge. Maggie wanted to go in the library. It is an interesting old converted home. She liked browsing so I took the opportunity to walk Gretchen on the grounds.

We stopped in a couple of shops that caught Maggie's interest. In one she bought scarves for her mother and aunt. She wandered through the antique/second-hand shops that shared the old 5 and 10 store. She liked the old furniture. "Maybe we could outfit the camp with antiques or dedicate a couple of rooms at the castle to how they used to look." I saw a few interesting things, too. One was an old Philco Bakelite radio. When she caught up with me she was carrying a large brown paper bag.

"Find something?" I asked.

"It's for you," she said. "Don't worry, I didn't spend much." It was the radio.

She bought a few things in a mostly used bookstore: old postcards and a pictorial history of the town put out by the historical society. "This is pretty cool, ever read it?" she asked. I admitted that I didn't know it existed. As we drove about I pointed out a few landmarks, but mostly I noted where something used to be: the second theater, a once fancy hotel, the bowling alley, the roller skating rink, the ball field where I'd played.

Dinner at the Barcelona was early. Two couples were at the bar; otherwise, we had the place to ourselves. "I'm starved," Maggie said, "How about sharing a bottle of wine? I want pasta and lots of bread. Carbs."

When we got back to the camp, TCM was airing "Laura." Thirty minutes into it I fell asleep.

We had done what we had planned to and more in Cherry Ridge. I dropped the plow off the truck. We had a hearty breakfast at Millie's. We stopped briefly at Serendipity Manor. By 1:00 I had let Maggie out at her home and I was on my way to check in at the office.

Two weeks later the bad news came. Both Mel and Chub called within seconds of each other. Maggie spoke with Mel; I spoke with a sobbing, heartbroken Chub. "Icky's dead, Chris. I went by this morning as I have every day. I found him hangin' in the attic. I failed him, Chris, I didn't see it comin'. I thought he was goin' to be okay, but I guess he just didn't want to live anymore. Me and Marnie will call his aunt and make the arrangements."

Maggie said Mel offered a little more information. They had found a note. In hand printed letters it said:

To my frend Chub. Pleez take care of Missy. He is a good cat. His food is in the pan tree. I didnt hirt that laydee. I didnt hirt nobody never. Im go in to see momma. Good by Gerald.

Chapter Ten

Maggie hugged me with tears in her eyes. "I didn't know him but I feel so sad."

"Yeah, I wish we had had a clue. It was always hard to know what Icky was thinking. To be honest about it, no one really cared to find out."

"Curt told me had planned to ask me to give Icky a regular maintenance job at the manner. He thought it would do him good. It would have. Maybe if . . .

After a pause I said: "Meghan, this is about the eighth, maybe the ninth person I have know who has committed suicide. People I have conversed with, broken bread with."

"Really, that many?" she replied.

"Yes, my great uncle who wanted to avoid a drawn-out death to cancer, a neighborhood kid who hung himself when I was about 12 and on and on. One was a guy in the service who was about to be outed for being gay. He gassed himself."

"Stress, despondency, hopelessness. They are all silent killers."

I laughed a gallows laugh. "Do you know the Theme to M.A.S.H?"

"Sure," she said quizzically, "Everybody does. Why do you ask?"

"Do you know any of the words to it?"

"I didn't know it has words. I don't remember hearing them."

"The movie version did. I may get it wrong but it started something like this: *Through early morning fog I see visions of the things to be, the pains that are withheld for me. I realize and I can see that suicide is painless. It brings on many changes and I can take or leave it if I please. I try to find a way to make all our little joys relate without that ever-present hate but now I know that it's too late.*"

"I used to think it was funny to think there was a line that went 'Suicide is painless, it leaves you numb and brainless.' I don't anymore. It *is* painful for those left behind.

"Do you ever think about suicide, Chris? I mean ... "

"I know what you mean, Maggie. I think about suicide, but not in that way. You know I can get into deep mire when I feel I might have been better off never being born. But I have never thought about ending it on my own."

"That's good to hear. You know, Chris, somehow, you never learned that you don't have to feel guilty about things you can't control. You don't have to feel guilty about your mother, your childhood, your marriage or being picked out by Scottie to get the money. You don't have to feel guilty because you have more than others. You don't have to feel guilty about your depression. None of those things are your fault. You only have to take responsibility for you own actions, and you do. Somehow you never learned that it is okay to be happy. I pray that that is getting a little easier for you.

Coming Together Begins

We didn't attend Gerald Stone's funeral. We did what we could for Icky in life. We could do nothing for him in death. Arnie wondered aloud if there was any evidence of something other than suicide. I had wild thoughts that the Cross murderer or even Broadhurst had something to do with it. Icky's demise could be a way to end the investigation. I had a feeling that as time went on the notion that he indeed was the murderer could take hold of public perception.

Without disclosing these ideas, I asked Mel his thoughts. He said it was clear-cut suicide. The doors were locked from the inside. When Icky didn't respond, Curt forced entry. Missy the cat led Curt to the attic where he found Icky hanging from a length of rope. A wooden stool lay on its side below him. A penknife he presumably used to cut the rope was on the floor beside the coil. The note matched other things he had printed. At Chub's insistence, the area was dusted for fresh prints. Only Icky's were found. It was likely that no one other than Icky and his mother had been in the attic in many years.

No one was directly accountable for his death; nevertheless, it was evident to me that had Icky not been put under duress by external forces he would still be peddling his bike. The responsibility for the added duress rested heavily on "by the book" Broadhurst.

Mel e-mailed me "The Citizen Ledger" obituary he had written about Icky. It was both elegant and eloquent. It ended with Matt 25:35-40:

For I was hungry and you gave me food, I was thirsty and you gave me drink, I was a stranger and you welcomed me, I was naked and you clothed me, I was sick and you visited me, I was in prison and you came to me. Then the righteous will answer him, saying, 'Lord, when did we see you hungry and feed you, or thirsty and give you drink? And when did we see you a stranger and welcome you, or naked and clothe you? And when did we see you sick or in prison and visit you?' And the King will answer them, 'Truly, I say to you, as you did it to one of the least of these my brothers, you did it to me.

Mel also sent me his editorial for the same edition. He intended to read it over the airwaves. Without mentioning Broadhurst's name, he called on citizens to pressure the mayor and council to investigate the leadership and conduct of the Cherry Ridge Police Department.

I responded saying: "Bravo! Well said on all accounts. Watch your back my friend. There may be repercussions. Keep close to Chub."

Two days later, after the paper came out and Mel spoke on the radio, Curt called me. "Someone slashed Mel's tires and broke the newspaper's windows. The guys are investigatin' it as vandalism. You and I know who's likely behind it. Whaddya want me to do?"

I told him to put the Serendipity security aside and shadow Mel as much as he could. Mel might not like it, but Curt's presence might prevent further incidents. Despite too many donuts, Curt could still take on most any two men and, if it came to it, he knew how to use a gun. I told him I would send in reinforcements from outside to spell him. Mel was resistant. I told him to think of Ella and his staff. They could suffer what the media calls "collateral damage." The next day we quietly sent three agency bodyguard-types to Cherry Ridge. There were no more incidents.

Given his actions and the rumors the Logans had passed on about Broadhurst, I asked Mary Stuart, Arnie's assistant, to do a background check on him. "Not just Internet stuff; network however you can. In particular, find out why he left the feds. Go through Auracle. Maybe the D.C. area people have some sources. Use whatever other resources you need, spend what you need to."

April was a beautiful month. I was eager to see Serendipity Manor and the blossoms at the camp. Maggie wanted to meet with the decorating team. She wanted to "plant shrubs and flowers and maybe some veggies" at the camp. However, we had a pending editorial board meeting for Auracle. I was still keeping my hand in with the crew's output. There were meetings for this and meetings for that. We had so many people coming in and out that we were already crowding our still-new space.

Most of all, we were getting close to launching our multi-million dollar grant event, surprisingly much as I had described it in the Ridgeview Motor Inn to Vincent and Maggie. The difference was that we would provide up to ten grants of up to $5 million and up to a hundred grants of $1 million. The person or group proposing the grant would get an additional 5%.

Under different circumstances, Magnus would have been the natural vehicle for the program. While it was now stabilized, we didn't think Magnus was up to the task. It would come into play once the awards were in place. Magnus would be in Cherry Ridge and would be the overseer and evaluator. In the interim, we had a team establishing the legalities, the process, the schedule, a means to evaluate submissions and a means to make the grants widely known. There was much more involved than I had imagined. I was learning that it was expensive to give away money. Nevertheless, I was eager for the launch. It was our first large-scale initiative in philanthropy. I was eager to see the ideas generated.

I was advised that our wide-open door would get crammed with nutty submissions. Fringe politics, fringe science, Utopian schemes, fantasy. I was okay with that so long as no reviewers got too casual and tossed out the good with the weird and bad. I wanted a second pair of eyes on every submission; and I wanted a senior person to spot-check the rejections. I was also reminded that kids would likely enter their ideas. "Out of the mouths of babes," answered that. It would be great if a kid's idea made the cut.

Mid April finally brought the report on Broadhurst. It had taken a while. It was worth the wait. Mary Stuart told me she had called an editor with Auracle Media's Virginia TV station. She had met him over drinks when the Auracle crew had been in Saratoga Springs. He had contacts inside the government from his prior employment in D.C.

I asked Mary to summarize the findings in her own words. She started by saying that much of what she had was hearsay, but Robbins, the editor, had confidence in his sources. What Mary told me was this:

Allegedly, Charles W. Broadhurst had been a narc snitch while in college. His ardent work led to a job with the DEA. He was subsequently with the ATF, Homeland Security and the FBI. It seemed he couldn't keep a job but always managed to find another one. Apparently, at least two claims of sexual harassment and one of excess force had been lodged against him. Each seemed to precipitate a job move.

There was also a formal charge of domestic violence. That preceded his divorce from his first wife after two years and no children. He had quickly married Heather Lemmon, the Cherry Ridge girl who was working as a secretary in his D.C. office.

According to Mary (and Robbins), the final straw for Broadhurst occurred just before he reached 20 years of federal employment. There was something about planting evidence. He went on extended leave, put in his papers and retired.

His history "escaped" the village council when he was hired as Chief of Police. His employment by the feds and the ties of his wife to Cherry Ridge were enough to make him the desired candidate.

I thought about what I should do. I conferred with Arnie. Then I had Lynn e-mail Mary's report to Mel, the mayor, the town council, the county D.A., the county sheriff, the regional FBI office and half a dozen other officials. Let the chips fall where they may. They fell quickly and buried Broadhurst.

Within 24 hours, the village council convened. Allegations were brought forth that went beyond our background report. Feeling they were not alone, several citizens voiced their own grievances. Some were petty and vindictive; others were more substantial.

Chet Lemmon, Broadhurst's father-in-law, protested until he saw the proof about Broadhurst and Sgt. Watson. That happened when Officer Perkins was summoned and crumbled under questioning. He presented the explicit telltale photos. Lemmon resigned from the council.

The following day the council held a public meeting wherein the mayor announced the firing of Broadhurst, Watson and Perkins. Another officer was allowed to resign. The County D.A. began a full investigation of the department and was looking into criminal charges. The sheriff sent in a senior deputy to temporarily run the force. Icky and numerous others were being avenged.

Late April meant my 40th birthday. No two ways about it, it was the onset of middle age. I try not to commemorate the passing of time. More often than not, it feeds my despondency. I hoped those around me would let the day slide by unnoticed. Fat chance. Like most offices, ours had a vibrant grapevine. I decided to find some excuse to be elsewhere on April 29.

Thirty-nine, single, lonely, bored, and just getting by—my state of mind and being of a year ago—sounded depressing. Forty, single, rich and with newfound friends, purpose and activities sounded far better. I thought, add in Maggie and life was pretty great. What did I mean, "add in Maggie?" The money was the catalyst but Maggie was the difference.

It was time for me to accept that she meant more to me than everything else combined—even if our relationship advanced not one iota beyond where it was. She brought something I had not known before into my life: true joy. I enjoyed every minute I was with her—even when she had me on skis or trying to dance. Despite our down times, our bond transcended.

I was trying to live this sunnier, more productive outlook when I stopped by the O'Connor house on a warm Saturday afternoon. No one answered the doorbell. Gretchen, hearing Perky, ran into the backyard. Kay was there alone. I said," You are getting around quite well, I see."

"I am indeed. This new ride of mine is great," she said, meaning her new electric scooter chair, "and my therapy is progressing. Come sit and talk with me. The sun is warm." She explained that Maggie was running errands. "How is it going with you? I hear you have a birthday coming up." So much for keeping it quiet.

"Yep," I sighed.

"Why the sigh? It is just a number along the way. You have lots of years ahead of you and lots to be grateful for."

"I don't know about the years but, yes, I have lots to be grateful for. The money makes a difference but it brings a burden and it doesn't solve all problems."

"But you could have something to be more grateful for than money if you tried."

"What's that?"

"True happiness with my daughter."

"What do you mean, Kay? I'm grateful beyond words for Maggie."

"Chris, you need to see she wants more, needs more and you do, too."

"Kay, I ... "

"Hear me out, Chris. I know I'm meddling. You are both adults and can make your own decisions. But you have no parents and Meghan only has me. So let me say my piece and then you can tell me to butt out. Meghan does. You two may be 'in this nice place' as Meghan calls it, but it is not the *right* place for either of you. You have fun together, you rely on each other. Meghan even says you are actually *dating*. As if you haven't been for months! You're a good man, Chris, but Meghan needs a *complete* man for herself. You need a *complete* woman in your life. You need family."

"What are you getting at, Kay? Are you saying I should propose marriage to Maggie?"

"If that is what you want to do, then do it with my blessing, but at least take your relationship to the next step."

The next step. "Are you suggesting what I think you are suggesting?"

"Do I have to spell it out for you? How many nights have you two spent together? What's happened? Nothing or so I gather. If you haven't slept together, the frustration must be killing both of you. You act like shy teenagers, afraid to ask for a dance. Start acting like adults in love. You are, you know. She'd give her life for you, and I know you would do the same for her. Anyone can see it. Why put it off, why risk losing it? You could, you know. Grab hold of each other and hang on while you can. If your difference in age is holding you back, forget it. She's not a child. It isn't any more difference than there was between Tom and me. Forget about 'thinking it through,' forget about baggage, let your feelings out. Take Meghan off the pedestal and put her in your bed."

I was stunned. In my mind, Kay was the prototypical Catholic mother. I admired her for it. But now this, this, this ... I was at a loss for words to describe it or respond. The best I could say was, "Are you sure she feels that way about me? She's never encouraged me."

"That's not her way. Are you wearing pants or a skirt? Do you love her?"

"Yes, of course I do." I had said it out loud.

"Then tell her. Carry her off to Cherry Ridge if you want to, or anywhere else. I know you will make her happy and you will never do better."

Fortunately, the Mustang carrying Maggie pulled into the driveway. "I've come to love you like a younger brother, Chris, but I would rather have you as a son-in-law."

Maggie smiled as she approached us. Innocently she asked: "What have you two been talking about?"

"The beautiful day, Meghan," she said, "And how much we have to look forward to this summer. Do you want to go in and watch the game?"

Instead of watching baseball, I cajoled Maggie into going to a batting cage.

Thus far Maggie had every reason to think I was athletically deficient, so I admit I wanted to show off, show her I could do something, something manly. I bought a bunch of tokens and handed her half. "Go to it, slugger," I said.

She chose a bat, adjusted her helmet and stepped up to the plate. She had played on her high school team. She had good form; well, she had good form no matter what she was doing, even just standing still. She missed the first pitch and let out an unfeminine grunt. I hoped she wasn't like those noisy women tennis players that punctuate every swing with bestial noise. The second one she grounded hard up the middle. Her timing was good but she was lunging. I was reluctant to say anything.

When her ten pitches ended I stepped in. I swung half-heartedly at the first pitch; still, I caught it solidly. I put in some effort into the next four. "That's pretty good," she said. I switched to the right hand box and whacked four of the five remaining pitches even harder.

We moved to the higher speed softball pitches. This time I went first. I about matched my first effort. Maggie is nothing if not competitive, so when she stepped up to the plate she was going to kill the ball. "You're lunging, Maggie. Can I show you?"

She was biting her lip. "I haven't done this in a long time," she said.

"You are getting too far out in front. Widen your stance and let the ball come to you. 'Glide and guide'," I chided. I demonstrated what I meant. It helped.

I left her side and went to the hardball cages. At 39, I could still get around on a 70 mph fastball but nothing more. The curveball cage wasn't much trouble either, since I knew what was coming.

Maggie was standing behind me for my last few swings. "How often do you come here?" she asked me. I had been there nearly every day since the weather allowed them to open. "Not that often," I lied.

"Then how come the ticket guy knows your name and asked after Gretchen? And you brought your own wooden bat!"

"Well," I said, "Some guys like to hit golf balls. I'd rather hit baseballs."

"Chub told me you were a pitcher. He didn't say you could hit."

"That was a very long time ago," I said.

"We can have a catch some time. Dad and I did so almost every summer night when I was a kid."

"Sure, if we are here," I said, "But if we are in Cherry Ridge we simply 'play catch'."

On the Monday before my birthday, Paul Randolph called to tell me he had run test flights with the chopper and it was fit to fly. He was still excited about all the unique nuances he had found. Apparently he had been crowing to his old buddies about what he was piloting. He asked if I minded if he flew it home to spend the rest of the week with his family. It would be a good test over a longer distance. Naturally, I agreed.

I called into the office about 8:45 Friday morning with the intention of saying I wouldn't be in. Lynn answered. I asked for Vincent. She said he hadn't come in yet. I asked for Maggie. Same answer. She then said she and Lindsay were the only ones there. "Where is everyone, did I miss a long weekend? Is there a problem?" What I didn't ask was: was there a chance a birthday plot was afoot?

"I don't know exactly where they are. There is no problem here. Yesterday Vincent told me that if you called in I am to tell you to be at

Cooper Park by 10:00 AM. If you didn't call, I was to call you at 9:00. It's not quite that now."

"Cooper Park, why, what's there?" Cooper Park was close by. Sometimes Gretchen and I walked there. It wasn't much: a couple of worn softball diamonds, an asphalt basketball court and few benches. I relaxed a little. That would be no sight for a birthday bash.

"Sorry, Chris, I don't know."

"And if you did you wouldn't tell me would you?"

"Ah, Chris, I don't know how to answer you."

I called Maggie on her cell. "Good morning, Chris," she said brightly, "Did you get the message? I will pick you up in a few minutes."

I repeated what Lynn told me and asked her what it is all about. She said, "You're breaking up, Chris, I forgot to recharge my cell."

I tried Vincent. His phone went to voice mail. I tried Maggie again. My call went unanswered. I figured I better finish getting dressed before she arrived. When she did, she wouldn't tell me anything. "It's a surprise," she said. Damn, my birthday, I thought. I hate surprises. Why Cooper Park?

It was a school day morning, so other than a dog and its walker there was no one in Cooper Park. As Maggie pulled up along the curb she said, "Wait for it, Chris, we are about to break a dozen laws."

"Wait for what? What laws?" She sure had me puzzled.

"Relax, you'll see. It shouldn't be long."

"I said: "Please tell me what's happening. You're making me anxious."

"Don't be," she said as she took me by the hand, "It's a good thing."

I heard kind of a whining, then over the treetops came a helicopter. My helicopter. It even had SERENDIPITY written on its side in purple, uh amethyst, lettering. It settled down quickly on one of the ball fields. "Surprise! Go, get in before the cops get here," Maggie said. "Gretchen and I will meet you at the party. Happy birthday."

Paul Randolph beckoned me into the chopper. The chopper was far less noisy than most and I could easily hear him say: "Buckle up. We need to get out of here quick." He handed me a headset and we were off. I looked down to see Maggie taking pictures and waving up at us.

Paul wished me a happy birthday as we whooshed away. He talked to me over the head set. We were up in the air more than an hour. Paul took me over parts of the Mohawk and Hudson Rivers before following the Northway. I was able to see the Berkshires to the east and the foothills of the Adirondacks to the north. It was all exciting and beautiful. Finally, he set down on a horse farm near Saratoga Springs. "It's your friend Swann's place. Have a good time. Enjoy your birthday party."

Nearly everyone I cared about was there. Even Chub, Marnie, the Reeves, the Burnetts (who almost never left the radio station) and Mathis. There was plenty of good food. There were desserts from Willy Logan. There were games and much laughter. For maybe the first time ever I stayed to the end of a party. It was at once the first and best birthday party of my life.

Maggie drove me home. I was on such a high that I wanted to invite her in and seduce her. My courage was high and it seemed like the right time. What better way would there be to cap such a great day?

I assumed Maggie would walk right in. Instead, she stopped at the door. She put her arms around me and gave me a warm kiss. I was encouraged until she said, "I'm sorry but I have to get home."

"Oh," I said, "I thought our evening was just beginning. Is something wrong?"

"No, I want to stay, especially tonight. It is just, you know, I have this thing and I am not feeling very well." I was baffled until she said, "You know, the moon thing that comes around every month." "Oh," I said. I had to settle for a few warm kisses and caresses. The time wasn't right after all, but I had more confidence than ever that it was not far off.

Chapter Eleven

Conclusive Evidence

Maggie and I shared a week of extra warm glances and stolen kisses. Wordlessly, we were building up to the weekend when we were going to Cherry Ridge. I was almost certain the Walls of Jericho would be crumbling. I got my hair trimmed. I shaved every day. I stood erect with my shoulders back as Nanna had told me so long ago. I added a smile to my appearance. It was there when I got up in the morning and stayed through each day. Instead of my past marginal doom and gloom and preoccupation with the past, I had a sense of hopeful expectation. I wondered if it showed?

I was eager to get away for the weekend. I asked Maggie if she wanted to leave Friday morning. I hadn't finished the sentence when she said yes. We planned to stop by the Manor, have lunch at Millie's, visit with Mel and the Burnetts and then settle in for the weekend in our woodland refuge. A romantic weekend I hoped.

On the drive out we talked while a CD of old radio shows played. Slowly I had made a convert, or at least a tolerant partner to my listening. Actually, Maggie found some of the dramas quite compelling. The allusions of many of the comedies were very dated and sometimes impossible to get; but I think she had become a fan of Jack Benny. Much of his humor holds up pretty well.

We talked about how good things stood with Serendipity's number of growing activities. I told her I was thinking of trying to hire Greg Mathis permanently or maybe establish a partnership with him. It would still be several months before he finished his work on the castle, but I had begun to think that having a talented construction engineer on board could be a good thing. He could evaluate building projects we might sponsor. Maybe we would get into renovating other buildings and houses and maybe build some new ones for those coming to work in Cherry Ridge. It wouldn't all be philanthropy, but it could be fun and worthwhile.

We talked about Vincent's imminent marriage to Melanie, her brother Dylan's college graduation and possible engagement, and her mother's improved health. Not only had Kay recovered from her stroke, she was stronger and more vibrant in every way. Some new tests, a different diagnosis and new treatments suggested she might regain the ability to walk.

Maggie told me that Leo was going to retire as director of the 911 center. With their four children grown and scattered around the country, he and Liz were thinking of selling their house and living with Kay. The three were so close that it seemed like the thing to do.

I learned for the first time that neither Leo nor Liz was a blood relative to the O'Connor's. Leo was Tom O'Connor's adopted brother. They had enlisted in the Marines together and been partners on the police force. Tom had introduced Leo to Liz.

I asked Maggie how she felt about all the changes. She said simply: "Fine. If it is what they want it will work out." She bit her lip, a telltale sign that it may not be entirely "fine."

Our first stop in Cherry Ridge was for gas at Ed Peck's. Maggie wanted to use the rest room. To his credit, Ed kept his cleaner than most. When she came back to the truck she said, "I didn't see a single girlie magazine or any punchboardy thingies." Laughing, she added, "I didn't ask about condoms."

We went up to the castle. There was a flurry of activity. The Miller kid was working, and he shouted out "Hello, Mr. St. James" when he saw me. I called out: "Tell your boss I want you to show me around, will you?"

"Me?" he said, "I sure will." He went over to his foreman who looked at me, shrugged, and nodded. He seemed to say something like "Sure, whatever; he calls the shots."

The kid knew his way around the place. I liked getting a description from the ground level instead of a contractor who might feel a need to exaggerate. Howie Miller told me he liked construction because each day you could see what you had accomplished. He was learning the rudiments of some trades and he thought he would have a job until the place was finished.

"Do good work and maybe you stay on after that," I told him. "There will be ongoing work to be done." That would be great, he said.

Curt arrived Midway through our tour. He had come to know the place well, too. He said he tried to get through every room at least a couple of times a week to look for hazards and security problems. He said he had run off a few kids trying to sneak in at night and caught a couple trying to steal some equipment. A few things were missing, otherwise there had been few problems. Curt was trying to earn his pay.

I asked him to join us for lunch at Millie's. He was happy to. The warm weather had brought back the regulars and then some. The place was busy. Still, Millie found time to greet Gretchen and take our order herself. When she had, she said: "Chris, do you remember that odd English guy from last summer? Just before the balloon festival? I told you about him and then he vanished. I never did find out who he is. Well, guess what? He's back."

I hadn't seen him, but I definitely hadn't forgotten him. It troubled me to learn he had returned. "When did you see him?"

"He's been in the last three mornings. Different outfit, and he looked scruffier, but it's the same creepy guy. There's something about him that makes my skin crawl. I wish he would patronize some place else."

"Describe him for Curt, will you Millie?" I asked. She did.

"Oh, yeah," said Curt. "50-ish? I almost ran into 'im yesterday mornin' when I was in here."

When Millie left I asked Curt to discreetly see if he could find the visitor and to call me if he did. "Sure," he said, "but what's he to you? Do you know 'im?"

"No, I don't know him." I said. "You will think I am crazy, but I do think I know who he is."

"Who?" Maggie asked.

I used my hands to tell them to keep their voices low. I drew closer to them and whispered: "I think we are on the trail of Cassandra Cross's killer."

They both became wide-eyed. Maggie asked: "He's her ex-lover, Chris? How do you know? Or is he the hit man from out of Scottie's past?"

Curt was bewildered. He hadn't been in on our speculative conversations. "Ex-lover, hit man? What's this? Broadhurst never said anything about any real suspects 'cept Icky."

"That's because Broadhurst's investigation was lazy and half-assed. He had access to much the same information I have, but he didn't pursue it. It was easier to try to pin it on Icky. Here's what I think."

I proceeded to go over what I knew. I had to go over some of it a couple of times before Curt got it, but when he did he said: "Son of a bitch, excuse me, Miz O'Connor, but it adds up, just like in the movies."

Maggie, who had preferred the spiteful lover scenario, said, "You didn't make a couple of those connections before. That wasn't fair."

Curt said he'd check out the motels and service stations and see where that led him. He said he would call me as soon as he knew anything.

Maggie, Gretchen and I went to the newspaper office to see Mel and then upstairs to see the Burnetts. Each shared a little information with us; otherwise they were no more than courtesy calls. The Burnetts were especially happy that the new broadcast tower would be operational in another week. I praised the new website they had designed. They had begun to put audio from the station on it.

Curt called while we were there: "The guy left Milt's not long after I got there. I got his name, Perry Ransom, probably a phony, and the car make. Nevada plates. That'll be easy to spot. I ain't never seen Nevada plates around here. I still got a couple of friends on the job so they put out a call on the car and they are runnin' the number. I'll call ya when I know more."

We reached the parking area outside the camp house a little after 4:00. I looked down the hillside to see a new addition on a flat space on the property. "Is that what I think it could be, Maggie?"

"It's your birthday present from me and Vincent. He had it set up the last time he was out here. Don't worry, the buildings stayed locked. Do you like it?"

"I sure do, I love it!" I exclaimed. I now had my own batting cage!

It wasn't 20 minutes before I was inside the cage. It was woven mesh so there was plenty of natural light, but there was also a covering for use in foul weather. And lights, too. There were two pitching machines: one for softballs, one for hardballs. Both could be adjusted for speed, spin and time between pitches. It was by far the best toy I ever owned.

Maggie stayed with me a few minutes, and took a few swings. Then she took Gretchen in for her dinner. I swung away until I felt strain in my obliques. Time to quit. I was weary on my way to the house, but I was still swinging a bat as I walked. I was like a little kid returning from a day at the sandlot. I put the bat against a post as Julia opened the door for me.

"Look at you," Maggie said, "You're all sweaty. You need a shower. Gretchen has eaten. Our dinner is underway."

"But it's good sweet, sweatie, oops, I mean good sweat, sweetie." She laughed.

I said, "Thanks so much for the cage. It really is the best."

I took my time in the bathroom. I shaved for the second time that day. There were often weeks when I wouldn't shave twice. When I emerged from the shower I heard light jazz. I didn't know if it was coming from Julia, a CD or the radio. Whatever the source I liked it. As I applied some deodorant and a hint of aftershave I could hear Maggie talking to Gretchen. I couldn't make out the words, but I did hear her lovely giggle. She seemed happy. I put on a clean t-shirt and fresh slacks. It had crossed my mind to go commando but . . .

"Dinner is ready," I heard. Maggie had dimmed the lights and put candles on the table. "This is your belated birthday dinner," she announced.

As I approached the table I said, "Everything looks beautiful and delicious but not as beautiful and delicious as you."

"My, isn't that provocative," she said. She let me take her in my arms and kiss her deeply. Her thin t-shirt and mine were all that was between her breasts and my chest. Her breasts heaved and I could feel her heart pounding.

An electric minute passed until she barely whispered: "We really shouldn't let this dinner go bad. We have all night."

I slowly released her. I found myself trembling as I poured the wine. I offered a toast to myself. "Here's to middle age," I said.

Our conversation was simple:

Maggie: "I know Gretchie shouldn't have pork loin so I have some chicken thighs for her. . . There is no cake but there is pie. Cherry. Your favorite, right? I had Willy's boy put it in the truck while you were talking to Chub, I mean Curt. We should call him Curt, shouldn't we?"

Me: "This wine is good. I am glad you chose white. Red can give me a headache. Something to do with the catecholamine. . . This pork is fantastic."

Maggie: "The 'cat of coal of mine?' What language is that?"

Calvin

When we finished eating, Maggie said she had opened a bottle of Scottie's top shelf brandy. We moved over to the couch, kicked off our shoes and sipped it. I think we were both thinking it was time but then I thought of Gretchen. She needed to be walked before we could settle in for the night without interruption. Maggie offered to do it. "The wine and brandy have gone to my head. A few minutes in the clear air will do me good."

I watched the two of them go outside. The sun had set but there was still light in the sky. They had barely passed out of view of the open doorway when I suddenly heard a scream and Gretchen's deepest, angriest growl. Something was terribly wrong.

It didn't occur to me that there was a loaded handgun still in its drawer. I simply ran through the open door to the deck. Before me on the gravel was a tall, red-haired man holding a knife to Maggie's throat. Gretchen was a few feet away snarling.

"Stop," I said, "Don't hurt her. I will give you anything you want."

The man shouted: "I want the kid. Now."

"Please! Let her go! You've come to the wrong place, Ferguson. There's no kid here," I screamed.

"Don't play me. Sure as I'm bloody standin' here, I'll slit her bloody throat."

I saw the bat against the post. Before I could grab for it or say anything more, Gretchen hit the assailant with her full force. This was no backyard play tactic; this was Gretchen enraged. The knife ripped at Maggie's neck as the assailant was knocked back. He swiped at Gretchen, cutting her across her shoulder. She pulled away yelping then prepared to charge again. "Gretchen, no!" I screamed. Maggie spun and kicked hard at her attacker. She fell to the ground but her kick jarred the knife from his hand.

With the bat now in my hands I rushed forward onto the gravel intending to slam the bastard to kingdom come. Out of nowhere a gun appeared in his hand. He fired toward me and I felt a searing in my side. I swung with all I had as the gun went off again. The shot hit me in the hip but I still connected. I slumped to the ground face first. Three or four seconds later I heard a third shot. I turned in time to see Maggie holding the gun. She screamed: "Chris, Chris!"

Gretchen came to my side whining. Maggie followed. "I love you," she cried reaching for me, "Don't you dare die on me!"

She pulled off her tee-shirt and pressed it on my side wound. "Hold this to your side. We have to stop the bleeding."

"You're bleeding yourself Maggie! I will be okay." It was false bravado. I tried to rise but the pain was intense.

"Stay still, you're not okay."

"Julia, I screamed. Call 911, call Curt Simmons. Open the gate!"

Maggie ran inside. I could hear talking. She came back with towels and her phone. She pressed a towel against my hip. I tried to hold one against Gretchen's bloody shoulder. She was whimpering from the pain. I began to get woozy. Time seemed frozen. There was the sound of a siren. Then flashing lights and Curt peering down at me. I remember saying to him: "Bring Gretchen, she's hurt. Take care of Maggie, help Maggie."

They say I went into shock.

I thought that there was an unwritten law that when you come out from under anesthesia the first face you are supposed to see is that of a beautiful, smiling angel of mercy. Somebody was in violation. The first face I saw when my head cleared belonged to one of the butt ugliest nurses I had ever seen. Bearded and scarred, he even had bad teeth. But he did smile. "Welcome back, Mr. St. James. Do you know where you are? You are in the Cherry

Ridge hospital. You are going to be fine. You were shot but the doctors took care of it. Here, sip on this."

"Where's Maggie? Is she okay? How's Gretchen?"

"I'm here, on this side Chris." She took me by the hand and kissed me on the cheek. "Gretchen has been stitched up. She's hurting a little but she will be okay. I think she is more upset that she doesn't know where you are. You lost a lot of blood but you are going to be okay. You ruined my new shirt. The bullet in your side passed through but they had to remove the one in your hip. The surgeon said you came through it fine."

"How bad did he hurt you, Maggie?" There was gauze on her neck and a bulge on her collarbone.

"I'm okay. Just two more scars for my collection."

"You sure? You look really beat. I'm sorry for getting you into this. I should have done something sooner. When can I see Gretchen?"

"As soon as you are strong enough. You need to rest, Chrissy. They gave her a shot for the pain and she is asleep in Curt's car. It's only been a few hours. You can see her in the morning. Mom and Sean are on their way here. Paul's bringing them. He left as soon as I called him."

"That's good. What about him, Calvin Ferguson?"

She bit her lip. "Is that who it was? I don't know. I think he's here, still in surgery. He's the one you asked Curt to find, the one who killed Cassandra Cross, right?"

"Yeah," I said, "I'm not sure why he came after us, but I'm pretty sure that's who he is."

The nurse said: "You should let him sleep now, Mrs. St. James. Why don't you go down the hall and get some coffee?"

"No." Maggie said, "I'm staying right here."

Whatever the nurse gave me worked. He'd called her Mrs. St. James. I was out for the next several hours.

Maggie was missing when I came to. I was thirsty and I needed to pee. I found the call button and a different nurse, a much more feminine one, came quickly and assisted me. She asked how I was feeling and she changed my dressings. There were three: one on my hip where they extracted a bullet; one on my side where a bullet entered; and one close to my spine where it exited. I asked her how my wounds looked.

"Like they should at this point. Dr. Banfield is really good. In time all you will have is two dots where the bullets entered. There was more tearing where the one exited, but it will heal real good, too." She pulled the sheet further away to look at my feet.

"What's wrong with them?" I asked, "They kind of burn."

"You have some abrasions, nothing serious. They said it was from being barefoot on gravel. The doctor will be in shortly. And the police want to speak with you as soon as you feel up to it."

Dr. Banfield came in about 30 minutes later. "Looks good," she said. "How's your stomach? Headache? You can eat a little bland food and have water. It probably sounds odd, but you are one lucky guy. You took two bullets at close range and neither did serious damage. Just missed your spine. You will be damn sore for a while. We'll keep you here for a few days. The main thing we want to watch for is infection."

"Thanks, doctor, "I said, "Can you tell me about Maggie? She wouldn't tell me much about her cuts."

"She has about a two-and-a-half centimeter cut on her neck, not deep. And a six-centimeter slash at an angle across her collarbone. It went to the bone. Straight cuts. We cleaned and stitched them. They will both heal fine and there shouldn't be much of a scar.

Your dog will be fine, too. We called Phil, my husband. He's a veterinarian. He came right over. We gave him what he needed and he took care of her here. First dog ever treated in this hospital, but your friends were pressing us hard. Phil said her thick coat probably kept the damage down. He also found a welt on the side of her head. He thinks she was kicked or hit with something blunt. He's checking the x-ray now."

"When can I see her?"

"Well, if you are feeling up to it and you promise you won't do anything to pop your stitches, we can probably get you in a chair later today. Okay?"

"Yeah, I guess so. How's Ferguson doing?"

"All I can tell you is that he's here in ICU. I didn't work on him."

Before Maggie came back, Curt came in. "You're lookin' good, buddy. You sure scared me last night. I'm really sorry I didn't find the guy sooner. I was almost to your gate when I got the call. I was comin' to see if he'd come your way … "

"It's okay, Curt, we managed. You got there in time to save us. Is that my blood on your shirt? Have you been here all night?"

"Yeah, yeah it could be. I guess I should get home, shower and change. Could be Miz O'Connor's, Gretchen's or the other guy's. There was a lot of it. Mel's been here, too. He wants to come in as soon as he can. I kind of pushed my way in."

"What do you know about the other guy, Curt?"

"Only that you three really put 'im down. If he did do in the Cross lady and then attacked Miz O'Connor, he got what he deserved."

I slowly asked: "Maggie shot him, right? She didn't say anything."

"Yeah, she did. She's one tough lady. The way I got it is you dropped him with your bat and the gun flew loose. He was crawling for the knife or the gun but Miz O'Connor got to the gun first and shot him. Got him in the chest. Didn't kill him but she stopped him. He was out when I got there. Nothin' I could do for 'im. Nothin' I wanted to do for 'im to be honest. The EMT guys brought him in. I brought you, Miz O'Connor and Gretch in with my Jeep."

"How she's coping with it? Shooting him, I mean."

"Ella Reeves grabbed her when she came down to the waiting room. She broke down crying. We got one of the ER nurses. They are treating her for shock. They'll set her up with a psychologist as a precautionary measure. The doc said she should have a session and at least one follow up. There is a possibility of a delayed reaction. You know, kind of a PTSD. Oh, and her mom and her brother are with her now."

Maggie's history of recurring nightmares from her car accident came quickly to mind.

"Don't worry," Curt said. "We'll take care of everything. I'm going to go now. If the sheriff knows you're awake he'll be comin' in. I'll check back later and see ya tomorrow."

"Thanks, Curt, you are a good friend."

They brought me some kind of gruel to eat and some juice, apple I think. I talked to the sheriff and another investigator. They were both patient with me. I could tell they were trying to match what they had learned from Maggie and seen at the scene with what I said. The sheriff wanted to know why I thought the assailant was Calvin Ferguson and I told him. It took a while.

He told me I was right about him being Ferguson and that my conclusions made sense to him. They had gotten a positive ID on his prints. They had found his car with his gear in it on the logging road. Nevada plates. It appeared he had walked up the road and then made his way to the shadows of the camp building. When Maggie came along, he took the opportunity to take her as a hostage. They were holding off on making charges until they knew whether or not he would pull through. They were also checking for outstanding warrants on him.

After the sheriff was satisfied, Kay, Sean, Vincent and Arnie all came bearing flowers and balloons. And Vincent added a big container of cashews. They all seemed relieved to see me a long way from death's door. Maggie and I assured them that Gretchen and we were doing fine. Since we were, I asked Vincent to call Curt and together take Kay and Sean on a tour of the village and the manor. They were all adamant about staying over for at least a day.

A little later Maggie and I finally went to the waiting room to see Gretchen. It was a tearful reunion. She acted as if we had been gone for weeks. She was confused and neither of us wanted to let her go. She and Gretchen were going to stay with Mel and Ella.

Things can sometimes work differently and certain rules can get broken in a small town. Between them, Mel and Curt knew most of the people who worked at the hospital. They pushed to have Maggie admitted for observation and treatment of shock. She resisted but they told her it was best for her and what I would want. She gave in when they told her they would arrange for us to share the same room.

I finally pressed her to tell me what happened before I came out the camp door. She said: "I think he was hiding by the storage sheds. I didn't hear him coming. He was suddenly just there. He was strong. He grabbed me hard and I felt the knife. He said something about us hiding the kid. I guess he meant Cassandra Cross's little boy. I told him I didn't know anything about him. When Gretchen lit into him the first time he kicked her. I guess that is when you heard us. I tried to get loose. It all happened so fast. I think you know the rest. I don't want to think about it."

"I'd come over there if I could." I said. Instead, she got up, pulled the screen and laid herself down beside me.

Mel Reeves, being both friend and doing his job, came by in the afternoon. He asked if I was up to taping an interview. I hesitated. He smiled and said he could use the one he already had.

"What do you mean, Mel?"

"From last night. Listen," he said. He punched his digital recorder. My voice came on: "Where's Maggie? Tell her I'm sorry. Tell her I love her. I want her so ... " Mel stopped the recorder.

"It gets much juicier after that," Mel laughed, "It's amazing what a few drugs will bring out in a person."

"You wouldn't ... "

"No, of course not. But I couldn't resist having some fun with you."

"Maggie was there?"

"Of course I was," she said.

I did the interview. Mel set up the story, then asked leading questions. It was complicated telling him how I had come to my conclusions about Calvin Ferguson. I had to start with how I had come to suspect that Cassandra Cross was actually Cassandra Burke, Angus' Ferguson's granddaughter and heir to his estate. Then I told him how Millie Logan had told me a stranger, possibly English, had appeared in town just prior to her murder, then disappeared right afterward.

I told him how I had learned that Ferguson's son, Calvin, might be able to claim the estate if Cassandra was dead. I told him I was suspicious of him given his record and his estrangement from his father. The clincher for me was when I realized the likely attempts on Angus Ferguson occurred when Calvin was not imprisoned.

Somehow he learned about Cassandra's plans to come to Cherry Ridge. I said I thought he already knew about Cherry Ridge from his father or his mother. I thought that intending to murder his father, he might have brought down the helicopter, thus killing Miles Randolph. I figured he thought Miles was ferrying Scottie from the compound. We will probably never know that unless he recovers and talks. In any event, we can surmise that he arrived ahead of Cassandra and then killed her in a manner to suggest some kind of maniac. Which I guess he was.

When he reappeared, it scared me. I couldn't figure out why he had returned. It was what Calvin hadn't known when he murdered his niece that almost did in Maggie, Gretchen and me. Instead it did him in.

It had to incense him when he learned that Cassandra had a boy who would inherit from his mother. He set out to find him. Something, maybe from information about the breakup of the estate, led him to conclude, wrongly, that I had the boy.

I told Mel, that unlike movies and TV shows, I couldn't tie a neat, tidy bow around all the facts. I said I think the way I added them up makes sense, and that maybe the professionals would fill in the holes.

Mel asked if we wanted to talk about the preceding night's incident. He said it was heroic how we had taken on a killer wielding a knife and a gun.

I said, "No, Mel, we don't want to talk about. You can get the facts from the police report. Lives were lost to Calvin Ferguson and, as I understand it, his is hanging by a thread. I have no regrets about our actions of last night, but there was nothing heroic about it on my part. We were simply fighting for our lives. On the other hand, it was Gretchen who could have run off unscathed.

Instead, she attacked Ferguson and that gave Maggie a chance to get free from him. If there was any heroism, it lies with Gretchen."

Over the next few days there were many callers both on the phone and in person. Vincent and Arnie went back to work but Kay and Sean stayed for three days. Maggie showed them Scottie's Camp and much of what it held. By then my pain had subsided to a tolerable level so I lobbied for my release. The evening before it was granted I expected Maggie to keep me company. I was waffling as to whether or not a hospital setting would be an appropriate place to ask her to marry me.

Instead, it was Curt who arrived. He had brought a deck of cards and invited me to play gin rummy. We had not done so since we were kids. "Remember, Chris, when we would sit in that old shed and play cards for hours at a time? That was always fun."

I hadn't thought about that in a very long time.

"It was in those years that you helped me to read better. Remember? We were eight, nine, ten."

"I remember the card games, but what do you mean about reading?"

"You must remember. I was always falling behind in school because I couldn't read well. When it was just the two of us we'd get out baseball cards and you'd help me read the backs of 'em. Then you'd have me read comics out loud and sometimes the sports pages and sports magazines. You helped me figure out the big words. You never made fun of me and I was never embarrassed like I was when I had to read out loud in school. Then that one summer I got through 'Tom Sawyer' and 'Robin Hood.' They are still my favorites. You told me to mark the words I didn't know and then you'd help me with 'em. You couldn't a been a better friend, Chris."

"I remember now, Curt. It seems so long ago. They were good times."

"Yeah. . . Chris, I'm really happy you've come back home. This town needs you."

"Curt, I ... "

"Let me say somethin, buddy. I got my kids and my family through Marnie, but my folks are in Florida and my sister is in Texas. You were sorta like a brother to me and now that you're back that feelin' has returned.

I know lots of people around here and I guess some of them are my friends, but not in the way we were. And for my part, that ain't gonna change, whether you stay here or not. I'll always have your back."

"Thanks, Curt, you had my back when we were kids and I think you've shown that in spades all over again. I hope I can do the same for you.

Legacies of Cherry Ridge

"I gotta tell ya, a few people are jealous of what you have and how they figure you got it. But I ain't. I think Ferguson made the best choice he could have. Maggie told me what a burden you feel having a ton of money. How the demands are increasing on you and how she and your staff try to protect you from some of it. I'd never thought about it in that way but she made good sense."

"Maggie told you that?"

"And some of it to Mel, too. And more. She wanted us to know because she says you need people you can trust. She's a great gal, Chris. She really loves you."

I said quietly: "She means everything to me."

"You are going to marry her, right?"

"If she will have me. And as soon as possible."

"You don't have doubts, do you? She'll have you in a New York minute. She as much as said so."

"She did?"

"Yeah, I sorta asked her in a clumsy way and she said you hadn't asked her. That's all she is waiting for, buddy."

"Well, we do have to get past this recent stuff, then ... "

"You're, what, procrastinating! I don't see what you have to get past. Defending yourself against Ferguson was natural and right. If anything it should make you feel even closer. Don't you feel nothin' bad about any of it. Maggie's okay and you will be feeling good soon. You two belong together. And I promise you both, for the rest of my life I have your back and hers. Whatever, whenever. That was gin. Now pay up. You owe me $22.50."

The next day Curt picked up Maggie, Gretchen and me and drove us "home." Our little family was reunited.

We learned that Calvin Ferguson had been transported to a city hospital. His recovery remained uncertain. The bullet to his chest had not killed him, but the blow to his head had him addled and at severe risk. No one seemed to know how he had remained conscious and threatening after receiving it. I couldn't be sure, but I think the bat hit his shoulder first, and then connected alongside his head. I took a bit of solace in it being his more severe injury. If he died, the burden would be more on me than on Maggie.

The following Wednesday Maggie got back to work via conference videoing. Being busy and seeing familiar faces helped her cope. We tried to return to where it had been before, but I sensed a *sub rosa* lack of closure.

Dr. Banfield removed Gretchen's stitches. In about a week it was obvious her coat was growing back in. She was getting back to her old self. Nevertheless, each time she was near the doorway to the camp house she grew wary. She hadn't forgotten what had occurred there.

At first I needed to carry a stick when walking. It wasn't that there were any problems with my bones or joints. It was that a sharp pain would throw me off balance. Still, each day Maggie and I walked hand in hand around the grounds with Gretchen nearby. We talked about everything except what was really on our mind.

For Once in My Life Call Me Joshua

I had a late afternoon appointment on the day I was to get my stitches removed. Maggie said she had something to do so I went alone. Afterward I stopped at the florist and bought one dozen white and one dozen red long-stemmed roses. I had already rehearsed what I would say when she asked me what the occasion was. I would simply say: "No occasion, just because I love you."

I came home to find the table set just the way it had been for my belated birthday dinner. I could smell something good cooking. Lasagna? There were dimmed lights and candles. Once again I said everything was beautiful. Maggie suggested I looked sweaty from the sun—nice sweaty, she said—and that there was time for a shower before dinner. It sounded like a good idea. It was refreshing and relaxing. I was feeling unusually mellow. When I turned off the water I heard Stevie Wonder singing:

For once in my life I've got someone who needs me,
someone I've needed so long.
For once unafraid I can go where life leads me
and somehow I know I'll be strong.
For once I can touch what my heart used to dream of
long before I knew someone warm like you
could make my dream come true.
For once in my life I won't let sorrow hurt me,
not like it's hurt me before.
For once I have someone I know won't desert me;
I'm not alone anymore.
For once I can say this is mine, you can't take it.

As long as I know I've got love I can make it.
For once in my life I've got someone who needs me.

When I finished toweling off I reached for my clothes. They weren't there. Hmm, I thought I had brought them in with me. Maybe I left them on the bed. I put my skimpy summer robe on and walked barefoot into the main room. "I forgot my clothes," I announced to no one in particular.

"No, you didn't," Maggie purred back. She had crept up behind me and slipped her arms around my waist. Stevie Wonder was still singing. She must have put him on a continuous loop.

I turned around and we embraced. She said: "You have an advantage over me. I have never seen you totally naked, but you've seen me."

"I have?"

Remember that night when I was in the pool in the motel? When you stood watching me from the doorway?"

I pulled back a bit. "Uh, yes, you knew I was there? I shouldn't have done that."

"I was glad, I wanted you to see me—like that. I wanted you to want me—like that. I went to bed naked and left the door unlocked, hoping you would come to me. You wanted to hold me and make love to me, didn't you? You want me now, don't you? I will make it easy for you."

She drew closer. Despite her forwardness she was trembling. This was something she had never done before. Still, I was trembling more. Her arms encircled me and I found myself holding her firmly. I loved how her height allowed our bodies to mesh together almost as one. I ran my hand up her back and gently cupped her neck. Our kiss was long and deep. Neither of us wanted it to end. When it finally did, she said: "Talk to me. Tell me how you feel. Whatever you say, I want to hear it. I won't run away from you. Not ever."

As if I would let her.

She was fidgeting with a button on her transparent blouse. Her voice became mellifluous, like purling water. "You know you want me."

"You know I do ... "

"And? Keep going. You are a writer, you can do better." She had opened the button. "I bet you do much better with Alexandra."

"Who?"

"Good answer. She's gone. Forever. Right?"

"Yes, I can't imagine being with anyone other than you. I can't imagine my life without you." She was working on a second button.

"A little better, you're getting there." The second button was freed.

She was wearing nothing underneath but a hint of lilac. She took my hand and put it on a third button. Her eyes never strayed from mine. My fingers couldn't manage the button. It was what I had been dreaming about, but I was fumbling like a novice teenager.

"I, I don't want you to be with anyone else, ever." I looked down and somehow I had managed to loosen the final barrier. She pulled her blouse open and said: "My eyes are up here, Chris, use your hands." I was being seduced by God's greatest creation and I was savoring every second of it.

The second kiss was even longer than the first.

"One more step, my Chrissy, just one more. One question." She loosened her skirt and it fell to the floor. She took a step back so I could take her all in. She turned around very, very slowly. "Do you want what you see?"

I reached for her and kissed her neck. I kissed the scars on her back. I reached around her and cupped her breasts with my hands. I whispered: "Will you marry me, Meghan O'Connor?"

Her green eyes were wet as she turned again to face me. She said: "There aren't words to say how much I love you, Christopher St. James," she said softly. She slipped off my robe and lowered her hands to around my waist. "Like I said a long time ago, all you ever had to do was ask."

Epilogue

It is now a year to the day since I awakened in Cherry Ridge ignorant of what the coming days and months would bring. When I awoke today, Gretchen was again at my side, asleep. But to my other side was my new bride, Meghan K. O'Connor St. James. Both were lightly snoring, sounds I had come to appreciate.

So much has happened! Our wounds have passed into history except when my butt is the butt of jokes.

Serendipity Manor is nearly a reality. St. James Research and the Magnus Foundation will soon be moving in, along with others. The new pool, the exercise center, the ballroom, the theater and restaurant will soon be ready. It looks like Maggie's mother Kay may be coming to live in the Manor and manage its daycare center. Who knows? Uncle Leo and Aunt Liz may not be far behind.

Dylan is heading to law school with no worries about the cost, and courtesy of Scottie Ferguson, via his new brother-in-law, both he and Sean are driving Mustangs like their sister's. Sean is still uncertain about his future, but as I have gotten to know him better I am confident it will be a good and useful one.

Even Vincent and Arnie are thinking about the lifestyle that international philanthropy based in Cherry Ridge presents.

If Maggie and Dawn Randolph have their way, which they will, Serendipity will also soon be home to a new grade school with Dawn at its helm.

There is a wonderful farm near the edge of the village. I haven't yet told Maggie, but if I have my way, soon it will not only be home to Gretchen's Health and Refuge Center, it will be a working farm where kids in need can spend their summers.

At the same time Maggie is "nesting." She can't wait to find and renovate an old house to be our "proper" Cherry Ridge home. She peppers me with questions about raising and educating kids.

As for me, I am learning to fly a helicopter. Not the big thing left by Scottie, but a little trainer Paul Randolph induced me into buying. Well, "learning" is a bit of an exaggeration. I have gingerly held the controls in my first flight.

I am enjoying the exploration of Scottie's Place. I found a secreted pond—the one that must have drawn Scottie and my dad—and I discovered a secret of the cave. And then there is the beginning of a memoir I found at

Scottie's place. I dearly want to unravel the mystery that his legacy embodies. Given the last year, I imagine other mysteries to be solved lie ahead.

Anxiety and depression are never far away from me but their hold on me has weakened. I still take the meds, but my real therapy has come from the happiness I have found. I still have many unanswered questions. I still have philosophical issues about many things and I still am not certain that Scottie chose the right person to expend his fortune. I still do not know if it is right for me to remake Cherry Ridge but I think that is what I am doing.

A year ago I was nearly alone, frequently depressed and seldom joyful. Now I have renewed friends, new friends, new challenges, and new interests. Most of all, I have Maggie at my side.

I awoke today, like every recent day, knowing that I can and will do something good.

CPSIA information can be obtained at www.ICGtesting.com
Printed in the USA
BVOW040913071211
277744BV00003B/27/P